David Wooldridge

From Darkness
to Retribution

From Darkness
to Retribution

Chapter 1

CAVE COMPLEX SOUTHERN TEXAS

Deep inside a cave complex, lay the outline of a young woman; motionless but breathing. There was no light, just an inky blackness. The air was damp with a strong smell of ammonia. The floor seemed to move as thousands of insects from cockroaches to a variety of beetles scurried around in an endless search for food. Some thought they had struck gold as they crawled over the face of the body which appeared to be covered in a moving blanket. The face twitched. A hand moved involuntarily to brush away the invading pests. As more took their place the body became more agitated until fully conscious it suddenly sat bolt upright.

The body was that of a young woman, mid-twenties with long blonde, rather bedraggled hair and a face that would turn heads. She shook her head and rubbed her eyes, her brain desperately trying to work out why her eyes were open but seeing only a deep black void. As she felt around, her fingers quickly found her rucksack. Clutched tightly to her she opened it, and fumbled around inside in search of her phone, but instead, her fingers found a bottle of water and a sandwich. Despair overwhelmed her.

Glancing at her Apple watch she selected the "find my phone" app. Several feet away in the darkness, a small light flashed and then quickly went out. Gingerly crawling towards where she had seen the light she searched with shaking hands through the moving floor of insects. She pressed the app again and saw the light just a few feet away. Clutching the phone in both hands, she sobbed silently. With practised fingers, she opened it up grateful to see a full battery indicator but then despair as she saw there was no signal. Switching on the flashlight app she shone it around. The light danced off the walls of the cavern and showed just two small openings. Trembling as the predicament she was in began to dawn on her, she shouted for help but the sound just echoed around, seemingly coming back to her with a vengeance.

"She began to scream."

***

Shaded from the blazing Texas sun, two men stood at the cave entrance. Bizarre looking, they were both wearing protective white overalls like to a forensic suit, caked in dirt and debris. One was carrying a large flashlight, the other, many yards of string coiled up around his elbow and hand; one end was tied to a large boulder, a short distance up a small slope. Having placed the items on the ground, they removed their overalls,

shook them hard and folded them roughly. From their pockets, they took out black-rimmed sunglasses, which they put on in unison. The items they had left on the ground were retrieved and giving each other a nod, they stepped out into the bright sunlight.

Small beads of sweat appeared on their upper lips and forehead as they made their way up a small slope towards their car. Behind them, a broken sign hung precariously by just one nail at the entrance to the cave which showed signs of multiple shotgun holes. The words "Do Not Enter" had been scrubbed clean. In their place, painted amateurishly in red with drops of blood dripping down, were a skull and crossbones.

The landscape bore little interest to the two men. They had lived and worked in Texas all their lives and the gently rolling hills which were covered in small clumps of grass, shrubs and wildflowers with a few scattered Cedar and Mesquite trees, barely warranted a glance.

The taller of the two, Ryder, was dressed in a short-sleeved white shirt and pale slacks with a necktie loosely positioned under the collar of the shirt. With strong facial features, suntanned skin, and perfect teeth with the physique of an athlete, he could have been a model. However, his balding head and a swept-over tuft of hair, which he continually adjusted, ruined the image. Whilst his overall appearance slightly outweighed his baldness, it was his voice that was most memorable. Following a childhood illness of tonsillitis, the infection had left him with a high-pitched voice characteristic of a whinging child. The voice matched his character perfectly. His companion, Brad, short and stocky, seemingly with no neck was similarly dressed but with a bola tie; he was the epitome of a pugilist. A nose, well used to being the recipient of a well-aimed fist and a cauliflower ear which showed signs of being bitten and mauled. A missing front tooth, circular shaped scar from a broken bottle together with a mouth that never smiled and small bloodshot skin erosion indicated the signs of a heavy drinker. This altogether, signalled a man best to be avoided.

Ryder reached the boulder where the string had been tied. He undid it and finished off by coiling it around his arm. As the pair approached their car Brad selected the boot opening on his car fob. The boot of the large black sedan, positioned at the top of the slope, sprang open. Brad threw in the large flashlight while Ryder dropped in the string and overalls. They both brushed off the dust from their trousers and shoes and climbed into the sedan. Taking out his mobile from his pocket, an old flip top type, Ryder selected a pre-programmed number and then waited. A voice, short sharp and showing no emotion said only 'Is it done?'

Sounding nervous, his high-pitched voice sounded as if his testicles had been clamped into a vice, Ryder replied, 'Yea.'

'No evidence or interference?' 'None, just as you said.'

The phone went dead.

'Miserable bastard,' Ryder said as he threw his phone onto the back seat. He nodded to Brad. 'OK let's go. Can't stand this place.'

Looking back at the cave, Brad said with no real feeling in his voice. 'Poor cow. What a way to go.'

As the car drove off, a small red hire car could be seen partly hidden in the undergrowth.

Chapter 2

25 YEARS EARLIER, SADR CITY, BAGHDAD

The orphanage lay in Sadr City to the Northeast of Baghdad. Well known locally for the pitiful conditions that existed inside, the residents were mostly mentally retarded and unlikely ever to be found a home.

Mustafa Hussein was 15 years old and had known no other life but the orphanage. One of 16 orphans in the orphanage, he had been there the longest. As he rocked gently in his cot, the sound of the chain attached to his wrist and the bars, rattled in time with his slow rhythmical movement; he waited. Dressed only in a nappy he showed signs of gross neglect. His weight was that of a 5-year-old. Abandoned before his first birthday by his family as soon as they realised it was another mouth to be fed with the prospect of a lifetime of caring.

Mustafa's mental health had never been tested and no help had ever been given to him. He could not read or

6

write, had a very limited vocabulary, and just survived day to day. He knew the routine and his rocking gradually increased as he sensed that breakfast was nearing and his chance to sit for a short time in the sunshine. He knew after eating he would feel relaxed not realising that the drugs in the food would ensure he was compliant and quiet until the evening meal. The process would be repeated as it had done every day of his life.

The room the orphans shared resembled a large gym, which it had been many years before. Wall bars were still attached to the walls. Dust and dirt-covered pieces of discarded equipment piled in a corner. Around the room, the other boys, in a similar state to Mustafa, moaned gently. The sound of the moaning and the rattling of the chains was both eerie and disconcerting. It increased as they heard a familiar sound from the main door as it was unlocked.

The so-called manager of the orphanage, a plump short man, bald with untidy stubble and a stoop, entered the disused gym. He was grovelling. Behind him, two men dressed in the traditional style of a long gown (the thaws) with headwear of fabric hats (shmack) pushed past him. The taller of the two took out a white handkerchief from his pocket and held it to his face, hoping to mask the smell of unwashed bodies and faeces. It did little to help, causing the man to gag. His companion, a brute of a man who looked like what he was, a bodyguard, had no such reaction.

'Let me choose Master. This is no place for you,' he said in his native Iraqi Arabic.

The tall man nodded, turned away and left the room.

The bodyguard walked around the room, now silent as the occupants realised something different was happening. When he reached Mustafa he stopped and stared at him for a long

time. 'Can he talk,' he asked the manager.

Bowing in subservience he replied, 'No master, maybe a few words but he has little understanding.'

'Can he be trusted to do exactly as he is told?'

'Mustafa has never been out of the establishment for 14 years. He knows nothing of the outside world. He follows his routine obediently and has never caused any trouble.'

'If you are wrong or lying, there will be repercussions the like of which you cannot imagine even in your worst nightmares. Do you understand?' shouted the bodyguard which caused the occupants to shake.

The rattling of the chains increased as fear of the unknown and the change to their routine caused panic to spread.

The manager answered as he too shook with fear. 'Yes, master I understand.'

'And if anyone comes asking questions, you know nothing. He just escaped one night. Is that clear?'

The Manager fell to his knees, hands together as if in prayer.

'I understand, I understand,'

'Have him cleaned up and ready to leave within the hour,' the bodyguard said as he handed the manager a wad of notes. He turned away and left the room.

Mustafa stood, shaking with fright. He was at the entrance to the orphanage, a place he had no recollection of and looked out on a street he had never seen before. He jumped when a large object, making a noise he recognised through the walls of the orphanage but had no idea of what it was, stopped in front of him. The car door opened, and the manager pushed him towards it.

Mustafa not knowing what he was supposed to do, stood, still shaking violently, and began to howl. He hardly felt the needle enter his upper arm, just the faintest of pricks. He swayed slightly and then as he began to fall was caught by the bodyguard. Mustafa was thrown into the backseat of the car as if he weighed virtually nothing. The door closed and the car drove off.

***

Lt Freddie Fordham, a ginger-haired, freckled-faced Officer on his first tour of duty in Iraq was much respected. His easy relaxed nature and care for his men led to him having a reputation as an Officer to be trusted. He was not a big man, of average height and build and could not be described as handsome, just average looks. That said he had always been a hit with the ladies having enjoyed many relationships which had ended abruptly when he had met his current wife.

They expected twins within a few weeks, and he was keen to get back home having just 2 more weeks left of his current tour of duty. Back home he was confident that he would be promoted to Captain. In all likelihood, he would be posted to a training establishment, even Sandhurst, where his experience on the front line could be best utilised. This expectation pleased him. It would mean he could settle down for a few years as a family man, helping bring up the twins with his wife Sophie, before the army required his services elsewhere.

A hearts and minds patrol through the backstreets of the capital was a routine event. Each soldier had pockets full of candy and although they were all armed, they kept their

weapons pointing down in submissive fashion. The brief was simple. Make friends with the locals. Smile, charm the children, kick a football with them if you can and where possible use the little Arabic you know to greet the Elders and the women.

Lt Fordham was in his usual central position within the troop. Although he had carried out similar roles in the past, he was enjoying the experience. The locals had been friendly, the children chased after them holding out their hands for any candy and although the temperature was in the low 80s, the gentle breeze was sufficient to keep the atmosphere bearable.

***

Mustafa came round from the drugs seated in a chair. He fidgeted and tried to stand up having never sat down in one before, only to feel a slap across his face and told to sit still. A slender man with jet-black greasy hair and a nose that filled most of his face shouted at him. 'Keep still you stupid little bastard, if this thing goes off, we are all in for it.' The man sweated as he continued to strap the suicide vest to the poor unsuspecting orphan.

Mustafa had been naked nearly all his life so material touching his body was alien to him and frightening. He tried to stand up again but this time he was slapped even harder. 'You sure this idiot is the right candidate?' asked the man.

'Once we have the device fitted and he is given just a mild sedative, he will settle down,' answered the bodyguard.

A young man, barely old enough to shave rushed into the room, and shouted excitely. 'Patrol along the market road heading this way, about 15 minutes.'

The bodyguard smiled. 'This will be the one. Finish up, give me the phone, and set him loose. We can monitor the route of the patrols from the rooftops and Mustafa here can wander into their path.'

＊

'You have any spare candy Billy?' asked Lt Fordham, 'I've run out.'

Billy, a young infantryman searched through his Bergen and brought out a small bag of sweets. Looking embarrassed he handed them over to Lt Fordham.

'Keeping a few back for yourself were you Billy,' said the Lt with a smile. 'No worries, I'll just take a handful. We have just about finished now anyway.'

He took a few, giving the rest back to Billy.

Two hundred metres away, Mustafa wandered around the streets in a daze. Confused and highly agitated he did not understand the world around him. Since leaving the orphanage, his sanctuary, his life had been in turmoil and now this. He fidgeted not understanding the funny vest-like thing with wires and lumps and bumps in it and the large white smock that covered his entire body.

He tried to remove the device around his chest, but it was fastened too tight and he had no idea how to undo it. Looking around bemused, he saw a group of men coming towards him with children around them. The children all seemed to be happy, smiling and taking something from the men. It looked like something to eat, and Mustafa was hungry. He hadn't eaten all day so wandered towards the men his hand held out.

***

Lt Fordham was about to give his last piece of candy away to a rather overweight greedy young boy when he saw Mustafa. Noting his drawn and ashen face, eyes sunk into their sockets and desperately stretched out his hand in a begging motion, the Lt withdrew the sweet from the fat boy, offering it to Mustafa.

On top of a building which overlooked the market area, the bodyguard watched Mustafa, hand held out, approach a uniformed officer. 'This could be a big one, an Officer,' he said with a grin. He checked the signal on his mobile that was linked to the one connected to the suicide vest strapped around Mustafa. He took a last look and then dialled.

The signal from the mobile phone triggered the electrical impulse to the blasting cap, the Detonator. The pale yellow, solid organic nitrogen compound, TNT, exploded. The force of the explosion sent the 50 ball bearings and over 40 nails, sewn into the vest, in all directions at over 3000 m/s.

A high proportion ended the life of Lt Fordham in an instance, his body torn into numerous pieces. Billy was partly protected from the main thrust of the blast by Lt Fordham's body but three ball bearings and two nails tore off his right arm. The small overweight boy had turned away crying when the Lt had refused to give him a sweet.

Running back to his home he was behind a large wooden pole supporting a market stall when the vest exploded. He escaped without a scratch. Mustafa's body disintegrated apart from his head which ended up several yards away. The look on his face was one of surprise but calm. The tension had gone, and the eyes no longer showed pain and sadness, as if he was at peace at last.

Chapter 3

FOREST OF DEAN, SOUTHERN ENGLAND.

The expensive, German-manufactured up-market saloon, travelled at breakneck speed and seemed impervious to the heavy rain falling in its path. At the wheel, the middle-aged driver, Isabel, looked anxiously at her passenger, a heavily pregnant young woman.

'Hold on Sophie honey, just a few more minutes.'

The young woman groaned in agony clutching at her stomach. 'Please hurry,' her accent and light-coloured skin hinting of a heritage of Indian descent.

The country road they were on wound its way between a forest of trees allowing the lights of the car to create a myriad of patterns. Leaving the lights on full beam, Isabel ignored the flashing lights and blaring horns from on-coming motorists. Ahead, a set of traffic lights signalled green and changed to amber as the car neared. Isabel put her foot down hard on the accelerator and cursed as they changed to red. The car shot over the junction. Out of the corner of her eye, she saw a car swerve violently narrowly avoiding a collision. A sign ahead indicated one mile to an A&E.

The entrance to the Hospital was via a large, landscaped roundabout, planted with a large variety of flowers and evergreens. An annoyance to locals who felt their hard-earned taxes should have gone to improving the maintenance of the elderly hospital which was in dire need of repair in all departments.

As Isabel approached the roundabout at speed, two slowmoving cars approached the entrance. Without hesitation she mounted the edge of the roundabout crushing a row of newly planted dahlias and overtook the two cars before skidding to a halt, causing both cars to break heavily. Blaring horns greeted her as she exited the car and ran up the steps and through the entrance, quickly scanning the area and searching for an orderly. A cleaner who was mopping the floor glanced up at the bedraggled soaking-wet figure depositing large pools of water over her newly cleaned floor.

An orderly appeared looking concerned as Isabel shouted at him, 'A Gurney, now.' Not waiting for a reply she ran back into the pouring rain to be confronted by an angry motorist.

'Have you lost leave of your senses; you could have caused...' He stopped as he looked into Isabel's deep blazing green eyes. The man's anger turned from bewilderment to submission as he looked into a face full of strength and character. He quickly turned aside as an orderly pushed a Gurney towards the car.

Isabel and the Orderly helped Sophie onto the Gurney as the man reappeared brandishing a large golf umbrella which he held over Sophie, protecting her from the rain.

'Thank you,' said Isabel to the man who sheepishly nodded back saying a weak, 'Sorry.'

Panting heavily Sophie cried out, 'They're coming.'

As she looked up Isabel saw a Doctor, she recognised hurrying towards them. Squeezing Sophie's hand, Isabel tried to sound reassuring, 'It's OK honey, the doctor is here now and they will be taking you straight into the delivery room.'

'It's Isabel, isn't it,' said the Doctor as he reached them. Isabel just nodded.

Looking at Sophie, the Doctor, turned back and shouted through the pouring rain, his voice reaching a young orderly who was just at the entranceway. 'You, here now, hurry.'

The young orderly ran down the steps joining the other orderly. Together they quickly pushed the Gurney up the slope, positioned in the middle of the steps, and through the entrance. Not stopping to slow down as the wet Gurney slid over the floor, they made their way down a corridor to the doors marked Operating Theatre.

Concerned, the Doctor touched Isabel gently on the shoulder. 'She's in good hands now.' Moving quickly up the steps and into the Hospital, he made his way to the Operating Theatre.

In the entranceway to the hospital, Isabel stood still, the water pooled at her feet. She felt cold and drained feeling the first wave of shivering affect her. The cleaner, a toughlooking woman with a face wrinkled by years of hard work and the frown of someone who fussed and worried over nothing, looked up from her work.

She sighed heavily at the floor she had already cleaned once, needing to be mopped again. Hurrying over to Isabel, ready for an argument she shouted at her. 'Haven't you ever heard of a bloody umbrella you moron? I've already cleaned this area and now look at the mess you've made.'

Looking directly at the woman, water dripping down her face, Isabel said nothing initially, letting the silence linger creating tension. People in the waiting area, having heard the outburst from the cleaner turned to watch the action.

In a voice spoken with no hint of an accent but one that instantly commanded respect, Isabel looked the cleaner in the eye. 'Lady, I have just heard that my son has been killed in Iraq following a suicide bombing. The news caused my daughterin-law to collapse and possibly at this moment be delivering twins 6 weeks early. So please excuse me if I don't give a fig for a bit of water pooling on your floor.'

Isabel took the mop from the cleaner, moped the floor and squeezed it into a bucket. She handed the mop back to the cleaner as a ripple of applause gathered momentum until the waiting room of over 20 people clapped together. The cleaner looking embarrassed turned and walked back to her work.

The clapping lasted until the Doctor reappeared. 'There is a warm waiting room where you can dry off. I will get one of the nurses to bring you a towel and I assume a cup of tea would be in order.'

Isabel nodded and followed the Doctor. Looking back to the people in the waiting room she mouthed the words, 'Thank you'.

Chapter 4

The waiting room was sparsely furnished. A two-seater sofa was next to a small wooden table on which were a few out-ofdate medical journals and several glossy magazines. The walls, painted in magnolia were decorated with boring paintings of landscapes. A water cooler with paper cups stood alone on a desk in the corner.

Isabel sank into the sofa and dried herself as best she could with a towel the nurse had brought in. Her mind was racing. Sophies collapse at the news of her husband's death left Isabel shaken and immediately concerned for the safety of her and well-being of the unborn twins. She had had little time to absorb the devastating news of the death of her son and now the shock began to set in and she started to shake at the enormity of what had happened. 'Oh, my beautiful boy, I will miss you so much.'

Her thoughts were interrupted by a young nurse who appeared carrying a cup of tea. 'I have made it strong with two sugars, thought you might need a boost.'

She sat down beside Isabel putting a comforting arm around her. 'I am so sorry to hear about your son,' she said with feeling. 'I will find out what's happening in the operating theatre and let you know.'

Giving Isabel a final hug she left the room glancing back as she looked at the wet and distraught figure sitting on the sofa.

***

As Isabel sat alone her thoughts drifted to her son. Freddie had been a delight to her and Ernie. Full of life and easy going he had never been in trouble and although not possessing any particular gifts or talents was, as his school report read, a good all-rounder.

His decision to join the Army had not come as a surprise. Initially, he had been rejected for Officer training due to his youth and lack of experience in worldly matters. This had not deterred him. Taking the rejection as a signal as to what he needed, he had packed a rucksack and explaining to his concerned parents his plans, had set off to hitchhike around Europe and Asia.

Freddie returned after 4 months, unrecognisable with a beard, long hair and burnt to the colour of ebony. He regaled the adventures he had had and his parents noticed a significant difference in their son. Now displaying a greater air of confidence, a maturity that betrayed his age and a determination to succeed in joining the Army. This time his application was successful. He went to Sandhurst to begin Officer training.

Freddie had found the training tough but enjoyable. A naturally sociable individual, he mixed easily with the other recruits, who despite the variation in backgrounds from Generals sons to recruits like himself, warmed to his easygoing nature.

He had always been popular with the opposite sex and had learnt a great deal about the ways of the world on those matters during his time abroad. However, he had never any plans to settle down telling his parents that his career came first, and a married life and a family could wait for a good few years. How wrong he was, thought Isabel to herself as her mind continued to trace the journey that had led her to this tragic point in her life.

Weekend passes from Sandhurst were few and far between during the initial months of training. They depended a great deal on the progress the recruits had been making as a group. Any individual could upset plans for a weekend break with some minor indiscretion.

Ginger Wells was a close friend of Freddie and had struggled from day one. He was a likeable young man but had a temper that went with his mop of bright ginger hair, that although now shaved close to his scalp, still shone the colour of gold. He had trouble accepting the petty rules that governed the recruit's lives. Inspections of every aspect of their rooms, beds and kit layouts that had to be perfect, toilets scrubbed clean, and even their toiletries inspected.

Ginger never saw the point of these trivial rules. It was an inspection that failed, which led to the weekend passes being cancelled. The other recruits were resentful and gave Ginger a hard time, blaming him for the loss of privileges. Although Ginger had contributed to the failure he was not totally to blame and took the moaning of the others with a shrug of his shoulders.

Freddie had planned to visit his parents that weekend, looking forward to spending time with them for the first time in several weeks. After ringing them and explaining the problem, he returned to the tasks the recruits had been given. A full kit inspection, followed by a five-mile run in full combat gear, followed by another inspection until the duty officer was satisfied. Told they could now leave the camp for what remained of the day, Ginger and Freddie decided to grab a coffee at a local vendor in the nearby park and just chill out. The park was busy. Summer was coming to an end, but the weather had not yet shown any signs of Autumn appearing. The trees in the park were still in full bloom, the sun was warm, and people walked around in light clothing, many lying out on the grass areas picnicking. The large pond with a variety of wildlife is being fed bread from excited youngsters. The scene was idyllic apart from a small group of youths on bicycles.

Showing disregard for the peaceful surroundings, they rode without care scaring youngsters and causing families to shout angrily, only receiving shouts of abuse back together with gestures, which portrayed an unpleasant meaning.

Freddie and Ginger were seated on a bench enjoying the sun and sipping away at the coffee they had purchased from a street vendor. Although in civilian clothes, they stood out as military. The short haircuts and general demeanour were a betrayal of their occupation.

The leader of the group of youths that were enjoying a day of creating a disturbance saw the two young army recruits. Gesturing to his colleagues they made their way over, stopping directly in front of them.

Without saying a word, the leader dropped some coins into the coffees held by Freddie and Ginger. 'That's your pieces of silver for training to kill women and children,' he said and then spat into the coffees.

Ginger reacted, getting up quickly he pushed the individual who, in falling, collected the other members of his group. Now in a tangle of bikes, the youths extracted themselves, standing up menacingly.

Freddie realised that if there was to be a fight, a possible police intervention, their careers could be over before they had started. It was an impossible situation. The youths were acting aggressively and spoiling for revenge, their so-called leader urging them on. Ginger was showing every sign of taking them all on.

Freddie often recounted the moment when his life changed. From seemingly out of nowhere a young, beautiful woman appeared. Taking the arms of Freddie and Ginger she spoke in a calm voice, 'So sorry I'm late, if we hurry, we might just catch the film before it starts.'

Pushing through the youths who weren't sure what to do, she pleasantly bade them a good day as she led Freddie and Ginger away. Being from a military family she explained later that she realised the situation the two men were in. If they decided to fight, they could have ended up in serious trouble as recruits were expressly forbidden from indulging in any form of activity with the local community that might bring the Army into disrepute.

That moment was a favourite talking point within the family for years afterwards. The young woman who had intervened and possibly prevented a fight was Sophie. Freddie often spoke in wondrous tones about how fortunes and life can be changed in an instant by the smallest of happenings. 'If Ginger hadn't messed up his kit layout, those youths hadn't threatened us and Sophie hadn't been passing at exactly that time, life would have been so different,' he would regale to anyone prepared to listen. Isabel often thought of that speech and how it applied to so many individuals around the world.

The relationship between Freddie and Sophie developed rapidly. Soul mates, they were inseparable and when Sophie announced she was pregnant, marriage was inevitable. The wedding was a simple affair, spoilt by the attitude of Sophie's widowed mother who, having lost her husband in Northern Island during the troubles feared her daughter was making a mistake marrying an Army man.

When Freddie left for Iraq, with Sophie expecting the twins at the end of his 6-month tour, Isabel was becoming increasingly concerned about Sophie's mental health. Her frequent visits to the cottage were used as an excuse to escape the continued gripping of her mother. However, Isabel's concern was that Sophie was beginning to display signs of deep depression. Fears over Freddie's safety, a difficult pregnancy as the twins grew, her visits were not a happy social occasion. When Sophie received the news of the death of her husband, she slumped into near unconsciousness seemingly giving up hope of any future life.

**

Isabel snapped out of her daydreaming, coming back to reality with a start. How long had she been in what to her was a near trance, she wondered and what on earth was happening to her Daughter in law and the twins? She finished the now lukewarm cup of tea and stood up pacing the room, beginning to have a feeling that all was not going well.

In the operating theatre, there was an air of concern. The scans clearly showed the twins but the Doctor was finding it difficult to work out how to move them around for a normal birth. Deciding that a caesarean section would be the best option he spoke quietly, not to upset Sophie, to the theatre sister.

'Sister please contact the Anaesthesiologist, tell her it's urgent.'

The Sister, a highly experienced midwife, glanced up at Sophie and nodded to the Doctor before hurrying out of the theatre.

The Doctor looked at Sophie, concern in his eyes that the woman was showing no signs of distress or emotion as if she was in a trance. 'Don't worry Sophie, everything will be fine,' he said with more confidence than he felt.

The Sister reappeared with the Anaesthesiologist, a very young-looking woman, who quickly set up the required equipment for an epidural, adjusting the drip rate. Having scanned Sophie's medical documentation, she stated all was OK and ready to go.

The Doctor made the first incision, a 20 cm cut just below the bikini line and then another into the womb. Sophie lay completely still as the Doctor placed his hands in her, moving them around to gain a purchase on one of the babies. He froze. 'Something is wrong,' he exclaimed moving his hands gently around. 'Oh my God they are co-joined. How did we not see this on the scans?'

Turning to the Sister, he asked urgently, 'I need your help to move them into a better position. Feel beside me and try to locate a head.'

Placing her hands alongside the Doctors together they gently maneuvered the twins into a better position.

'I can feel a head but wait...' she paused as if unable to believe what she too was feeling, 'They are joined at the top of the head,' her voice sounding disbelieving.

The Anaesthetist looked up in surprise. 'Everything is fine here, can I help?'

'Please,' answered the Sister, 'can you go to the ICU and tell them to bring the largest incubator they can find and get another nurse in here.'

The Anaesthetist left the theatre in a hurry as the Doctor and the Sister finally managed to maneuver the twins into a position for extraction.

'Right gently as you can, let's get these beauties out of here,' said the doctor as sweat began to appear on his brow.

Together they gingerly lifted the twins, each holding one of the babies as another nurse wheeled in an incubator.

She plugged it into a socket and checked the dials. 'All set, how can I help?' she asked.

'Help the Sister transfer the babies to the Incubator while I finish stitching and take care of our new mum,' the Doctor said with a satisfying smile on his face.

The Sister and the nurse gently carried the babies, both amazed at the site of co-joined twins.

'A first for you I dare say nurse. Certainly is for me,' the Sister said smiling as they carried the babies and gently lowered them into the Incubator. The nurse quickly wheeled the incubator to the ICU making her way down a corridor where staff lined the way hoping for a glimpse of the twins.

The doctor went to Sophie who was still lying unmoved, eyes closed breathing quietly. He looked at the monitor which showed normal blood pressure and pulse. 'Well, Sophie you have two beautiful children, a boy and a girl.' He held her hand but there was no reaction.

'Right, let us get you moved into a ward and give you some time to recover.'

'I have a bed ready for her and an orderly is on the way,' said the Sister.

'Efficient and organised as always, thank you, Sister. That was quite an evening, I think it's time to get cleaned up and call it a day. A specialist team will be here tomorrow to look after the twins, which is time enough for Mum and Grandma to see them. Not sure how

27

difficult the operation will be but they seem healthy enough.'

An orderly arrived and Sophie was wheeled out of the theatre, still showing no signs of a reaction to what had happened.

Leaving the Operating Theatre, the Doctor and the Sister moved to a side cubicle where they removed their scrubs and cleaned up.

Turning to the Doctor, the Sister had a quizzical look on her face. 'Doctor, I know what we have experienced here is unique to both of us but did you also notice another peculiarity?'

'No, I was too overcome by the enormity of the occasion. Why, was there something else?'

'Yes, I'm not certain but I think we have just witnessed a first. Wait until they are cleaned up then have a look.'

***

Alone in the waiting room, Isabel sat quietly, her mind switching between the loss of her son, the worry for her daughterin-law and her concern for the well-being of the twins. Her thoughts were interrupted by an alarm going off and the sound of feet rushing down a corridor. Her instincts told her it was related to Sophie. She felt helpless and just sat waiting for what seemed like an eternity until the door to the waiting room opened and the Doctor walked in.

He had a sombre expression on his face and tears in his eyes. Struggling to find the right words, his voice heavy with emotion, he said, 'My dear I have bad news and extraordinary news,'

Isabel got to her feet unsteadily and reached out to the Doctor's outstretched hands.

'Is it the babies?' she asked, an anxious expression on her face.

'No my dear, they are well although there are some complications.' Hesitating he added, 'I'm afraid we have lost Sophie. We don't know why, it was as if she just gave up after the twins were delivered.' He paused as Isabel began to sob.

Isabel sat back down on the sofa, her head in her hands. 'Poor Sophie, she loved Freddie so much, they were soul mates. When she heard the news of his death, she just collapsed as if her world had fallen apart.'

Sitting quietly with tears in her eyes she looked up at the Doctor. 'You said extraordinary news.'

'The other news is that the twins appear to be fine but are co-joined at the head. It is only a small area so we have no idea yet how serious it may be.'

Isabel looked up in alarm. 'Co-joined. Oh, my goodness.' 'We have a specialist team arriving tomorrow morning and your Grandchildren, a boy and a girl, will be transferred to a specialist hospital in London.'

Isabel wiped away her tears as she tried to compose herself. The Doctor then took a deep breath and continued. 'There is also one other surprise which I will let you see for yourself.'

He stood up and lead Isabel from the waiting room.

'We believe that what you are about to see may be the first time it has ever been witnessed in this country and possibly the world,' he said as he led her to the ICU.

In the ICU a group of nurses in protective clothing and masks were gathered around an incubator. There was an air of excitement as the Doctor and Isabel arrived. Standing behind the glass partition, the Doctor gently taped on the screen which attracted the attention of a Senior Sister in a dark blue uniform. She turned, acknowledged the Doctor, and then spoke to the nurses who then left the area. With a big smile on her face, the Sister wheeled the incubator over to the glass partition.

The twins were lying side by side with just their heads touching. Isabel gasped in shock as she saw them for the first time. 'I can't believe it, is this possible?'

'Seeing is believing my dear, co-joined at the head but nothing too serious. We believe they may be sharing a small part of their brain but there are some wonderful specialist surgeons who I'm sure will be able to successfully separate them. It will mean they will be in intensive care for several months.'

'Yes, I can appreciate that but it is the other difference which is extraordinary. One with a blue ribbon around his wrist is the colour of Sophie, a beautiful light olive colour and the other with a pink ribbon around her wrist is the colour of my son, white.'

'That, my dear is possibly a first, co-joined twins of a different colour.'

Looking at Isabel as she stared in wonder at the twins, he gently asked, 'Have you decided what to do? Will you be putting them up for adoption or ...'

Isabel looked up sharply at the Doctor. 'There is no question. They are my flesh and blood. I would not dream of letting anyone else bring them up. I have a comfortable home and am financially secure, and once they have been separated, I can give them all the love in the world. They are so beautiful and I can already feel that I love them with all my heart and soul,' the tears running down her face.

She looked once again at the twins, smiling through her tears. 'Thank you so much for all you have done Doctor. Now I must organise two funerals and prepare my home for the two new arrivals.'

Chapter 5

HE REFUGE, the sign over the door to the Thatched Cottage swung lazily in the light Autumn breeze. Isabel, dressed in what she called her "comfy clothes", loose fitting jeans, comfortable walking shoes, a cloth cap and her favourite Berghaus jacket. She glanced as always at the sign and smiled. She and her late husband, Ernie, had named it after purchasing the cottage nearly 15 years ago as a weekend refuge from their busy lives running a small but successful Art Gallery in London. Now, on the edge of the New Forest, 'The Refuge' was the home for Isabel and the twins.

She opened the heavy oak panelled door, quickly turned off the alarm before carrying in two heavy bags full of shopping, and with an expertly well-practised backward kick allowed it to close with a satisfying clunk.

She stood for a moment, relishing the smells which seemed to vary every time she arrived home. Today it was the smell of paint from her studio after she had finished her latest oil painting of the cottage mixed with the remnants of the twins' attempts at cooking; burnt toast and overcooked bacon. She smiled and walked down the carpeted hallway and glanced occasionally at the various pictures on the wall.

She stopped as always at the photo of Ernie, beautifully framed in silver to match the colour of his hair. She missed him so much and regretted that he had never met the twins. How he would have loved them. Both are so different. Francesca is pretty, clever and smart. David is athletic, energetic and full of playful mischievousness. How could it possibly have been 7 years since they came to stay?

The operation to separate them was heralded as a great success. Fortunately, all the excitement the event had created in the media had now been forgotten and the twins were accepted in society without any fuss or favouritism.

Isabel walked into the kitchen, recently modernised and the hub of the home. A central breakfast bar with stools which could be raised or lowered was next to the bar. One slightly lower than the other, neatly stowed under the counter. The other was higher and casually pushed aside as if discarded in a hurry. 'Sums up the twins' she thought. She repositioned the stool and glanced at that side of the breakfast bar, untidy with crumbs and utensils left on the bar. The other side is clean and tidy. 'So different, but inseparable,' she thought as she smiled to herself.

She placed the shopping on the Corian work surface and started to put the contents into the large double fridge freezer unit. Once finished she began preparing ingredients for their evening meal, Chicken Curry, the twin's favourite when the phone rang. She moved to the hallway where her landline phone was, frowning slightly as calls to that number were rare.

She answered the phone warily, having heard about all the scam calls that were prevalent at the moment.

'Good afternoon, Mrs Fordham speaking,' she said prepared to put the phone down if she thought it was a scam call.

The voice on the other end of the phone was female, polite, and well-spoken. 'Good afternoon Mrs Fordham, I'm sorry to bother you but this is Miss Driscoll, the twin's teacher.'

Slightly agitated, Isabel's first response was automatic. 'Are they OK?'

'Yes, please don't worry, I'm sure it's nothing serious but we have had a disturbance in the classroom which the twins seem to be at the centre of.'

'Well, I must admit to being somewhat surprised. I know the twins are not perfect, just full of life but really can't imagine them causing a disturbance,' said Isabel sounding slightly more defensive than she had intended.

'I was hoping you could come over to the school so we can discuss it. Are you available now?'

Isabel nodded to herself. 'If you don't mind waiting, I can be there in about 20 minutes. I assume the twins are with you?' 'Yes, they are sitting here quietly. Thank you, see you shortly.'

The phone went dead and Isabel returned it to the cradle. Feeling a little worried she made her way back to the kitchen catching a glance at herself as she walked past the large mirror in the hallway.

'Maybe I should smarten up a bit. Ditch the old hat, brush the hair and god forbid put some make-up on.'. The face that stared back at her was complex. Not pretty but attractive, not eye turning but always gained a second look, strong yet compassionate and those green eyes, almost hypnotic.

Back in the kitchen she quickly finished off the last of the preparations for their evening meal and then climbed the staircase to her bedroom. The room was one of her favourite places in the cottage. Attractively decorated in a soft purple with contrasting curtains and her favourite pictures painted by herself, hung on the walls which gave the room a warm and inviting look. But most of all those wonderful memories of the fun she and Ernie had shared.

Shaking her head to stop the daydreaming she made her way into the en-suite. The luxurious wavy brown hair, just combed, she put on the minimum of makeup, a light brushing of mascara, a touch of lipstick and a spray of her favourite perfume. A last glance in the mirror which made sure she looked presentable, she returned to the kitchen collected her bag and car keys then set the alarm before she left the house with thoughts of what problems lay ahead.

Chapter 6

Isabel arrived at the school and approached the chaos of dozens of parents and children in what appeared to be a reunion of long-separated families. Children and parents hugged and kissed and the younger ones regaled the day's activities. Isabel waited by the entrance impatiently for cars to leave and for a parking place to become vacant. Eventually one appeared and she expertly manoeuvred into the space. Switching off the engine and quickly unbuckling her seat belt she excited the car making her way through the tsunami of children who hurried out of the school's grounds. Isabel eventually arrived at the entrance doors, the oncoming tide seemed to have suddenly vanished which left a quiet and empty corridor miraculously appear ahead of her.

Hurrying down the corridor she ignored the numerous pictures drawn by a variety of age groups and considered to be the best of their class. Above all these were pictures of the Governors and below them the schoolteachers. Amongst them is Miss Driscoll. A rather stern-looking-middle age woman head of year 2. Isabel had never met the teacher but had heard that she was a no-nonsense woman, unmarried who lived with her invalid mother.

***

Finding the classroom at the far end of the corridor, Isabel took a deep breath, knocked gently on the door and walked in. Sitting in seats behind their desks were the twins. Francesca was smart in her uniform, purple jacket edged in green over a clean white shirt and neatly tied tie. She looked upset. Next to her sat David, similarly dressed but with his tie loosened from his neck. He looked relaxed.

Miss Driscoll stood as Isabel entered the room, holding out her hand in greeting. 'Thank you so much for coming Mrs Fordham.'

'Isabel please, much less formal.'

'Agreed, I'm Clarissa although I hope the twins can keep that secret from the class,' she added with a genuine smile on her face.

Isabel returned the smile warming to the teacher. 'I'm sure the twins will be discrete.'

She sat down next to Francesca and gave her a cuddle which bought a tear to the young girl's eyes. 'I'm so sorry Gran I didn't think we were doing anything wrong.'

Isabel looked over at Davy. 'Hi Gran, like Fran said we didn't think we were doing anything wrong, just having some fun. I'm sorry.'

'Well this is intriguing,' Isabel said, turning to Clarissa.

'Let me explain,' said Clarissa as she stood up and made her way to sit by Isabel. 'The twins have somehow come up with a game whereby Francesca thinks of an item, like a doubledecker bus, whispers it to her friends and then Davy who is sitting across the other side of the classroom, guesses it.

She paused and looked at the twins. Francesca was still tearful while Davy remained impassive.

Continuing she said, 'The trouble was that even during lessons the other children would whisper items to Francesca and Davy would write the answer down on a notepad and show the class. It created a great deal of laughter.'

'May I ask, apart from this tomfoolery, have the twin's behaviour and their progress has been acceptable?'

'Beyond question. I must admit that David is at the centre of any action going on in the playground even amongst the older boys. He seems to be the one the others turn to for games and leadership. Academically,' she paused, 'well, he is average. However, that cannot be said about Francesca. She is well above her age group. Highly intelligent, resourceful and an absolute pleasure to have in my class.'

Isabel looked at the twins. 'Please leave this with me. I can assure you that however the trick is played, I'm sure I can persuade my very cheeky Grandson to reveal all. I will be in touch.'

Both Clarissa and Isabel stood and shook hands. 'Thank you so much, Isabel. It's been a pleasure to meet you.'

'Likewise,' said Isabel as she led the twins out of the classroom.

Together they made their way back to the car, both twins looking sheepishly at one another.

Chapter 7

The drive home was in silence as the twins sat in the back seats. Davy looked casually out of the window, while Francesca sat head bowed. Once back inside the cottage the twins went to their bedrooms, changed out of their school clothes, and made their way to the kitchen. Isabel made them a cold drink and then took some fruit scones out of a cake tin. Cutting them in half she spread strawberry jam on them before putting them in front of the subdued twins.

They all sat quietly at the table, Isabel waiting for them both to explain. Eventually, she said,' OK I'm sure there is an explanation for what happened so who would like to start?'

The Twins looked at one another.

Davy smiled at Francesca, 'Gran I don't know what we have done wrong. Surely, we are like all sets of twins. I can sometimes know exactly what Fran is thinking. It mostly seems to work me to her and occasionally the other way round but if she is ever worried or needs help I just seem to know.'

'That's right Gran, I'm sure all twins can do the same. We were only having some fun, there is no trickery.'

Isabel looked at them both. 'I'm a little confused. Twins do not normally have a connection as you suggest. I have heard that occasionally they may think the same thing at the same time but are not able to communicate as you have just said. Are you sure there is no trick to this?'

'Honestly Gran,' the twins said together. 'Let us prove it,' said Francesca, 'If you get a pack of playing cards Gran, then we will show you.'

Isabel left the kitchen and made her way to the study at the end of the hallway. The room was old-fashioned with wooden beams across the ceiling and oak panelling as part of the decoration on the walls. A beautiful mahogany desk with a roll top and inlaid desktop was positioned near an old-fashioned log fireplace. The room, a favourite of her late husband's, had seldom been used since his passing. She opened a small drawer at the side of the desk taking out the well-worn pack of cards. Next to it was a homemade crib board and a small notebook with a worn-down pencil. Unexpectedly her emotions overcame her and Isabel started to reminisce. 'So many fun games,' she said to herself as she picked up the notebook looking through the pages of scores under her headings Piggy and Piglet. These were the nicknames they had given each other after a visit to a farm during their honeymoon. The memories came flooding back, tears welled up in her eyes. Her Ernie was such a wonderful man. Not handsome, rather short and ordinary looking but such charisma. A man who could

41

listen, understand, and seem to make the world seem like a better place when he spoke. No temper, no side, just normal but exceptional in his own way. She stood looking down at the cards when she heard a movement behind her. 'Are you OK Gran, you have been in here for ages and you have tears in your eyes?' Francesca said as she walked into the room.

Wiping her eyes and picking up the cards, Isabel hugged Francesca. 'Yes, I'm OK darling, just a flood of memories when I saw the old crib board.'

'I remember you telling us about the games you played with Grandad and how he usually won.'

'Yes, but of course I let him,' she laughed.

'Of course, Gran, boys and men are such wimps, they don't like it if they lose.'

'Well said young Lady. Now let's sort out this so-called telepathy of yours.'

Back in the kitchen, Isabel up the pack of cards and gave them to Francesca.

'Right then Gran, I'm going to pick a card, and show it to you but of course not too old clever clogs over the other side of the table. He will then, in his showy-off way, tell me what the cards are.'

Francesca picked out a card, the 7 of clubs and showed it to Isabel making sure she kept it hidden from her brother.

'OK brother dear what card am I thinking of?' '7 of clubs,' said Davy sounding bored.

Isabel surprised. 'So, what's the trick?'

'As I have said it's not a trick Gran, I just know what Fran is thinking.'

Isabel began to feel the first signs of alarm bells ringing. 'Right, I want you, Davy to go in another room and we will try it again.'

Davy shrugged his shoulders and walked into the study. 'Is this far enough away Gran?' he shouted, laughter in his voice.

'Yes you cheeky monkey,' said Isabel as she picked out a card and showed it to Francesca; the 10 of Diamonds.

'The 10 of Diamonds,' came the shout from the study.

Alarm bells now rang at full volume in her head. Isabel tried to think of an explanation but could see none.

'Now I will try,' she said. Picking out a card but keeping it to herself she waited. 'Nothing,' from the voice in the study.

She called Davy back from the room and the three of them sat for a while in silence.

Isabel shook her head as if in bewilderment. 'This must not, under any circumstances, be allowed to go public. You are to tell your friends at school that it was just a trick that you had come up with between the two of you for some fun. You are not under any circumstances to do this trick again. Is that clear?' 'But why Gran, it doesn't seem to do any harm. We were just having fun,' interrupted Francesca, still not certain what they had done wrong.

'My darlings let me tell you what happened when you were born,' said Isabel as she got up from her seat at the table and walked around the kitchen.

43

'The local press heard the story of twins being born joined together at the head and that they were different colours. The word spread until there were dozens of people from different newspapers crowding around the hospital. Every time I visited you I was besieged by reporters shouting questions at me wanting to know what was happening, what colour skin you were Davy, black, olive or brown.

She sat down beside Francesca, putting her arm around her.

'The questions never stopped. Would they be joined together for life; how would I cope etc? They even tried to follow me home and I had to take different routes each time to try to ensure they didn't find out where I lived. So now imagine if word got out that the famous co-joined twins could read each other's minds.'

She moved over next to Davy and cuddled him. 'There would be no peace. All our lives would be continually monitored by the press. Questions, requests for interviews and even possibly TV shows asking for appearances and proof that you can read each other's minds. Please believe me when I say it would ruin our lives.'

'Wow, Gran we never had any idea that could happen, all from a bit of fun. We are really sorry,' said Francesca.

'You have gone very quiet Davy. Have you any questions?' asked Isabel.

'Just one Gran, what does besiege mean?'

There is a moment of silence before all three burst into laughter.

***

Isabel's studio was situated at the southern end of the house guaranteeing a plentiful supply of heat and light for most of the year through the large sliding French windows. It overlooked a spacious garden of well-stocked borders surrounding a wellmanicured and lush-looking lawn. At the centre, a small fountain driven by solar cells guaranteed a cost-free energy source. The studio was her sanctuary. A place where she could escape the stresses of bringing up the twins singlehanded at her age. Not that they were any trouble she thought, just wonderful children demanding a great deal of her time.

She shivered slightly as the sun began to set and its warmth gradually subside. Still light enough she continued putting the finishing touches to a landscape that she had been working on for several weeks.

Putting her brushes down in frustration knowing that the picture was lacking any depth or character. Since the bombshell of the twin's telepathic connection, she had found it difficult to concentrate on any meaningful task, concerned that the story would somehow come to light.

Isabel got up from her painting, made her way to the phone in the hall and searched through her personnel directory until she found the number she had been looking for. After dialling, she heard the call go through to a receptionist who transferred her to the Surgeon who had separated the twins, years before.

'Mr Clifton speaking, is that Isabel?'

'Yes, how are you?' said Isabel, concerned that she might be overreacting to what she was about to request.

'Extremely well, and you and the twins?' 'We are all very well, thank you.'

'So how can I help?'

'There has been a development with the twins that I would like to discuss with you. I was hoping I could bring them up to London.'

'If I'm not mistaken, they are due their annual review in a few months so let's bring it forward. I will get my secretary to arrange a date and get back to you. Look forward to seeing you all soon.'

'Many thanks,' said Isabel.

Putting down the phone she said, thinking aloud, 'I do hope Mr Clifton has an explanation. If he hasn't and the twin's telepathy is permanent, I can see a great many problems ahead.'

Chapter 8

The twins were excited when they heard about their trip to London. Although knowing they would be in for a few boring hours as the team of specialists looked them over and carried out what they regarded as childish tests; looking at funny shapes and describing them, memorising names and numbers and co-ordination exercises. Once that was over they knew the fun would begin; a trip to the London Zoo followed by a visit to Madam Tussauds, a meal in China town and then a sleepy train journey home. But first, the Black Cab journey to Whitechapel from Paddington Station and to what Francesca described as the inquisition much to Davy's annoyance as he had no idea what it meant but decided to play along as he nodded in agreement.

'You don't know what it means, do you?' teased Francesca.

'I do,' replied Davy looking away and thinking rapidly, 'it means to grill something.' 'Like what?'

'I don't know, a sausage or something.'

Francesca burst out laughing. 'Funnily enough my dear brother you are partly right. An Inquisition is a form of grilling, not of sausages but of people. Asking questions.'

'I knew that, I was just being funny.'

'Of course, you were,' said Francesca with a grin.

Isabel smiled to herself over their banter, thinking that this journey may be a waste of time. The twins were so normal in every way and apart from this so-called telepathic connection, were just great youngsters with very bright futures in front of them.

When they reached the hospital, Isabel paid off the taxi and the family made their way to the reception area. Behind the desk, an elderly, white-haired lady smiled in greeting and confirmed their appointment then directed them to the waiting area for the Neurological department. Isabel felt slightly tense. Although this was an annual visit to ensure the twin's progress was on track after the invasive surgery to separate them, the worries of the telepathic connection between them and the possible media frenzy, should their secret get out, played heavily on her mind.

She was brought out of her trance by a sister calling her name.

'Mrs Fordham.'

'Here,' she answered rather hastily, possibly portraying her anxiety. 'Calm down,' she said to herself as the three made their way following the nurse to the surgeon's office.

'How lovely to see you all again,' came a warm friendly greeting from Mr Clifton. Shaking hands and pointing towards three comfortable chairs. 'Please all take a seat.'

'Thank you and also for seeing us so promptly,' said Isabel.

'Not at all. Our star patients must be given some priority.

Now, before we go through the usual tests you said you have some concerns over a personal matter concerning them.'

Taking a deep breath, Isabel explained the telepathic connection between the twins. 'May we give you a practical demonstration?'

'Of course,' said Mr Clifton sounding intrigued.

Taking a small notepad and pencil from her bag Isabel asked the surgeon to write down any number.

'Does it matter how long?' he asked.

'No, and it doesn't have to be a number. A word, an animal, anything as long as it's pretty simple for my brother's sake,' Francesca interjected, which caused them all to laugh, apart from Davy, who just glared at his sister.

'OK,' said the surgeon writing down a six-figure number, 438925, then handed it to Francesca who had her back to Davy.

'438925,' said Davy almost immediately.

'One more try,' said the surgeon, this time writing down the first line of Ba ba black-sheep.

As soon as the piece of paper was given to Francesca and she looked at it, Davy answered.

'How extraordinary,' the surgeon said as he looked at the twins. 'However, there may be an explanation and one that I hope will alleviate your concerns over this becoming an issue if news got out.'

Going to a large cabinet situated behind his desk he produced a model of a skull that had the sections of the brain inside, divided into removable parts. Taking one part out he pointed to the frontal portion of the temporal lobe and speaking directly to the twins told them. 'This is where you guys were connected and inside this area is something called the Amygdala. The name comes from the word almond because it has its shape, so let's call them the Almonds.'

The twins stared in fascination at the model as Davy gently rubbed the area of the operation site, 'Seems so unreal,' he said.

'It does. Interestingly, you have two, one on either side of your head next to the places where you were both joined. So basically they could talk to one another.'

He paused and smiled at the twins. 'These almonds are essential to your ability to feel certain emotions and to perceive them in other people.' Getting out a sketch pad and pen he drew a simple diagram of the area. Pointing to the sketch he said, 'These little devils are also important if you are ever frightened as it will trigger a response, like make your heart race.'

'That's incredible,' interjected Francesca. 'I haven't mentioned this before, but I was once being harassed at school by some moron and out of nowhere came Davy.'

'I just knew there was a problem. I assumed it was normal for twins and never thought any more of it,' said Davy.

'So that was the almond triggering a response in Francesca and somehow Davy felt it. The explanation could be that when we separated you some of the billions of nerve cells could somehow have been transferred between the two of you.'

'Why is it that it seems to be mostly one way? Davy can feel Francesca's emotions but not the other way round,' asked Isabel.

'That's not quite right Gran. I can if I concentrate. Sometimes I can get some form of message to Davy, but it doesn't happen often. Probably because his brain is filled with nonsense anyway,' she laughed Davy gave her a lopsided grin.

'It could have been that the nerve endings were closer to Davy than Francesca and gave a stronger response but although this is a very unusual occurrence, the good news is that I believe this to be only a temporary one.'

He picked up the skull and returned it to the cabinet. Continuing he said, 'As you both grow and get into puberty, your hormone balance will begin to overcome this problem, I feel sure.'

Isabel looked relieved. 'I was concerned that we might have to face the rigours of the press, like before, if this news got out.'

The surgeon smiled. 'I suggest until this extraordinary gift they have corrects itself, discretion would be advisable.' He dialled a number on his phone and the sister who escorted them in entered the room.

'I have everything ready for the tests,' she said. The twins stood and both extended their hands to the surgeon. 'Thank you,' they both said in unison, laughing as they left the room. 'Thank you so much, Mr Clifton,' said Isabel sounding relieved. 'It is a relief to know that in a few years, they will both be truly normal.'

'I feel confident that will be the case,' said the surgeon as he extended his hand. 'I will look through the test results and if all is OK, I won't bother you. Safe journey home.'

Chapter 9

Isabel sat at her easel and completed the picture of the landscape she had been painting, content that she had finally captured the true character of the setting. The relief of hearing that the twins should be OK in a few years had been reassuring and allowed her to regain her old self-confidence. She just had to hope that before then, no instance occurred that would highlight the twin's special gift. She was about to be disappointed.

***

The semi-detached house in a smart leafy neighbourhood was like many others in the street. The small front garden had a short, tarmacked drive which led out to the main road. To one side a square lawn with a few flowering plants and the odd child's toy left abandoned as if in a hurry which was normally the case for the Foster family.

Despite all her efforts Rose Foster seemed to always be behind the preverbal drag curve mainly because her husband, Reginald, was old school; 'a woman's place is in the home and housework is her calling,' he would often be heard regaling to colleagues. But with two young children and no help from him, Rose, a person who had drifted into a soulless marriage, struggled. Attractive with an hourglass figure that she worked hard to maintain she was, however, not the motherly type.

Her only interest seemed to be in getting her two young children out of the house and to school as soon as she could. A coffee morning with friends and then a visit to the local spa and the gym were on her agenda and the sooner Reginald and the children were out of her hair the better.

'Reg, for the third time, your breakfast is on the table and you're running late,' she shouted up the stairs.

'Mum,' came a winning voice from Matthew her 6-yearold, 'these cereals aren't making the same crackling noise as yesterday.'

'Just eat them, they are exactly the same as the ones from the box you opened yesterday and Tammy, "her-5 yearold", will you please hurry up and finish yours.'

She turned as a man, red in the face and showing a wellrounded paunch hurried down the stairs. 'No time for breakfast must rush.' he said breathlessly.

'Might be a good idea if you removed the shaving cream from around your ear.'

Reg quickly wiped away the cream, grabbed a warmish cup of coffee, took a quick gulp and hurried out of the door.

'Love you too,' said Rose under her breath.

Reg struggled to fit his paunch behind the steering wheel, then cursed when his mobile rang. Recognising his boss's number, he cursed again under his breath as he searched vainly for the end of the seat belt, eventually managing to retrieve it. He took in a deep breath, fastened it and then as calmly as he could, answered his phone. 'Hi Sir,' he grimaced when he heard the angry voice of the CEO on the other end of the phone berating him for not being at the meeting which had already started.

'Look I'm sorry, the traffic has been dreadful. I will be there in about 15 minutes. Please apologise to our clients...' Before he could add any more lies to the tale, the line went dead.

'Bugger,' he exclaimed in frustration feeling a wave of breathlessness overcome him. Slamming the gears into drive, he accelerated quickly out of the drive, narrowly missing the small wall, marking the boundary of his property.

***

David was walking with friends along a pathway paralleling a main road. Ahead of them by some distance was Francesca with her friends.

She was holding forth telling a story about her chemistry teacher. 'He was such a numpty. During the experiment he was meant to say it smelt like a whiff of tarts, instead, he said it smelt like a whiff of farts. Honestly, we all just collapsed in laughter.'

As they approached a junction she stopped as she heard Davy's voice shout out, 'Fran stop.'

She turned around seeing Davy a hundred yards behind. He waved to her, gesturing for her to come back to him. 'Hold on girls, must see what brother dear wants.'

The other girls stopped except for one, Rachael. 'I'm not waiting, see you in class,' she said as she carried on.

In his car, Reg was breathing with difficulty. He suddenly clutched his chest and tried desperately to control the car. As he slumped forward his foot pushed on the accelerator pedal and the car veered across the road. His last vision was of a young girl's terrified look on her face as his car hit her sending her over the bonnet and onto the path. The car bounced off of a small garden wall and stopped with its bonnet embedded into an elm tree which shuddered under the impact but remained stoical.

As Francesca and her friends rushed forward, the scene that met them stunned them into silence and shock. The car alarm blared loudly, and steam came from under the bonnet. Rachael was slumped on the ground with blood coming from her mouth but having no signs of life.

A young woman ran from the other side of the junction and quickly took charge. 'I'm a nurse, please stand back.'

She went to Rachael and felt for her pulse. 'She is still alive, someone call an ambulance but nobody move her.'

Davy was running to the scene. Without stopping he took out his phone and dialled Treble 9 requesting an ambulance giving details of the location. 'Ambulance on its way, should be here in a few minutes,' he shouted to the nurse as he arrived.

Pushing his way through the shocked pupils he went straight to Rachael. Speaking quietly, he bent down next to her giving her words of encouragement as he gently held her hand. 'Hang in there Rachael, help will be here in a few minutes. You will be fine.'

She opened her eyes and seeing Davy there tried to smile but grimaced as pain from her fractured ribs shot through her body. 'Is my face damaged?'

'No you are still, what should I say,' he said smiling, 'a real corker.'

He felt her squeeze his hand, 'I should have listened to you.' The nurse went to the driver's side of the car and switched off the engine. She checked Reg's pulse. 'I'm afraid he is dead,' she said quietly.

Sirens could be heard in the distance, and as they rapidly approached the scene changed as fire crews and ambulance paramedics took over. They moved Davy aside as they carefully attached a neck brace to Rachael and gently lifted her onto a Gurney.

Moving away from her, Davy glanced up at Francesca who was staring at him with concern on her face. She mouthed the words, 'How did you know?'

He shook his head as he put his index finger to his mouth to silence her.

***

Back at the cottage Isabel sat in mesmerised silence as the twins recounted the events of the day.

'Apparently, Rachael, although badly injured and in intensive care, will pull through but it may take over 6 months before she is fully recovered,' explained Francesca.

'But we have to ask the question. Was this just a coincidence or did you, Davy, have some feeling that something was about to take place?' queried Isabel.

The two women looked at Davy as he struggled to answer. 'I just had this overwhelming feeling that made me tell Fran to stop. It was as if I were some form of Guardian. Sounds unbelievable but that's how it happened. If only Rachael would have stopped as well, she would have been OK.'

'Agreed, but more importantly, if Fran and her friends had ignored you, this could have been a far worse tragedy,' said Isabel taking a sip of her tea. 'What are your friends saying about you stopping.?'

'They put it down to an amazing coincidence. There was more chatter about how Davy rushed to the scene and comforted Rachael. He was heroic,' added Francesca.

'Well done Davy,' said Isabel as she touched Davy on the shoulder. 'Can I ask you though, do you get these feelings often?'

'Not often Gran but when I do, the feeling is so overwhelming I have to take action.'

'Well, let's hope you don't have to take action too often!'

Chapter 10

At home in the kitchen, Isabel and Francesca had just finished their coffee when they heard a distinctive clattering as the noise from a pair of football studs on the slate-tiled floor could be heard approaching. Davy walked in. His bright red and yellow football jersey and yellow socks made Francesca stifle a laugh.

'Are you sure you don't want to come shopping with us brother dear instead of playing that stupid game where you kick a bag of wind around trying unsuccessfully to put it between two posts and into a net,' teased Francesca.

'No, but thanks for the invite sis,' he answered going over to the fridge to take out a bottle of sports aid drink. 'And as you well know my team could not possibly do without their star player,' he added, taking off the top of the bottle and having a large noisy gulp.

He grinned at the two women and then gave a satisfying, cheeky burp. 'And as this is an important match I will have to be at my very best, which for me isn't very difficult,' he said giving the ladies a wink. 'You go and enjoy yourselves and think of me sweating it out on the pitch for the honour of the school.'

Isabel coughed as her coffee went down the wrong way. Laughing she said, 'I'm sure we will spend most of our time walking from shop-to-shop thinking of nothing but you on that football field,' giving him a returned wink. 'Right young lady, let's go and have some fun.'

***

Rushing along the platform, carrying the afternoon spoils, Isabel and Francesca just managed to board the train when the whistle was blown for departure. Making their way through the carriage, occasionally making apologies to the passengers as their packages took their toll on elbows and feet in the passageways, they eventually found their seats. The other passengers looked up and smiled as the two, panting slightly, sat down. The small commuter train eased its way out of the station on the double track to follow the coastal route to the main station.

The view from their seats was boring, to say the least, just a rock face flashing by while the other side of the carriage had a view through passing trees over rolling fields to the sea. Not that either Isabel or Francesca was too concerned. Four hours of shopping together with an occasional coffee stop visit and a favourite meal of fish and chips had left them both sleepy. Although the journey was just under the hour, the gentle rhythm of the train over the gaps in the track, together with the slight sway had them both asleep within minutes.

***

Several miles ahead and on top of the cliff face, above the railway track, three youths were engaged in a game of dare. The leader of the group, a skinny lad with jet-black unkempt hair and a bad case of acne which dominated his face, was a bully. He relished in the title he had given himself of "Governor." Daring each of the others, in turn, to move as close to the edge of the cliff as possible, he taunted the youngest of the group, a pale-faced ginger-haired lad who feared heights to, "show some bottle."

The young lad teetered on the edge before being violently sick, throwing himself to the safety of the ground. The other two laughed calling him a variety of derogatory names. Plucking up the courage and with snot running down his face, mixed with the tears of humiliation, he shouted back at the Governor challenging him to, 'show some bottle'. The self-elected governor gave the youngster a quick kick in the ribs, then sauntered towards the edge and, displaying more confidence than he felt, peered over the edge.

Several hundred feet below he saw the Rail-track and felt the first waves of nausea. He wavered and began to lose his balance. Turning back he moved away from the edge but as he did his left foot slipped. As he felt himself begin to fall he clutched at thin air crying out

61

desperately. The other two rushed over and grabbed his flailing arms and pulled him back as best they could. As he struggled to regain his balance, his foot settled on a large boulder buried in the rock face just below the cliff edge. He used this as a foothold to push himself up, along with the help of his gang and reached the safety of the solid ground.

The boulder that had saved the governor's life had not moved in several hundreds of years. But nature has a rule: action and reaction. It was the reaction that moved the boulder. Initially, it moved just a few inches but in doing so loosened other smaller rocks that had been its companion and now allowed the rock to break free. To begin with, its movement was slow but as gravity took charge, its downward journey accelerated and gathered other rocks on its way.

Engineers many years before had anticipated the small chance of a minor landslip and had fastened netting along the base of the rock face to protect the track. They had fixed the netting with large bolts drilled into the rock at regular intervals. Most were well embedded, but some protruded out a few inches. It was just one of these bolts that the rock hit. Instead of being captured by the netting the rock bounced off the bolt, hit the rail track and shattered into several pieces. Although individually they would not have caused a great deal of a problem, together they created a major obstacle capable of derailing a train.

Chapter 11

The football game had proved to be a disaster. Already two nil down and the first half still not over, Davy thought it was the game from hell. His teammates kept berating him as he missed opportunity after opportunity, tackle after tackle and even a penalty. He shook his head trying to clear his mind of the nagging feeling that seemed to dominate his thoughts. The half-time whistle was blown and as the players walked off the pitch, the coach, a no-nonsense bull of a man shouted at Davy, 'Buck your ideas up kid or you're off.'

In the changing room, Davy sat by himself, and the nagging feeling grew stronger. As the coach started to give a team talk, Davy suddenly got up and moved quickly to his locker. Grabbing his phone, he dialled Francesca's number.

A voice shouted from inside the changing room. 'If you don't join us now Fordham, you're off the team.'

***

In the train carriage, Francesca was jolted awake by her phone ringing. Shaking her head to wake herself up she glanced at the screen and saw Davy's number come up. Answering she said, 'I suppose you want to know what we are...'

'Just listen Sis,' Davy interrupted, 'stop the train.'

'Say that again, I thought you just said stop the train,' said Francesca suddenly realising that several occupants of the carriage were now staring at her. 'Don't be daft, I can't do that.'

'Get Gran on the phone now,' shouted Davy, loud enough for the occupants of the cartridge to hear and to wake Isabel.

'What's going on?' said Isabel sleepily.' 'It's Davy... '

'Somebody wants her to stop the train, bloody idiot,' shouted a slightly inebriated young man slurping from a can of beer.

Francesca handed her phone to Isabel. 'What's this all about Davy?' said Isabel as she put her hand over the phone to try to stop her conversation from being heard.

'Gran, just pull the communication chord, you need to stop the train now.' Davy's voice sounded stressed and worried. Isabel hesitated. 'Now gran,' shouted Davy.

Isabel looked for the chord spotting it over the other side of the carriage. She moved across to be confronted by the man taking a quick swill from his can.

'Not a chance old girl, you ain't stopping this fucking train....' he doubled up as Isabel's knee found its way into his groin.

'Don't swear at me young man,' she said as she stepped over him now bent up and in agony.

The other passengers stared at her in awe as she grabbed the communication chord, took a deep breath and pulled it.

In the train cab, Nigel Grayson was feeling relaxed. He had been a train driver, mainly on this route, for over 3 years. He loved his job and apart from youngsters occasionally messing around with the communication chord, the job was safe, reasonably well paid and had hours that suited him. Being a Friday meant he and the misses would later be at the local working men's club, a few beers, good nosh, a bit of karaoke and then back for what he hoped would be the icing on the cake.

His thoughts were shattered when the alarm light and bell, signalling that the communication cord had been pulled, flashed on his control console. 'Bloody kids, that's the third time in three weeks,' thoughts of his Friday evening being ruined flashed through his mind. He quickly and expertly cancelled the automatic braking before they had time to lock and took control manually. He cursed as he began to gently slow down the train. 'All that paperwork possibly interviews with the police, angry passengers and of course the inevitable delay getting home,' he thought to himself.

As the train rounded a bend, he had started to gently apply pressure aware of the chaos he would cause if he used it fully. Passengers and luggage falling all over the carriages, possible injuries and drinks spilt; the mess he would have to clean up and then of course all the possible claims for injury.

He looked up from his console and froze. Ahead was the rockfall. He slammed on the brake fully and started to pray. The train was still doing over 30 mph and was less than 100 metres from the rocks. He knew that if they hit them at any speed above a crawl that there was a very strong possibility of a derailment. The metal wheels screeched in protest as they slid on the rails.

In the carriages there was chaos. Those facing forward were catapulted onto those facing the rear. One old lady ended up in the lap of a young, good-looking man, who held onto her as the train started to slow. She smiled at him thinking how fortunate she was. The man drinking the beer, having just recovered from his groin problem, had been standing in the aisle and was thrown the length of it ending up in a heap by the toilet door.

Isabel managed to hold onto the communication chord which had stopped her falling but that had now broken free. She stood there, as the train slowed, holding it feeling very self-conscious.

In the cab, Nigel's prayers were answered as the train crushed the first of the rocks and moved a few others aside before coming to a halt.

Once the train had stopped and the passengers started to recover from the shock, the repercussions began.

A large black lady, brushed herself down having had a cup of coffee spilt over her, raised herself to her full height and rounded on Isabel. 'What the bloody hell were you doing. Some crackpot tells you to pull the emergency chord and you, like a soft pussy do....'

As she spoke, Nigel came through the adjoining doors looking flushed. He scanned the carriage seeing Isabel standing still holding the chord in her hand.

'Now we'll see some action. Going to get what you deserve bitch,' said the black woman.

'Not so fast Madam,' interjected Nigel. He went over to Isabel and took the chord out of her hand. 'I assume you were responsible for stopping my train.'

Isabel smiled sweetly, 'Guilty.'

'Yea, the stupid cow had a phone call from the God almighty telling her to pull the bloody chord,' shouted an old man rubbing his sore knee that he had caught on the edge of a seat as he fell.

'Calm down folks. This lady has just saved us from a potential derailment and I for one would like to understand how the hell she knew there was a rock fall on the track and stopped the train just before we hit it,' said Nigel looking around the carriage.

There are gasps from the passengers. 'I'm not joking folks, We were within a few feet of hitting them. So Lady, how the hell did you know to stop the train?'

Francesca came to Isabel's side taking her hand. 'I was the one that took the call from my brother. Apparently, he was out for a walk close to the track and saw the rocks on the line. He knew we were on the train so rang me to warn us.'

There was stunned silence as the news was absorbed. The old lady, now recovered from her encounter with the young man, stood up and started to clap. Slowly, the whole carriage joined her, many coming up to Isabel and Francesca to congratulate them.

The journey back to the cottage took several hours as clearing the debris from the track and ensuring the way ahead was clear and safe was a slow process. Not much was said as both Isabel and Francesca had decided that total discretion would be prudent and despite the many questions fired at them by the grateful passengers, they gave little away.

***

When they arrived back at the cottage Davy was waiting for them in the kitchen. Looking worried and keen to know what had happened as he had not heard from either of them since the incident.

'Why didn't you tell me what had happened?' he asked in frustration.

Isabel went over to him and hugged him, 'Hello to you too,' she said as she ruffled his hair. 'Circumstances were a little difficult as you can imagine, and we decided to keep our talking to a minimum to make sure there were no misunderstandings.' She filled the kettle up and prepared to make tea for them all. 'Let's have a cup of tea with chocolate biscuits and take it into the lounge and go over all that had happened.'

The lounge in the cottage was not a place they used very often. The twins had their own televisions and computers in their bedrooms and most conversations were held around the kitchen table at mealtimes. Almost the length of the cottage, the lounge was an impressive room. The grasscloth wallpaper, lightly embossed and patterned with thin goldcoloured branches on a light-coloured background covered one entire wall while the other three walls had expanded vinyl, lightly textured in a soft oatmeal colour. The overall effect was one of peace and tranquillity.

Alongside one wall was a large gas fire with a coal effect facial inset into a marble fireplace which had a selection of maruri doves and family photos on it. Surrounding the fireplace was a 3 seater sofa in grey leather and two large single armchairs to match. One entire end of the lounge was taken up by a mahogany dining table and 6 matching chairs. At the garden end of the lounge were two sliding doors that led out onto a paved patio.

In the lounge, Isabel sat on the large sofa and the twins in the lounge chairs. Cups of tea in hands, Davy on his second biscuit, all sat in silence for a while. Breaking the silence Davy piped up. 'By the way, we lost the match and I have been dropped from the team so I hope the story I'm about to hear is worth it.'

'Oh, it most certainly is,' said Francesca, 'but first what made you call me?'

Davy took another sip from his tea. 'I had this overwhelming feeling that something was wrong. I couldn't concentrate on the game, missed numerous opportunities to score, basically made complete pigs of everything, then had to walk away from the half-time talk to make the phone call to you.'

'Well, your phone call saved a very nasty incident,' said Isabel as she described what happened.

'So this is a new development,' added Isabel, 'you were nowhere near us, and yet you still had this feeling. Just glad that Fran came up with the reason for the call or we would have had a great deal of explaining to do.'

Sounding concerned Francesca said, 'So what do we do now Gran? If this happens again and the story gets out, we are going to become a laughing stock.'

'Now don't go mad at me but what would you think about going to see Father Jenkins and get some advice,' said Isabel, 'he might be able to think of something.'

'That old fuddy-duddy,' objected Davy, 'his sermons last forever, never get anywhere and have me snoring within 5 minutes.'

'I know you find him a real old bore but he has been a priest for many years,' said Isabel.

'More like centuries,' said Davy causing Francesca to giggle. Isabel smiled. 'There is no harm in trying, we have nothing to lose.'

'No just my sanity,' said Davy, 'we might as well give it a go at least we know he won't go blabbing our story to everyone, they would fall asleep before he got to the punch line.'

Chapter 12

The appointment at the church was early evening and the weather had started its journey from Autumn into Winter with a vengeance. The three pulled their coat collars hard around their necks as the wind channelled into a Venturi between the church and the trees, which pushed against them. As Isabel and the twins made their way up the gravelled footpath to the porch entrance, she reflected on the twins and how well they had developed into their early teenage years.

Francesca was a pleasure as a companion. Intellectual, worldly beyond her years and becoming a young lady who didn't appear to realise the impact she had on the young men at her school. With long honey-blonde hair, sparkling green eyes and pale but unblemished skin, her outward appearance and remarkable calm nature together with a wit and personable character made her an enviable package.

The only problem she had was her limp. Since birth, the displaced hip had never settled and despite attempts by surgeons to correct the slight deformity, none had been successful. Francesca had ignored the occasional hurtful comment from classmates and only really regretted the disability during sports. She found it difficult to run which meant most sports were beyond her ability. Swimming was her one outlet and in this sport, she could compete at a reasonably high level representing the school and could dive as straight as an arrow, much to the delight of her sports-mad brother.

In complete contrast, Davy was a sporting natural. Athletic and possessing excellent coordination skills he found all sports a pleasure, representing the school at the older age group level in football and athletics. Since losing his spot on the football team he had concentrated on track enjoying success at the middle-distance events. Tall for his age with brown eyes and black hair, he had a face that was not particularly handsome but had character. His olive skin had initially caused some caustic comments from some of the older boys which Davy had initially ignored but as the comments became more hurtful he decided to take action. Since the two older bullies had gone home with bloody noses, all comments had ceased.

So as Isabel led the twins into the church she felt proud of the way she had brought them up. Although slightly tentative as to what Father Jenkin would say, she felt no regrets. The three blessed themselves from the sandstone font which had suffered badly over the centuries and then genuflected before the Alter. Making their way up the aisle they passed the wonderful variety of monuments primarily to the initial beneficiaries The 15th-century octagonal carved seated figures under facial canopies with standing figures holding hands seemed to stare at them as they passed.

As they reached the alter to turn towards the office, where Isabel suspected Father Jenkins to be, she glanced up at the 15th-century carved wooden eagle lectern supported by figures of 8 lions. The site together with the ornate figure of Christ on the cross, the light streaming through the decorated stained glass windows along with the silence, gave her a sense of peace that she always felt in this church.

Isabel knocked on the office door and heard the rather gruff voice of Father Jenkins beckoning them in. The family entered the rather stuffy and untidy office, smelling the dampness that had crept through the Barnack stone and was fighting with the small oil heater. Offered seats in well-worn armchairs, they removed their coats and settled down as Father Jenkins, head down, ignored them, scribbling on a notepad. After several minutes he looked up, stared at them and turning to Isabel asked rather aggressively, 'So, what is the problem?'

Isabel was prepared for his intimidating nature. She, like most residents who lived in the neighbourhood and frequented the church, knew of his reputation. A Priest side-lined for his overly wayward views on the sanctity of marriage, abortion, adultery, and any deviation from the chosen path, together with a thirsty appetite for whisky, had led to this backwater.

As he spoke, Davy studied this face. He had not been that close to the Priest before to notice the blemishes on the skin and the numerous small burst blood vessels that centred around his bulbous nose and baggy eyes. But the thing that fascinated Davy most was the hairline.

He stared at it and began to realise that the top dark mop did not match the colour of the fluffs of hair protruding from the side. 'He's wearing a wig,' thought Davy and started to grin.

'We have had a rather unusual event that has happened and would like some advice,' said Isabel.

'Something funny young man,' interjected the priest as he noticed Davy's grin.

'No, sorry Father, just thinking of something funny.'

'This is not a place for humour young man. It is a place of worship, a place of contemplation, reflection and cleansing.'

'Yes Father, I'm sorry,' said Davy stifling a laugh. 'Now Mrs Fordham. Enlighten me.'

Isabel recounted the incident on the train, leaving nothing out and feeling slightly foolish as the story sounded more incredible in the telling. The priest listened, head in his cupped hands elbows resting on the table. He appeared to be half asleep and only seemed to wake up when Isabel stopped talking.

'The answer is simple,' he said forcedly as he stood and walked to a bookshelf. After a quick search and brushing away the dust that had settled on many of the books, withdrew a large red book. Going back to his seat he settled back down and started to rustle through the pages. Mumbling incoherently as he read, he took a quill pen and a small notebook, from a drawer in the desk. He dipped the pen into a small ink well sunken into the desktop. As he wrote, the scratching sound of the pen on the paper seemed to grate on the teeth making the family cringe. Davy stared in amazement, stifling a laugh as he watched the old priest mumbling and scratching away on his notepad.

After what seemed to be a long agonising 5 minutes, the scratching of the pen seemed to get louder and more energetic as the old priest wrote frantically, he suddenly stopped. Getting up he wandered around the office seemingly in a trance. As he glanced down at the notebook he mumbled the words he had written as if practising and rehearsing them.

Suddenly, as if out of a trance he walked quickly to the door. 'Well, come on,' he said in a voice brimming with excitement, 'follow me.'

Walking with exaggerated energy he led the family past the Alter, genuflecting hastily and down the aisle to the Font, the family hurried along behind him. At the Font, he bent down and picked up a small porcelain cup-shaped spoon which he filled with holy water. Raising it high above his head, as if offering it to the gods, he started a slow melodious chant, his voice surprisingly gentle and slightly hypnotic. Gathering impetus, the chant become more intense, higher pitched until a crescendo was reached, the echoing around the church almost deafening.

Suddenly there was silence as the priest stopped. Sweat glistening on his brow, he turned to Davy and without warning slowly emptied the contents of the cup over his head. 'There,' he said joyfully, 'the devil has been expelled from your body, you are cleansed. God bless the Almighty.'

Davy wiped the water from his face, then shook his head sending water drops over Isabel.

'You no longer have to worry,' said the old priest, as he reached out his hands towards Isabel.

Isabel wiped away the odd droplet and looked the old priest directly in the eye.

'Do you really believe a load of rubbish you have just chanted, that your show of unbelievable hypocrisy will have proved effective? We only wanted advice, not some ridiculous exorcism. Francesca, Davy we are leaving now.'

Taking the twins by their hands the three left the church. Davy glanced back to see the old priest in a form of trance, just staring into the font his mouth moving but no sound coming out.

Chapter 13

The first few months in the sixth form of their school showed a major difference between the twins. While Francesca found the work satisfying, rewarding and well within her capabilities, the same could not be said of Davy. He found the step up to A levels a challenge, frustrating and stretching his abilities. So, when his teacher, Miss Forrest, announced that she had decided to give them, what she termed a revisions test, Davy felt a sense of panic. 'Now before you all protest about not having been given any warning,' she said as she looked directly at Davy who swallowed his protest before he could say anything, 'it is just to make sure all of you have mastered the basics to date.' As she stood up from behind her desk at the front of the class, she collected a pile of question papers. Walking around the class she gave one out to each student in turn. Returning to her desk she announced that they had 30 minutes to complete the paper. emphasising that the questions were a culmination of all they had learned to date.

***

Miss Forrest was an exceptional teacher and individual. An ex-professional footballer whose career had ended after a crucial ligament injury; she had taken to teaching like the professional she was. Attractive with a sense of fun, she taught in an unconventional manner that kept her students always wondering what she would spring on them next. She kept her private life, totally private which led to rumours and speculation about her sexual preferences. This caused her some problems as she was often approached by both sexes from both senior students and other staff members. The truth was she was in a happy relationship with her long-term partner, and neither had any plans for marriage.

The class settled down to work out the answers to the questions. After 20 minutes Francesca stood and handed in her paper. She was followed at intervals by other students until only Davy was left still trying to work out the answers.

As Francesca sat patiently waiting for the results, she heard a question in her head. Startled she looked around and saw Davy giving her a sideways glance.

The question in her head was repeated. 'Sis, give me a hand, what's the answer?' The voice clearly belonged to Davy.

Still startled by what she had heard, she felt a rising sense of devilment. 'So brother dear, you want me to cheat on your behalf do you,' she said to herself. 'Right let's have some fun.' Thinking for a few seconds she said in her mind, 'The answer is B squared, times G to the fourth minus X to the third.'

After a short pause, she heard, 'Thanks Sis,' as Davy got up and walked to the teacher handing in his paper, just in time.

He walked back to his desk, a look of relief on his face and mouthed a thank you to his sister.

Miss Forrest spent several minutes going through the answers. Looking up and smiling, she said, 'Well done class, I can see that the majority have a very sound understanding of the

essential basics. I would like especially to single out Francesca.'
She looked directly at her causing Francesca to blush slightly.
'Her answers came quickly, neatly laid out and logically.'
Hesitating she looked directly at Davy. 'Now David Fordham,
please come forward as I would like some help in understanding
your answer.'

Davy looked up, confusion on his face. He looked over at
Francesca who had a mischievous grin on her face. She mouthed
the word, ' sorry.'

Standing in front of Miss Forrest he felt a mild sense of panic.
It began to dawn on him that his beloved Sister had played a trick
on him that she was about to enjoy and use against him for many
years to come.

'So David, please enlighten me on the first part of your answer
namely B squared and G to the fourth, how did you get that?'

Davy thinking quickly replied, 'Well Miss, B and G seemed to
be the key parts of the question and using all the wonderful
teaching methods you have given us I worked out that X was a
key element ....'

'Really,' interrupted Miss Forrest, 'would it interest you to
know that neither B nor G is mentioned anywhere in the
question and the whole point of the question was to find a way
to eliminate X.'

By this time the class were all in fits of laughter until there
was a gentle knock on the classroom door and the Headmaster
poked his head around. 'Heard all the laughter, is everything OK
Miss Forrest?'

'Yes fine Sir, just going over the results of a quick test.' 'Fine,'
he said and then stared directly at Davy. 'I thought young

Fordham would be in the thick of it,' before he closed the door and left.

'OK Davy, you can go back to your seat.'

As Davy made his way back to his seat, head down with the class still laughing, he heard Miss Forrest say, 'By the way David, I think the coach was wrong in dropping you from the team. You were the team's best player by far.'

The class stopped laughing and slowly the sound of clapping all around started.

***

Back in the cottage, Francesca was retelling the story to Isabel with Davy sitting with a bashful expression on his face. 'Oh Gran, although I felt a bit guilty, it was so funny, the whole class was in hysterics.'

'Yea, really funny Sis and I suppose you will be dining out

on this story for a few years to come.'

'Well actually brother dear, unfortunately, I can't. If I did I would have to explain how I could pass on that answer.'

Isabel, sat comfortably on her sofa had been listening to the story. 'I always thought that the communication between you two was primarily one way.'

'It was Gran,' said Francesca, 'I was as surprised as anyone when I replied, and Davy heard me. I really didn't think it would work.'

'So that's your story is it, Sis,' said Davy with laughter in his voice.

'It is Davy. When you walked up to Miss Forrest and handed in your paper. I was pleased it had worked but somewhat surprised.'

'I think it is just when I feel under pressure,' added Davy.

'Well, it looks as if nothing has worked to stop your so-called telepathy. The surgeon said it would go when you reached puberty. The Old Priest tried exorcism and that didn't work so I can only assume you will be living with this for the rest of your lives. So, all I can say is please, please be very careful.'

Chapter 14

The doors to the gym in the school were opened by the Head Master who greeted the parents and their siblings with a bright warming smile. 'Welcome to careers evening. I sincerely hope our staff can give you some ideas as to what we believe may be the future path for your children.'

He stood aside as the families walked into the gym, and took their allocated seats, neatly laid out in lines in front of the single desks behind which a teacher sat. Isabel looked at her watch noting that her allocated slot of 8.30 pm was just a few minutes away. She sat down along with Francesca and Davy and waited to be called forward.

First was Francesca. Miss Forrest was dressed in a business suit with immaculately coiffured hair. She stood up and greeted Isabel and Francesca with an outstretched hand. Gesturing for the two women to take the two seats positioned in front of the table she sat down and took a file from her in tray.

She glanced down at the open folder in front of her and smiled. 'Thank you for coming to this meeting Mrs Fordham. As you know we are here to give you a brief resume of Francesca's progress and to maybe,' she emphasised the word, 'give some indication as to the possible career opportunities that may be open to her.'

She glanced again at her folder. 'We have one more term to the end of the first year in the sixth form so next year is a key time when Francesca will be taking her A levels and I must say that I am confident that she will gain an A* in her chosen subjects.' Isabel looked towards Francesca and smiled.

The teacher continued 'Now, to her future. I believe she should consider Oxford University and then a career where her inquisitive mind and attention to detail could be best utilised, perhaps in research.'

'Thank you so much.' said Isabel as she shook Miss Forrest's hand. 'I'm not so sure my other twin will receive the same level of confidence.'

Francesca stood extending her hand to shake the teacher's hand too, then returned to her seat and gestured to Davy. 'OK brother dear your turn. I think she will be recommending a career in the local council, probably as a dustman's apprentice.' She pecked him on the cheek as he stood and moved towards the teacher's table.

'I suppose she was telling you, you will be the next Prime Minister,' said Davy with a smile. He walked confidently to the table and took a seat.

'Good evening, David.'

'Good evening Miss,' said Davy as the teacher put Francesca's folder away and picked up another one with

David's name on it.

She glanced through it and then looked up. 'Let me ask you,

David, are you enjoying the academic side of the school.'

Davy looked a bit surprised at the question and thought for a while. 'Well, sort of but I don't find it easy.'

'I must be honest with you. I don't believe you have a future within academia and think with your current subjects, Maths, Chemistry and Physics, you would waste a full year if you stayed on for those subjects. Your GCSE results were OK. You are an exceptional sportsman, Captain of the athletic team and considerable promise as a leader.' She stopped to let her words sink in. 'What do you think?'

Davy looked at Isabel who smiled. Putting a hand over his she said, 'I think we know that your passion lies in some future that involves action and adventure.'

The teacher nodded. 'I agree. I thought of maybe a career in the Armed Forces.'

Davy stiffened as tears began to fill his eyes. 'I'm sorry,' said the teacher, 'have I said something wrong.'

'Unfortunately, Davy's father was killed in action in Iraq before Davy was born,' said Isabel.

'Oh, I am so sorry, I had no idea,' said Miss Forrest. 'I can understand if that idea is not one you would consider.'

Regaining his composure Davy wiped his eyes. 'On the contrary, I think it's a good idea and well worth considering.' 'I believe you have the potential to become an officer. You do have the basic qualifications, namely sound GCSE's but they would be looking for a more rounded person. Someone who has experienced life.' She hesitated, looking at Davy for any reaction.

He looked at her intently hanging on every word. 'If you were in my position what would you do?'

'You must understand David, that anything I say is only my opinion, not a recommendation.' 'I understand that,' he replied.

'I would take several months off, travel as much as I could, Asia, Americas, Australia. Have adventures, meet different people, experience different cultures, then come home and apply to join.'

There was silence. Isabel looked at Davy who was deep in thought. 'Would I be able to finish this term, it's just another 2 months?' he asked.

'I'm sure that could be arranged but please don't rush into any decision. I would suggest you discuss this with your grandmother.'

Isabel and Davy stood up each extending their hands in turn to shake the teachers. 'Thank you so much for your advice. We will be in touch,' said Isabel.

They both turned and walked back to join Francesca.

Chapter 15

In the lounge, birthday cards, some funny, some rude but most just celebrating an 18th birthday were positioned at strategic places around the room, mostly on the ornate fireplace. Isabel sat on the large sofa and the twins on the floor surrounded by parcels, some opened and some yet to be opened.

'Your turn Sis, as you are the youngest,' laughed Davy. 'How can you say that, we were co-joined and delivered at the same time,' argued Francesca.

'Yes, but I was the first one to make any noise.'

'Agree with that and you haven't stopped ever since,' interjected Isabel.

Laughing she stood and moved towards the mantle piece. Behind one of the cards, she produced two envelopes and gave one to each of the twins.

Francesca opened hers first and let out a shriek. 'Driving lessons, wonderful Gran, thank you.'

'Oh Sis, you've spoilt the surprise, but thank you anyway, Gran,' said Davy going over to her to hug her.

Smiling Isabel said, 'Not so fast young man. Maybe you ought to open yours too.'

Davy obliged as he ripped open his envelope and gasped in surprise. 'Oh my God a flying lesson.'

'Thought you might enjoy some excitement since your socalled boring 3 months travelling around the far east getting up to who knows what.'

Isabel and Francesca both looked at Davy who went bright red with embarrassment.

'I'm sure over time Gran, we'll get all the juicy bits of information out of him,' said Francesca. She turned to Isabel and winked. 'What do you think Gran? Time to extract the truth from this creature who had confessed to nothing apart from, he had a good time.'

'Agreed,' said Isabel as she joined Francesca. They made their way menacingly towards Davy who was sitting on the floor.

'What?' he said as he glanced up to see the two women move towards him. They pounced on him pinning him down but his struggles in return were only half-hearted.

'Come on brother dear. Were there lots of pretty Taiwanese girls who caught your fancy?' said Francesca as she puts her long fingers into his armpits tickling him which caused a wave of laughter and protests from Davy. He held up his hands in surrender.

'You win Sis, you win, but no more than a few dozen,' said Davy rescuing himself from her clutches, 'just a few dozen.' The two women let Davy up. 'Right, now we have a few confessions albeit a bit tongue in cheek, what are your plans?' asked Isabel.

'Well Gran, I thought I might pop down to the Army recruiting office early next week after I have had my flight and then apply to join, hopefully, my dads' old regiment.'

***

After the twins had collected their presents and given Isabel a warm hug both saying how wonderful their 18th birthday had been, they both disappeared to their bedrooms. Isabel went to her drinks cabinet and looking at the seldom touched variety of spirits decided a small celebration of her own was in order. Taking up a bottle of Bacardi she poured herself a generous measure and then went to the kitchen. In the fridge was an opened bottle of Coke. Hoping it was still relatively fresh she added it to the spirit and returned to the lounge.

Putting on her favourite album by Frank Sinatra she settled down to relax, pleased with the way the twins had received their presents. As Frank started to sing My Way, Isabel felt a wave of nostalgia overcome her. Memories of her time sitting with her husband in this very room listening to music and often dancing to it, made her smile. But it was the words that Davy had said when she had asked him what his plans were. His answer 'Well Gran, I thought I might pop down to the Army recruiting office next week ....' had sent a chill down her spine. The words echoed those of her son, Freddie.

She glanced up at the picture on the mantelpiece. Resplendent in uniform and looking so proud, her son looked the epitome of a soldier. He had not been the best recruit on his course at Sandhurst he was classed overall as average. The prizes had gone to sons of ex-military men, Generals and Colonels but one prize had eluded them.

The recruits had decided on a prize of their own; the recruit they would most like to serve with. The vote had been overwhelming, Lt Freddie Fordham.

Isabel and Ernie had sat at the ceremony feeling a sense of pride as Freddie walked across the stage to collect his prize.

As he collected it he turned to look directly at his parents and mouthed the words, "I love you"

Isabel sat, memories flooding back to her. The picture in her mind of her son in uniform waving happily as he left for Iraq. The last time she saw him.

Chapter 16

The light aircraft, an ex-military Bulldog, made a perfect touchdown barely making a sound as the tyres just kissed the runway. While taxiing back, the passenger, a middle age man, overweight and red-faced held a brown sick bag to his face. Trying to be sick while maintaining some dignity, he turned away from the pilot, but the noise he was making was evidence of his distress.

He folded over the top of the bag and put it down on the floor next to a similar bag. 'Well,' he said with some embarrassment, 'it looks as if my dreams of getting a Private Pilots licence are up in smoke. First trip and sick as a dog even though the weather is perfect.'

The pilot taxied the aircraft into dispersal and parked next to several similar aircraft. Once the aircraft was shut down and the chocks put in place by a ground crew member, they both climbed out. The passenger collected the two sick bags holding them half-hidden behind him in a subconscious manner as the two walked back to the building housing the Operations area.

'Don't worry about it Ian,' the pilot said, 'it happens, but I have to be honest with you. I believe you would be wasting your money pursuing this particular dream. You could be spending thousands of pounds with us and not be able to pass the basic tests.'

'I appreciate your honesty, Bert. Must admit I had no idea what was going on in the cockpit. Even the simplest task you gave me seemed ridiculously difficult.' He laughed as he said, 'think I'll try the next thing on my bucket list, sky diving.'

Inside the flight operations area, Ian made his way to the bathroom where he deposited his sick bags into the bin, washed his hands and rinsed out his mouth. He looked at his rather grey-ashen face in the mirror. 'Well old boy, it's no Top Gun for you.' He laughed at his joke and made his way into the crew room.

Bert took the flight sheets from the young operations operative and signed the aircraft in giving details of flight time. 'Thanks, Billy,' said Bert to the young man who looked at Bert with something resembling awe. 'Looking forward to your next lesson. What is it, Spinning one?'

'That's correct Sir,' answered Billy, 'I've completed all the groundwork and studied the Student Guide so I'm well prepared.'

'Knew you would,' said Bert who smiled at the young man, 'I have another familiarisation flight shortly and then we will get airborne.'

Leaving the operations area he joined Ian in the crew room.

'Coffee?' asked Bert.'No thanks, not sure my stomach can take anything at the moment. Think I'll mosey along. Many thanks, Bert, you are a real gentleman.' They shook hands and Ian made his way out of the crew room.

'Sir,' said Billy as Bert walked back into the operations room, 'your next customer for the familiarisation flight has arrived. I've shown them into the briefing room and made them coffee.' 'Well done Billy but you said them. I thought it was just one person, a young man.'

'That's right but he has a lady with him. I think it's his Grandmother.'

'Really,' said Bert sounding surprised. 'OK thanks, Billy, I'll pay a quick visit to the loo and then join them.'

***

In the crew room, furnished with second-hand but goodquality leather chairs and small tables with chequerboards and cards on them, Isabel and Davy looked at memorabilia and trophies in a cabinet and pictures around the walls.

'Gosh Gran these trophies are from the World Air Rally

Championships in Italy and the Kings Cup Air Race.'

'Well, you should see these photos. A pilot dressed in flying kit next to a jet aircraft.' She looked at the notation on the bottom of the picture. "Squadron Leader Bertie Fordham Lightning Mk 6." 'There are other photos of different aircraft... '

She stopped speaking as the door opened and Bert walked in. Looking up Isabel felt a flutter in her stomach that she had not felt for years.

'Good afternoon, I'm Bertie,' he said holding out his hand and shaking Isabel's.

'Good afternoon, I'm Isabel,' she said managing to control her emotions. 'I was just admiring the photos.'

'Oh those, please don't take too much notice. The Company Directors like to have us show off a little. Embarrasses me somewhat.' He turned to see Davy still staring into the cabinet. 'You must be Davy, welcome.'

'Hi,' said Davy shaking Bertie's hand. 'Are these trophies yours?'

'Well technically they belong to the Flying Club, but yes they were mine.'

As he started to talk to Davy, Isabel studied him. About her age, medium height, silver hair with a strong, if slightly long nose but charisma that you could almost touch. He carried himself with an air of confidence, and those eyes were sparkling with intelligence and fun. She shook herself out of her trance.

'I hope you didn't mind me coming along. I just wanted to make sure my Grandson was in safe hands and it looks as if he is.'

'I believe so.' Bertie laughed, a rich no holds barred laugh that caused Isabel to smile broadly. 'I was an Instructor in the RAF and have flown with hundreds of young men and haven't lost one.'

'I'm so glad to hear that, as my Grandson is rather important to me.'

Davy stared at the two and smiled. 'Well, who would have thought it, a flame seems to have been lit here,' he whispered to himself.

Bertie and Isabel stared at one another for a few seconds before Davy interjected with a soft cough. 'Don't want to interrupt but when will we be getting airborne?'

'Yes right,' said Bertie. To Isabel, he said, 'Will you be OK here? We will be just over the hour. Help yourself to coffee or tea,' he said pointing to a hand-built stone coffee bar with an urn and jars of coffee and sugar. 'Milk's in the fridge.'

'I'll be fine, there is plenty to keep me interested,' she said waving an arm around the crew room. 'It will give me a chance to get to know your background,' she said looking Bertie directly in the eye.

'Please don't be too impressed. I've just been lucky. Now let's see what this young man has to offer.' He and Davy made their way to the crew room door. As they go to leave, Bertie looked back catching Isabel's eye. He smiled and left.

***

In the aircraft, Davy was spellbound as they performed loops and barrel rolls. The G forces, incredible views when inverted and the valley flying through the clouds gave him a feeling of such freedom that it was euphoric. When allowed to take control of the aircraft he felt as if he was part of it. He could feel and sense every minute movement, every subtle change in motion and corrected them automatically. Bertie sat beside Davy watching in silence. Could this be a young man with natural ability, so rare and something Bertie had only experienced twice before in all his years as an instructor?

As they walked back to the flight building, Bertie was silent as he listened to Davy babbling with excitement. 'I have never experienced anything like that Sir. It was the freedom, the magic of the cloud formations and flying between them. The G forces were such a weird feeling...' He stopped and looked at Bertie. 'What's up, Sir?'

'Nothing young man. Let's talk in the crew room with your Grandmother.'

In the crew room, Bertie made himself and Davy a coffee and sat down with Isabel. 'Let me say from the start that I never try to get anybody to sign up for flying lessons unless I feel confident that they can make progress to warrant their expenditure.'

He looked at Isabel and then Davy, 'As I mentioned before I have flown with hundreds of students, the majority military who have been chosen after going through extensive testing to see if they are made of the right stuff. However, there have been just a few who I have taught who have a natural ability. A true feeling for the aircraft that can never be taught. I believe Davy has that ability, rare though it is.'

There was silence as Isabel and Davy absorbed what Bertie had told them.

'So what you are saying is that my Grandson could become a military pilot,' said Isabel.

'If I were a betting man, which I am not, I would place money on Davy making it to the very top of the tier as a single-seat fighter pilot.'

Chapter 17

The impact that the flight with Bertie had on Davy was profound. That night he had laid in bed, his mind ablaze with the sights and feelings he had felt and witnessed. Thoughts of joining the army were quickly fading from his ambitions and a new avenue of adventure beckoned. The words from Bertie had surprised him. He had felt at home in the aircraft and hadn't realised that what he had experienced and reacted to was unusual. 'Surely everyone felt the same,' he thought.

Drifting into a deep sleep his dreams became vivid with visions of clouds rushing by, the world upside down as they performed loops and the wondrous views of a green and unspoilt countryside. He awoke, and the decision was made.

In the kitchen, Isabel was standing at the gas cooker, a pan of porridge gently bubbling on the gas ring when Davy burst in. His overly energetic entry made Isabel jump, and as he grabbed her round the waist, hugging her tightly he said, 'Gran I love you.'

'Well, you must have slept well. What's brought this on?' 'Your present, the flight.' He squeezed her as Francesca walked into the kitchen.

'What a lovey-dovey sight to greet me in the morning,' she laughed. 'What's got into my normal sleepy head, I don't do mornings brother.'

Davy turned and ran to grab his sister around the waist, spinning her around. 'I have decided on a career. I'm going to apply to join the RAF as a pilot.'

For a few seconds, there was stunned silence in the kitchen. 'This after just one flight in a light aircraft,' asked Isabel somewhat surprised.

'That's right Gran. I'm going to go to see Bertie and ask how much flying lessons would cost, and see if he can help prepare me for the interviews.'

'Well, I can help pay for the lessons...'

'No Gran,' interrupted Davy. 'I'm going to get a part-time job and pay for them myself. When I go for interviews I want to be able to show I worked hard myself to achieve my goals.'

***

The Cafe in the local village was small, only seating 20 people but was always full. Good coffee and homemade cakes are run by a matronly lady, large with a no-nonsense approach, running the cafe with military precision. The decor left a great deal to be desired. A mixture of second-hand settees, two booths with seats on either side of a small table and a random selection of chairs and tables. Somehow it worked. Not pretentious, just a simple cafe that served good food and coffee.

'What will it be, the usual, coffee and cake for four?' asked the lady to a group of 4 lads sitting at a table in the corner.

'Yes please,' replied Davy giving her a cheeky smile. 'Any chance of a cheese scone? Couldn't see one amongst the cakes.'

Winking at him she said, 'I'll check. Have a feeling there might be one or two in the back.'

'How come you always get your way?' asked a fair-haired lad. 'If I had asked that I would have been told, "What's on display is what's on display," he said mimicking the lady's voice, stopping quickly as she returned with a cheese scone and butter.

Placing it in front of Davy with a smile, she looked directly at the lad mimicking her giving him a hard look making him cringe and look away.

'Well, Scotty if you had the looks and charm of our Davy boy here, with that lovely olive-coloured skin,' said a pretty lad, nicknamed Madeline, speaking in a rather effeminate voice, 'you would probably get a cheese scone.'

Laughing, a butch-looking character with a crew cut and black stubble said, 'Now now Patty boy, we all know you fancy Davy but I have a feeling he isn't into your ways. Girls girls girls for our handsome lad,' getting a high five from Scotty. 'OK, OK,' said Madeline. 'Doesn't stop me dreaming. Now changing the subject before I get too flustered, how was this place you went to for the RAF?'

'Biggin Hill. Interesting. Was there for 4 days. Lots of testing, interviews discussions but have no idea how I did. Waiting to hear which should be any day now.'

'What sort of tests?' asked Scotty.

'Lots of team ones. We all wore overalls with numbers on our backs. I think I made a pig of one of the tests,' said Davy taking a bite from his cheese scone. 'I had to get my team across a water-filled trench. There was a rope hanging from a beam in the centre and I suppose we were meant to climb up the supporting poles, somehow get the rope and swing across. I just walked through the water followed by my team. The officers watching us seemed perplexed. So not sure what they thought...'

Davy was interrupted by his mobile ringing. Glancing at the dial he smiled to himself when he saw it was his Gran. 'Hi, gorgeous. How's my favourite Gran?' He went silent when he heard her reply.

'Right Gran, I'll be back soon.' 'You OK?' said Scotty

'Fine,' replied Davy. 'Will have to go. Gran has a letter for me from the MOD. Must be the result of my application.'

'Best of luck mate,' they all said as they stood, giving high fives.

Davy walked out of the cafe, cheese scone in hand and butterflies in his stomach.

***

The walk back from the cafe to 'The Refuge' was along a river bank through a wooded area. The path, a popular venue for outdoor activities, ran close to the river. Davy was in no hurry. He felt nervous about knowing that the contents of the letter his Gran had, would dictate his future.

He had been well prepared for the interviews, leadership and initiative tests by Bertie who had become a second father to him. Davy had passed his flying tests and ground exams without problem to gain his Private Pilots License. Thinking back he realised just how much Bertie had sacrificed to give him a great start and the chance of passing the selection system. He had charged him for just the fuel for the plane, and spent hours of his own time going over the many subjects Davy would face questions on airmanship, aerodynamics, meteorology, aircraft systems and Air law, plus others.

Unlike his difficulties during his time in the 6th form, Davy found these subjects fascinating and absorbed the information with enthusiasm. He also found the methods Bertie used to both teach and test, refreshing. Role play with Bertie grilling him on current affairs subjects, his views on racial equality, defence, and even politics. Bernie would get Davy to act as the teacher getting him to stand in front of a whiteboard and explain the fundamentals of all the syllabus subjects in detail. He was even given homework much to Francesca's amusement.

***

As he continued his leisurely walk along the footpath he reflected on the part-time job he had taken on to pay for the flying lessons; working in a jam-making factory. This had not been a particularly enjoyable experience. Davy had been subjected to racial abuse and bullying. He knew he didn't fit in. Good looking, a little over 6 feet tall with an athletic build, he spoke well, did not swear or tell vile jokes and didn't get drunk on Friday nights. The bullying had come to a head early on. Two colleagues had drawn a picture of a monkey with Davy's face superimposed on it and pinned it to his locker with the words 'Pakky Monkey, piss off back to the jungle.'

As Davy took down the picture, the two lads who had left it came up behind him. One, Porky, an overweight hulk of a man who intimidated others through his bulk and aggressive attitude stared at Davy. 'I designed that masterpiece, Pakky. So suggest you leave it pinned to your fucking locker,' poking Davy in the chest.

His colleague a tall stick thin individual with a nervous twitch under his right eye and who stumbled over his words, stood next to him grinning. 'Yea, took a lot of work and imagine....' He stopped as he tried to get the word out.

His colleague helped him out, 'yea lots of imagination.'

'I can see that,' said Davy crumpling the picture up into a ball before throwing it into a nearby basket, a great deal of imagination.' Davy turned back to his locker, 'Now if you don't mind, I need to get changed before my shift.'

As he turned, Porky slammed Davy's head against the locker causing a dent in the door. Davy slumped to his knees shaking his head. As the stars in his head began to subside he felt a knee kneeling on his back and a fist hit the back of his head.

'Give him a good kicking,' shouted the thin lad.

Porky stood up, taking a step back preparing to kick Davy.

Davy had spent years keeping fit indulging in a variety of sports but primarily Taekwondo. Over nearly three years of hard training, he had achieved a second-degree Black belt. He had enjoyed the regimented routines, the precision of the patterns and the total respect given to and from his training partners.

Davy had heard the thin lad tell Porky to give him a kicking so knew, as Porky stepped back, a foot would be aimed, possibly at his ribs. He waited a fraction of a second and then twisted onto his side, bringing his knee up to his chest. Keeping his toes curled back and with the heel of his foot, he struck out.

His aiming point was the top of the tibia just below the knee cap. He connected, hearing a crack as the pressure from the kick snapped the meniscus.

Porky stood for a while before the knee, holding his heavy weight, decided it could no longer support his bulk; he collapsed screaming in pain.

Davy got to his feet quickly and turned towards the thin lad who stood, looking shocked. 'I suggest you go and get a first aider and if possible a Gurney because your companion here will not be walking anywhere for a while.'

***

Coming out of his reminiscing, Davy continued his walk home, enjoying the warmth of the spring air and the newly flowering daffodils and snowdrops. On the river, two swans began their laborious take-off run. The noise of the paddling of their feet on the water, as they attempted to gain some form of purchase together with the frantic flapping of the wings and the clucking between them as if giving each other encouragement, filled the air.

Davy watched in fascination as eventually, they achieved take-off speed withdrawing their legs into their bodies like an undercarriage and majestically left the water in perfect formation.

'Is this an omen,' Davy thought. 'They were like fighter jets. Clumsy on the ground but then majestic once airborne.'

***

Reaching home he took a deep breath as he entered the cottage.

In the kitchen sitting around the breakfast table were the two women whom he adored.

Trying to sound more casual and cool than he felt he said, 'Watcha ladies, how are things?' the nervousness in his voice evident.

On the table in front of Isabel was a brown envelope with the stamp of the MOD across the top. Davy stared at it mesmerised.

Sounding tense, Francesca said, 'Well, are you going to open it and put us all out of our misery,'

'Please,' said Isabel, 'I seem to have been staring at this for the past hour.'

Davy reached over and picked up the envelope, toying with it but not opening it.

'Oh, give it here,' said Isabel.

Davy handed over the envelope and then turned to a cabinet fastened to the wall, taking out a large glass which he then filled with water. Taking a sip he looked again at the envelope as Isabel opened the flap carefully as if it was a precious document. Taking out the letter she scanned it quickly and then folded it up putting it back in the envelope. No expression showed on her face.

'Well!' said the twins in unison.

'Not much to say. Unfortunately...' Before she had time to say any more Davy, shoulders slumped, turned around and started to walk out of the Kitchen.

'Unfortunately,' said Isabel, this time with a voice that commanded attention, 'it looks as if Francesca and I will not be having the pleasure of your company for quite some time young man.' She paused as Davy turned to look at her.

'What do you mean Gran?'

'The letter says you are to report to the RAF College Cranwell in 3 weeks to commence Officer training and from there, if successful, Pilot training.'

A strange silence filled the kitchen as both Isabel and Francesca got up from their seats, tears of joy beginning to flow as they made their way across to Davy.

'I am so proud of you,' said Isabel.

'My little brother, an RAF Officer and Pilot. Who would have believed it,' added Francesca.

They stood together in a group hug, all three trying to talk at the same time until Davy suddenly broke away and with a loud 'Whoop' threw the contents of his glass of water in the air soaking all three of them.

Pandemonium then broke out.

Chapter 18

C offee houses in the local town near Francesca's flat in Oxford were few and far between. But Loafers near the centre was both popular and profitable. Always well stocked with homemade cakes and varieties of fresh sandwiches made to order. It was tastefully decorated in pale colours with a selection of abstract paintings which led to the local youngsters considering it a cool place to congregate in the afternoons. In contrast, the older generation chose the mornings when it was quieter.

Francesca sat in her favourite corner by a window that overlooked the local green where at its centre was an ancient oak tree, reported to be nearly 200 years old. She checked her watch. Over 10 minutes late she thought but smiled. Her brother was never much of a timekeeper.

Close by, four teenage girls were laughing and giggling. Francesca cringed at the constant use of the words, "like, so and basically". Isabel had instilled in her at an early age not to overuse these words in the wrong context and looking back now she realised what a wonderful Grandmother she had been, always setting an example to be followed. She was generous with her affections and love but strict when necessary, especially with her brother. Francesca knew that he would not have been the young man he now was without her love and guidance.

Her thoughts were interrupted by a peck on the cheek. 'Well you were on a different planet there Sis, dreaming of some new love,' said Davy laughing.

'Wishful thinking,' she said playfully, 'by the way, you are late.'

'Yea sorry about that. Duty calls and all that.'

'More likely it was some new love of yours that made you late.'

'Fair call Sis, but she is rather gorgeous. Let me get you a fresh coffee.'

'OK, but don't make a mess of that wonderful uniform.' Davy was dressed in his RAF Officers' blue with the rank of Flying Officer and his wings proudly displayed. He took off his hat with the RAF crest just above the peek and left it on the table. As he made his way to the coffee counter heads turned and the four girls went quiet.

'Two cappuccinos please.' he asked the young barista. She smiled at him and went to the coffee machine and after a few minutes returned with the coffee.

'How much?' asked Davy smiling at her. She blushed, looked around to make sure she was not observed and said, 'On the house for our magnificent boys in blue'.

Davy looked around and saw a Help for Heroes charity tin.

'I'll put the money in there,' pointing at the tin adding, 'Many thanks.'

He collected the coffee and made his way back to Francesca. As he passed the young teenage girls, two of them wafted their hands in front of their faces as if fanning themselves. He smiled at them and joined Francesca. 'Talk about making an impression.' she said.

'It's the uniform,' joked Davy

'Not the rather dishy young man wearing it,' laughed Francesca.

'Might have helped. So how is my genius sister, hopefully making good use of that first-class hours degree from Oxford? I hear you are working in a paint shop.'

'Not exactly you moron,' she said giving him a friendly punch on the arm. 'You know only too well that I am in the research department. At the moment we are working on some incredible new paint products that only glow in the dark under certain lights. Believe it or not, it's fascinating work,' she said. 'Yea, only kidding, I'm really proud of you sis,' he said as he added sugar to his coffee. 'Knew you would always find your true passion. But what about your love life? Still turning away every eligible young Bachelor.'

'Now don't laugh,' laughed Francesca, 'but I've joined Tinder and have a date in a few weeks. I've checked him as best I can and he does seem to be suitable.'

Suddenly Davy went quiet. He became very serious and tears appeared in his eyes.

Francesca thinking he was messing around said. 'What on earth is wrong, Davy, it's only Tinder.'

'I'm sorry, it's nothing to do with Tinder, it's just a horrible feeling that I won't ever see you again.'

'Hey lighten up Bro. Where did this come from?'

'I don't know it's just a feeling. I leave for the USA tomorrow morning for a Fighter affil' he said wiping his eyes. 'That means we go up against the best their Air force can throw at us. As the new boy it will be an amazing experience but I can't seem to overcome this feeling. Too heavy, let's change the subject. How's Gran?'

'You know our wonderful Gran. Fit as a fiddle, in the centre of village life and believe it or not has had a couple of dinner dates with Bertie.'

Taking a drink from his coffee and he tried to regain his composure. 'I'm not surprised. When they first met you could almost see the sparks flying. Good for her.'

'She sends her love by the way and understands why you couldn't pop in.'

'First port of call when I return.'

They chatted for several more minutes before Davy stood up, collected his hat and kissing Francesca, walked out quickly. Francesca sat there for a few more minutes contemplating what Davy had said. 'Not even you Davy can predict the future. He had better come home,' she said to herself wiping a tear away.

Chapter 19

I sabel felt happy. Francesca was home for a week's break from her job in Oxford. A few months had passed since she had seen either of the twins but the weekly correspondence by telephone from both of them kept her up to date with what was happening in their lives. The fact that Francesca was about to go on a Tinder date was proving a vibrant talking point between them. Isabel knocked on Francesca's bedroom door. 'Come in,' said Francesca. As Isabel entered, she savoured the flood of memories that this room evoked. Francesca's tears after her first boyfriend had dumped her, the excitement of the results of her GCSE then A levels. The time she decided to wallpaper her bedroom by herself only for it all to peel off in the middle of the night much to Davy's amusement. She looked around at the generation of photos. The twins aged 3 dressed identically,

Francesca on her first school day, a family photo at the beach and many, many more.

'Well, what do you think Gran?' said Francesca as she stood up from her seat in front of her dressing table mirror with a twirl.

'What can I say? A picture of loveliness. So where are you meeting this Tinder man?' laughed Isabel.

'His name is Philip and his profile said he is a very stable well adjusted individual, well-educated and looking for a long-term relationship. Probably a right moron like the last two I dated,' said Francesca as she collected her coat and car keys.

She had a final look in the mirror and gave her Gran a peck on the cheek. 'Don't wait up Gran, although I won't be that late. Love you.'

***

As always Francesca was thankful for the satnav in her car. She put in the details given to her by Philip of the pub they were to meet at. Knowing there was no chance of rain and the warm evening, she lowered the hood of her small but lively red sports car and headed for what she hoped would be a pleasant evening. How she loved her car. The feeling of the wind messing up her long blonde hair, which she always found liberating but knowing that a quick brush and a shake of her head would bring it back under control. The variety of smells and sounds she could experience would be masked in the enclosed capsule of a normal car. Nippy, easy to drive and park and a bit of a head-turner. Perfect.

The satnav took her the shortest route to the rendezvous point, allowing her to arrive a few minutes early. Putting the hood up and securing the car, she composed herself and made her way to the pub, a brightly lit establishment and by the noise emanating from inside, popular. The small covered entranceway split into two: one for the dining area and the other for the lounge. Opening the door to the dining area she was greeted by a young black man, smartly dressed in dark pants a clean white shirt with a bow tie but no jacket. His brilliant smile helped

Francesca relax as he took her name and led her through the dining area.

As they weaved their way between the tables, Francesca glanced around impressed with the decor, modern and stylish with subtle lighting, and soft music playing in the background. Nearly all the tables had either couples or small groups of men and women, all casually but smartly dressed, sitting at them. The chatter, although incessant was not too noisy as to be a distraction and a great deal of laughter could be heard. Francesca approved of Philip's choice of a meeting place. She now just hoped Philip was up to his Tinder profile.

The young black man stopped at a table in the corner of the dining area next to a large patterned window which let through the last of the daylight giving a warm glow to the atmosphere. 'Boy has this man planned the evening well,' thought Francesca to herself. She caught herself smiling as the young black man stepped aside allowing Philip to rise from his seat and introduce himself.

Her first thought was one of relief. His picture on the website did him justice as did the description he gave of himself. Average height, average looks nothing special. His handshake was firm but not too heavy and she caught a whiff of a pleasant smelling aftershave. His voice was soft with just a hint of nervousness but his eye contact was steady and his smile seemed genuine. Brown hair neatly combed and no hint of any stubble.

Helping her to her seat he settled down and after a short pause said, 'I don't know about you but I'm nervous. Your profile is something else. Oxford University, working in R&D, is extremely pretty. I didn't think you would be interested in someone like me.'

'I am nervous as well and as for the profile I didn't know what to put so my Gran filled it out for me and posted it before I had a chance to stop her.' They both laughed.

A waiter appeared and handed them both a menu, telling them his opinion that the Steak Diane was exceptional and highly recommended.

'Probably been told to push the steak as they are trying to get rid of it,' Francesca said with a nervous giggle.

'I bet you are right but I did see a few other customers take his recommendation and they seemed to be quite happy. Think I might give it a go,' said Philip.

'Yes, so will I.'

They both finished their meal agreeing it was excellent. They chatted amiably swapping anecdotes and funny stories. Philip explained how devastated he had been when his wife walked out on him and then the divorce which had left him lacking confidence and having to restart his life. He rented a small flat, lived alone and just worked as hard as he could as a car salesman to save enough to get back into the property market. Francesca felt comfortable in his company feeling that this relationship may have some potential. Philip had asked sensible, polite questions about her life and family.

He listened intently to her views on a variety of subjects gently arguing his point when not agreeing. Philip insisted on paying for the meal agreeing with Francesca when she promised to pay if they met again, which she hoped they would.

At the bar, Philip checked the bill, handed over his debit card and waited for the receipt. He glanced sideways and met the eyes of a dark-haired, tough-looking individual who was resting against the bar, a beer glass in his hand. The man nodded and

Philip took the receipt and rejoined Francesca. 'I don't want to seem pushy but I would love you to come back to my place for coffee and I promise just coffee,' he asked taking her hand. 'I really am one of the good guys.' He hesitated. 'I enjoyed your company so much and would just like to see the evening out and hopefully make arrangements to meet up again.'

Francesca hesitated, 'I'm not sure. Normally going back for coffee means more than just coffee.'

'Understand but I promise the minute you want to leave I will personally escort you to your car, not even holding your hand. Cross my heart and hope to die as we used to say in school.' They both laughed.

'OK, but just one coffee.'

'Brilliant. If you follow me, it's just a 10-minute drive.'

As they left the entrance to the pub Philip looked back and nodded to the dark-haired man seen earlier at the bar. Philip noticed Francesca glance at the man

'Just an acquaintance. Sold him a car a few months back,' said Philip,

'Shifty looking character,' observed Francesca. 'Yea, not my type at all but business is business.'

She followed Philip out to the car park where he got into a small family saloon. She walked the short distance to her car, and getting in followed Philip. On the drive, she went through the evening feeling pleased that she thought she may have found a man who appeared to fit her profile of a suitable companion. 'Just coffee,' she said to herself. 'Never know, maybe more we will see.'

Chapter 20

The flat was in a relatively new build. The first two levels of the six were affordable with the price and value rising as the levels rose. Philips flat was on the second floor near the centre and the floor was accessed via a lift. The overall appearance was one of a building well maintained and secure, this view reinforced by the barrier to the car park.

Philip drove up to the barrier taking out a swipe card which he swiped through the slot on the gate pillar. The barrier opened and after he drove through, he parked his car and walked back using the same card to allow Francesca through. Driving through she parked next to Philip's car, climbed out and waited for him as he walked back from the gate.

Outside the flats, there was a small pharmacy, a convenience store and a fast food chain. The area was well lit and a treelined pathway led to the entrance to the flats. Philip used his key card to enter the small lobby. Letterboxes for each flat were lined up against a wall along with a self-service machine containing a variety of snacks. They both climbed the two flights of stairs and walked along the internal hallway, well-lit with automatic lights triggered by motion.

Opening the door with his key, he stood aside and let Francesca in, and leaned around her to switch on the light. The first impression she had was one of tidiness. No clutter. Unusual for a guy she thought. She looked around the lounge area which was conservatively decorated if rather boring, all the walls a soft green pastel colour, few pictures and a window that overlooked a nearby road. There was a small settee and two lounge chairs which surrounded a coffee table with an artificial plant in the centre. A cabinet, close to the door had a lamp with a sandy-coloured lampshade over an ovalshaped brown base. This was matched with another one on a small table in the corner of the room. Off to one end was the kitchenette and from what she could see the tidiness extended to that area as well. At the other end of the room were two doors supposedly leading to the bedroom and bathroom.

'Take a seat, and I'll make the coffee. How do you the take yours?' said Philip as Francesca sat in one of the lounge chairs continuing her surveillance of the flat.

'White with no sugar, please.'

'Same as me,' said Philip moving into the kitchen and filling the kettle and getting coffee from a cupboard. Hidden from Francesca he took out his mobile sending a text that read, "Swipe card usual place. Give me 10 minutes."

The answer came back quickly. "OK. Boy, she looks hot!!!." Philip made the two coffees and then taking a small phial from his pocket emptied the contents into Francesca's coffee, stirring it before taking both cups into the lounge.

'There you go just coffee and not an unwanted advance in sight,' smiling as he placed the coffee in front of Francesca.

She smiled back and leaning forward picked up her cup and was about to start drinking when a buzzing sound on her phone indicated a text had arrived. Putting down the cup she took her phone out of her handbag, opened it up and silently read an almost unintelligible message. '"**f*e* n*." She stared at the message trying to work out what it meant.

'Everything OK?' asked Philip.

'Yes, just some crank message. Would you mind if I had a glass of water?' 'Certainly.'

He went to the kitchen as Francesca realised the message should have read "Coffee no" and probably from her brother being his usual overprotective self. Thinking it better to play safe, she switched the coffees around.

'Here's your water. Have you tried your coffee yet?' asked Philip as he sat down and took up his coffee, drinking it slowly and watching Francesca.

'Yes thanks, really good,' she answered.

'Great now we can relax and enjoy the rest of the evening.' 'Not sure what you mean?' said Francesca.

'Oh, you will, not long now. How are you feeling? 'Fine, how about you?'

'Really good,' he said but began to slur his words. 'What the fuck have you done you bitch?' The change in character shocked Francesca.

Standing up, she picked up her handbag and smiled at Philip. 'I don't think that language is appropriate from a man who spent the evening trying to impress me with his charm and his gentlemen ways. Good job I switched the coffees.' Under her breath, she said "Thanks, Davy.'

'It's not over yet.' Philip tried to stand but his legs gave way and he fell back into the chair. 'My friend....' he passed out before he could finish the sentence.

Francesca felt a rising panic. 'The man he acknowledged when we left the restaurant.' Thinking to herself. 'Time to leave.'

As she did there was a knock on the door. Moving quickly to the door she glanced through the spy hole, seeing the rough looking individual she had seen earlier, standing looking impatient.

He knocked on the door again. 'Phil open up it's Guy. You can't have started already.'

Francesca stood back from the door. She looked around. On the floor was a large thin rug which she positioned so it was directly in front of the door. After unlatching it she quickly bent down behind it. Taking one end of the rug she waited. When she heard Guy enter she took a deep breath and pulled the rug as hard as she could hearing a satisfying yelp as he fell heavily cracking his head on the cabinet.

Getting up quickly she moved around the door, eager to make her escape. Lying on the floor unconscious, Guy was motionless. Feeling concerned she felt for his pulse, relieved when she realised he was still alive. Rifling through his pockets she found his car keys and the Key card. 'Planned all along,' she thought.

Looking back at Philip lying unconscious on the floor. 'I think some revenge is in order,' she said to herself as she closed the door.

Taking out her phone she took pictures of both men. 'I'll post these on the website. That should put a stop to their plans.'

Moving into the kitchen, she rifled around through the drawers and found two large bars of chocolate. After taking off

117

the wrappings she put them into the tumble dryer situated in the corner above which was a microwave. Smiling, she went to the fridge and took out 8 eggs, put them into the microwave and turned it on full.

Hurrying through the lounge she checked that the two men were still unconscious before going into the bedroom and shivered at the thought of what might have happened to her. Looking through a wardrobe she took out two suits and then from a drawer, four shirts.

Making her way quickly back to the kitchen, she put the clothes into the tumble dryer and turned it on full. "Boy, are they going to be a mess,' she said to herself.

As Francesca turned she felt the full force of a hand slap her across the face. Staggering under the blow she saw colourful stars shooting around her head before she fell to the floor.

'Right Bitch. Now I'm going to get what I came here for,' said Guy as he grabbed Francesca violently by the hair and pulled her up off the floor. Turning her around he forced her to bend over the worktop. Struggling to free herself she felt her underwear being ripped off and then the sound of a zip being drawn and trousers falling to the floor. She gasped as he entered her violently, grunting as he did so.

In the microwave, interesting developments were in motion. The centre of the eggs was gradually turning from a liquid into a near-solid state. However, small tiny pockets of liquid in each egg were becoming superheated. They spontaneously exploded. The sound level approaching 130 decibels.

The sound of the exploding eggs was similar to small grenades going off in the enclosed space of the microwave.

Taken completely by surprise, Guy stopped in mid-thrust. 'What the fuck?' he shouted turning his head to the sound just in time to meet Francesca's wild swinging elbow.

The remaining exploding eggs drowned out the sound of his breaking nose. With blood flowing down his face from his broken nose, he staggered. His trousers, now neatly positioned around his ankles and with the help of gravity, he began to tumble, slowly at first then faster until, despite his waving arms trying to grab something, he hit the floor.

Francesca shook her head, straightened up and felt pain in her stomach where the worktop had dug into her. Looking around she saw Guy fall, his naked groin exposed. In desperation she searched around for some form of weapon, opening up various cupboard doors below the worktops. Under the sink, she found a selection of domestic appliances including bleach in a plastic spray bottle. Grabbing the bottle she aimed it at Guy and pulled the plastic trigger, but nothing happened. Realising the nozzle was set to shut she quickly turned it to open.

Guy, with discarded trousers and now virtually naked was getting to his feet. 'Right, you Bitch. No more fucking around. I'm going to make you pay for this.'

He lunged at Francesca who just pulled the trigger without aiming. The first spray of the liquid just soaked his hair but as she pumped the trigger blindly, the second entered his mouth. Guy stopped, trying not to swallow as the liquid began to burn. The next spray did the real damage. Francesca admitted to herself afterwards that it had crossed her mind where to aim but didn't really mean it, or so she said.

The liquid, meeting the delicate exposed skin took only a little time to burn, which Guy found out as the bleach met his genitals and the exposed foreskin. Still trying to wipe his mouth he didn't at first realise the significance of the slight warm glow begins between his legs. Francesca sent another spray in the same area and then rushed passed him as he began to rub his groin making the situation worse.

Realising now what had happened Guy panicked. Running and holding his crotch he rushed passed Francesca moaning as he made his way to the bathroom. Not waiting to see what happened, Francesca started to leave the kitchen but stopped. On a wooden board hanging from hooks was a selection of keys. She assumed some for the flat, others for Philips's car and maybe his office. Grabbing them all she quickly put them into her bag, and with a final look around the flat, left.

Outside the flat complex, she looked around for a drain cover. When she found one she pulled off the cover and dropped all the keys and the cards down into the black sludge at the bottom. Replacing the cover she made her way to her car.

In her car Francesca initially felt elated at having escaped but as she started the car and drove towards the car park exit, trepidation set in. The barrier to the exit was down and she had just thrown the cards away but as she approached the barrier, relief swept over her as it rose. Putting her foot on the accelerator she drove quickly through it and once on the main road started to relax but as the adrenalin slowly left her body she started to shake.

Tears appeared and flowed down her cheeks. 'My God what would have happened if I hadn't received that garbled text Brother dear, I Love You and owe you big time.'

Chapter 21

Francesca parked her car, made her way to the front door of the cottage and let herself in. She quietly shut the door and removed her shoes keen not to disturb Isabel. As she got to the foot of the stairs the phone in the corridor rang, and the noise echoed up the staircase. Pressing the answer button she spoke quietly into the phone moving away from the stairs into the lounge.

'Good evening Francesca speaking.' She looked at the number noting it came from the USA. Immediately she thought that Davy was calling her. 'Is that you Davy….' Before she could continue a voice interrupted her.

'No Miss Fordham, this is Squadron Leader White calling from the Air Attaches office from the British Embassy in Washington.'

There was silence. A tight fear gripped Francesca's stomach.

'Are you still there Miss Fordham?' 'Yes,' she answered quietly.

'May I ask if there is anyone with you?'

'Yes, my Grandmother. She is asleep upstairs.'

' Could you get her please,' the Squadron Leader requested. 'You're making me very nervous. Has something happened?'

'It would be better if your Grandmother was with you, please.'

Leaving the phone on the small hall table Francesca made her way upstairs, her brain racing. 'It can't be Davy', she thought, 'he sent me a text just a few hours ago.'

She knocked gently on Isabel's door and entered. Going over to her Gran, she shook her gently on the shoulder. Isabel stirred and slowly became awake.

'Hello, darling. Did you have a nice evening? said Isabel sounding sleepy.

'Gran, I have a senior officer from the British Embassy in America on the phone. He wants to talk to us both.'

'Oh my god something has gone wrong. It must be Davy,'

Isabel said suddenly becoming fully awake.

'It can't be,' said Francesca, 'I received a text from him a few hours ago.'

Getting out of bed, Isabel put on her dressing gown. Together they went down the stairs and Francesca picked up the phone and put it on speaker.

'Squadron Leader, I have my Grandmother with me.' 'Good evening Mrs Fordham.'

'Good evening Squadron Leader. Now I'm sure you are not calling from the States unless you have some important news for us,' said Isabel sounding more confident than she felt.

'Ladies, I am so sorry but I have dreadful news. Flying Officer David Fordham died yesterday in an aircraft accident.

We have only just had confirmation.' He paused to let the message sink in. 'The crash site was quite remote and it was difficult to find his body. We will make all the necessary funeral arrangements.' There was silence. 'Are you both OK?' he asked.

Francesca tried to reconcile the news with what she knew. 'I don't understand,' she said. 'I received a text from him just a few hours ago.'

'I hate to disillusion you Miss Fordham, but we have David's phone here. Most pilots leave their phones with the Operations Officer before they fly. David left his so he couldn't possibly have sent you a message.'

Francesca shook her head in disbelief. 'But I had a text. How could that happen?'

'I can't explain that I'm afraid. All I can say is that I am so dreadfully sorry. I will be in touch as soon as I have made the necessary arrangements. My sincere condolences.'

Sitting in silence, the two women, hug on the sofa finding it difficult to speak. The tears flow and the minutes pass until they eventually find their voices, reminiscing over memories of Davy, even managing the occasional smile and a gentle laugh.

Eventually, Isabel got up to make a cup of strong, sweet tea. 'I still don't understand what you were saying about a text from Davy when he was supposedly....' She stopped unable to finish the sentence.

'I don't understand it at all Gran, all I know is that if I hadn't had that text I believe my evening would have been an even bigger disaster than it was.'

Getting out her phone and scrolling through various Apps she said to Isabel, 'I'll find the message he sent and show it to you.'

She hesitated as the message App opened but showed no message. 'This can't be right. It was here, barely legible but said, 'Coffee no.'

She scrolled through the messages. 'It's gone. I can't believe it, it's just gone.'

***

Three weeks later at the Church, the mourners were gathered around the grave. The last post played by a member of the Royal Air Force band, resplendent in his dress uniform, echoed around the cemetery. The mourners, in black were dressed for the winter weather. As they breathed out, gentle clouds of vapour rose in unison to be carried away by the biting wind. Four Royal Air Force Officers from Davy's Squadron stood around the coffin. Dressed in their best blues they all shivered as they waited for the bugler to finish. As the last notes drifted away, the priest gave the final blessing and the four officers each stooped to pick up the strong cord, emblazoned with the Squadron crest, positioned underneath the coffin. Together they raised it up and then gently lowered it into the grave, dug earlier by the ground staff.

Isabel and Francesca stood side by side holding hands. Isabel had a dark vale over her head, Francesca nothing, her blond hair waving like a flag in the wind. She had decided that her brother would have wanted her to be as natural as possible and although grief-stricken, she found some comfort in still feeling that strong bond with him.

As the coffin reached the bottom of the grave, the chords, held by the officers were released and allowed to fall. The Squadron emblems resting on the coffin lid as a tribute to one of their own.

Stood to one side of Isabel, Bertie was in his Squadron Leaders uniform, three campaign medals proudly showing on his chest below his wings. As the coffin was lowered he raised his right arm in a salute, holding it there until the four Officers stepped back from the graveside and in perfect unison, saluted. He felt emotional. He had attended several funerals during his career. The price many paid for serving their country. He had even attended that of his son.

***

The memory of that dreadful episode in his life would always remain raw. He felt the rising anger every time he recalled the incident that had robbed him of his son and eventually his wife.

His son had done well during flying training. Not exceptional but competent. He had progressed through the various stages and was in the final phase, Weapons School, before Operational Conversion Training onto his operational aircraft.

The sortie should have been straightforward. Low-level navigation was flown with an Instructor through the Welsh valleys to find a variety of targets. The weather, as often in the Welsh mountain area, was unpredictable. The sortie had gone well up to the time the low cloud had been encountered. Following the operational procedure, the Instructor had pulled up through the cloud informing local control that they were climbing out of low level, nothing more was heard from them. The wreckage was found several miles away scattered around the side of a mountain.

The Board of Enquiry made some suppositions placing the blame on the Instructor's shoulders. They presumed that having climbed through the cloud and found clear weather on top, the Instructor had decided to press on hoping to find a gap in the cloud. Having found one he descended, not taking into account the safety altitude for the area and flew straight into the mountainside. Neither occupant had time to eject.

Bertie controlled his anger. He had flown hundreds of similar sorties in all sorts of weather and knew the golden rule. You do not descend through a gap in the clouds unless you know exactly where you are and never go below your safety altitude unless in visual contact with the ground. Breaking that rule had lost him his son. His wife never recovered. A nervous breakdown and a strong resentment towards Bertie for encouraging her son into the military led to divorce.

***

Back at the cottage the officers and mourners gathered. Isabel and Francesca thanked them for all they had done and for chatting about Davy. Francesca was comforted by hearing how popular Davy had been on the Squadron and highly thought of. 'The best first tourist we have ever had on the Squadron,' his Wing Commander had commented.

Isabel and Bertie were talking. Since that first meeting at the flying club, they had got to know one another well. Dinner and theatre on occasions and even a flight for her with Bertie which had left her less than impressed. 'Never again.' she said as they walked away from the aircraft, he carrying her two sick bags. 'Feet firmly on the ground thank you.'

Suddenly and uncharacteristically Bertie began a silent sob.

Isabel took his hand. 'I know what you are going to say. It's all your fault,' Isabel said.

'I have been feeling a strong sense of responsibility for Davy's death. If I hadn't encouraged him, coaxed him and virtually trained him to pass the Biggin Hill selection centre he might well be alive still.'

'Poppycock. You gave him a career he loved, a future he would have blossomed in. He lived for flying. He would come home from flying with you and talk about nothing else. That time you flew a formation sortie with him he was virtually bouncing off the walls when he came home. So Squadron Leader retired Bertie Fordham, let's not ever hear talk like that again.' She gave him a peck on the cheek, 'Now let's circulate. We have a lot of people to talk to.'

Francesca was with the Squadron Leader from the Embassy who had telephoned through the tragic news. 'Are you sure you want to do this,' he asked. 'It will be a traumatic experience.' 'I realise that,' she said, 'but Davy and I were so close and I want to visit the crash site, it's something I feel I must do.'

'OK, as soon as the investigation is complete and the wreckage cleared away I will let you know and send you the details. There is a small town nearby where we stayed when visiting the site. Reasonable hotel, some bungalows to rent, a car hire and a few good restaurants. I'm sure you won't have any trouble although the walk to the site from the car park is pretty rough.' 'I'm sure I'll manage,' Francesca said. 'Have they come to any conclusion you can tell me about as to the cause?'

'There is sound evidence, which I believe will be confirmed at the Board of Enquiry that he ran into a flock of geese. They blocked out the engine intake and smashed through the canopy probably knocking your brother unconscious, which is why he didn't eject. A million to one chance. Geese are not normally found that far south in Texas.'

'So it wasn't my brother's error?' 'No, he was just really unlucky.'

Peace and quiet descended over the cottage after all the guests had left. Francesca and Isabel sat in the lounge feeling the pressures of the day. Both had a drink; Francesca a Gin and Tonic, Isabel a Baracardi and coke. They quietly reflected on the day's activities and the conversations they had had, the information they had gleaned and the impressions of people they had met.

'I spoke to Squadron Leader White,' Francesca said, leaning forward to reach her drink from the table. 'He said it would be possible for me to visit the crash site. There are some reasonable hotels and the walk to the site although tough is manageable.'

'Are you sure that's what you want to do,' said Isabel, 'don't you think you have grieved enough without putting yourself through another emotional trauma.'

'I just feel I need to see where he died. It's really important to me. Why don't you come with me?'

'Why don't we compromise? You go, visit the site and I will join you maybe a week later. I'm getting a little old for tough walks in the summer heat, especially in Texas.'

'Sounds a great idea, Gran. I'll make the arrangements as soon as I hear from the Squadron Leader that I'm cleared to visit the site.'

Chapter **22**

TEXAS USA

The old warehouse was due for demolition. Built-in the late 1960's it had been a distribution centre for goods crossing the border into Mexico, just a hundred miles or so to the west. Situated to the north of the town in an industrial complex it had been swallowed up by the expansion of the fracking business which had revitalised the area. That together with a new Interstate and changes to modern distribution methods had left it a monument to past times.

The construction of the warehouse was typical of the day. A floor area the size of a football pitch, heavy steel girders and a roof bolted directly to the main frame to ensure that even the tornadoes in tornado alley wouldn't reduce it to rubble. A small upper gantry accessed by a single metal stairway led to an office that had been used by the owners to overlook the workers. Many illegal immigrants would work and sleep in the warehouse for a week and then return over the border to Mexico for the weekends.

The old warehouse did still have a few uses. The odd illegal rave is a refuge for the needy and, on occasion, a place for drug gangs to do their business away from prying eyes. But it was one set of prying eyes, that of a male prostitute, Wayne Leroy, that was centred on blackmail and a nice little payout. Wayne looked like what he was, dressed like a tramp and smelt like an unwashed bin man. A well-known snitch who would sell anything to anyone including his own body.

Entering the warehouse via a side door he climbed the staircase. He settled down on the floor of the office, then removed a modern camcorder from its case, stolen from a Japanese couple visiting the Davy Crockett museum. He knew he had a few hours before the exchange he had heard about, would take place. He took the time to examine the camcorder. The buttons were mostly self-explanatory but the part that took his attention was the SD card slot on the side behind a small flap. He searched through the case and in a small pocket inside found an SD card. He fitted into the slot and experimented with the controls until he found out how to transfer data from the camera drive directly to the SD card. He took some selfies trying out the recording and the low light settings until he felt confident in its use.

He looked around the office not bothering to hide his disgust at the smell of urine emanating from the corners of the room. Graffiti was plastered around every wall and on the windows which overlooked the ground floor were the words, 'Henrietta lost her virginity here.'

Content that he had everything under control, he laid down on the steel floor and positioned himself to be able to view the whole area. Nervousness showed as sweat began to slowly move down his forehead smarting his blue eyes which had black bags beneath them and across a stubbled, weak-looking chin. Wiping away the sweat with a hand seldom washed, with dirty blackened fingernails, he tried hard to control his erratic breathing.

Leroy was not certain of the details of the meeting but his source had told him two main players would be exchanging drugs for money sometime that evening. Filming the exchange and going to the police with the evidence would surely guarantee a reward. As he lay there waiting he heard an aircraft fly nearby, on final approach to the small municipal airport just a few miles away.

***

The only sound of the aircraft touching down was the soft kiss as the tyres touched the tarmac. The aircraft was an Embraer Brasilia, a 30-seat short haul, twin-turboprop aircraft. Sat in row 3 and beginning to feel the effects of jet lag, Francesca hardly felt the landing. She was relieved that the long flight from Heathrow to Dallas and then onto this small town in Texas was finally over. She just hoped that her grandmother would not suffer too much from the lengthy journey.

Collecting her single suitcase from the turntable she made her way through the departures exit searching for the car hire signs. She had pre-booked and with no one in front of her was quickly given the keys and directions to the parking bays where she found a red Ford Fiesta. Opening the boot she put her suitcase in and then instinctively went to the right-hand side of the car opening the door. She laughed when she saw there was no steering wheel on that side. Going back around to the left side, she climbed in and made herself familiar with the controls.

Francesca put the address of the small villa she had found on the internet and hired for 2 weeks into the satnav. Setting off tentatively she kept reminding herself to drive on the righthand side of the road. All went well until she came to her first roundabout. She froze trying to work out what way round she was meant to go. An angry horn from behind made her decide. Taking a chance, she set off and managed to circumvent the obstacle. As she progressed towards the villa, her confidence grew.

When she arrived at the villa, she was pleasantly surprised. The pictures on the Internet did not do justice to the pretty detached single-story home. Parking the car in the driveway she turned off the engine and after exiting the car stood for a while and just looked around the neighbourhood. Many of the villas were similar with a few being double-storied. All seemed to have the same neatly mowed, small front lawns. Modernlooking cars, many with roof racks and some with trailers were parked in the driveways. Two cars drove past going to their homes, children just collected from school. Waving at them, Francesca smiled as they waved enthusiastically back. What a lovely neighbourhood she thought.

Francesca took her suitcase from the boot and enjoyed the gentle warmth she felt from the evening sun. She went to the front door looking for the small key safe she knew would be close by. Finding it, she entered the code she had been given and retrieved the key and used it to unlock the front door.

The first impression she experienced was one of the villa being cool and clean. She could feel the air conditioning chill her as she walked in. The lounge, plainly decorated in neutral colours had the necessary furniture, fairly plain but practical. A two seater settee, a couple of comfortable looking armchairs and a small coffee table. A corner unit, with glass-fronted doors through which a variety of small ornaments could be seen, dominated one area of the room. Three rugs covered a small proportion of the floor, the rest was varnished timber. At the other end of the lounge was a dining area with a brightly polished wood table. Settings for six people were laid out with each place setting having a circular embroidered mat with cutlery for a 3-course meal. At the centre was a vase with brightly coloured artificial flowers. A large smart TV was anchored to one wall and below it, blinking lights showed from an internet box with the Wifi code written on a slip of paper, carefully placed by its side.

Francesca left her suitcase in the lounge and walked into the large open-plan kitchen. Looking around she noticed the microwave and smiled at the memory of the eggs. The Corian worktops of dark crimson looked new and the cabinets on the walls were made of solid wood with matching handles. Opening up one of the cupboards, she found a good selection of tableware. As she shut the door it closed gently under its own steam. Impressed, she moved to the other cupboards and found tea, sugar and condiments in one, and glasses of a variety of shapes and sizes in another. A breakfast bar, rounded at one end and attached to one wall protruded into the centre of the kitchen. Four matching stools were positioned around. However, the lighting in the kitchen was drab, with just a few overhead hanging lamps and nothing at eye level. The overall impression was one of a kitchen that had been modernised but not quite finished.

Checking the fridge she was grateful to see a small carton of milk, a loaf of bread, and some cheese. She filled the kettle and made herself a welcomed cup of tea. The teabags were of a variety she had not seen before, rather weak but better than nothing at this stage. She smiled at the advice Isabel had given her and had packed some good old English Breakfast tea bags. She sat down at the breakfast bar and sipped the tea when the doorbell rang.

Surprised, she made her way to the front door. On opening it she was greeted by an overly enthusiastic middle-aged lady who introduced herself as Agatha. 'So glad you found the key alright. I hope everything is OK. I'm the realtor and want to welcome you to our little old town.' She spoke as if she was running out of breath and Francesca had to concentrate to keep up with her.

'Yes everything is wonderful, thank you,' said Francesca holding out her hand to shake Agatha's. 'By the way, did you put the tea and milk in the fridge, if so how much do I owe?'

'Oh don't be silly young lady,' she said handing Francesca the hamper she was carrying. 'Here is a small food parcel, eggs, bacon and grits so you can have a good breakfast before you go shopping. Now is there anything else I can get you or help you with?'

'No I don't think so, thank you, that is so generous of you.'
'Just one piece of advice if I may. You are in the best part of town here. Some lovely shops etc. I would suggest you avoid going to the northern part as it is, to say the least, a little rougher.'

'Thank you, Agatha, for your sound advice.'

'I believe your Grandmother will be joining you next week.'
'That's correct. We plan to look around the area and then spend a few days in Dallas on our way back home.' 'Wonderful. Here is my card should you need anything just

give me a call.' After handing over her business card, Agatha bid a cheery goodbye and left.

Back in the kitchen, Francesca unpacked the contents of the food parcel into the fridge having no idea what grits were. She went back to drink her tea and decided it was far too weak, so flushed it down the sink and used one of her tea bags for what she considered to be a really good cup of tea.

On the flight over she had studied the route to the crash site and was confident she would be able to find it without too much difficulty. With this in mind, she retrieved a map of the area from her suitcase and settled down in the lounge with her fresh cup of tea and worked through her activities for the next day. When her tea was finished she returned to the kitchen and rinsed the cup out in the sink. With that done she collected her suitcase from the lounge and made her way into the bedroom suddenly feeling tired as the jet lag began to take hold.

She altered her watch to local time, surprised to find it only 8.30 pm. Leaving her suitcase on the bed she made her way into the en-suite bathroom grateful to see a walk-in shower with soap and shampoo provided. Despite her fatigue, she stripped off and was soon enjoying the hot water and the steam it created. Feeling refreshed she returned to the bedroom and opened her suitcase to take out her night dress. After she had changed she climbed into the inviting double bed and set the alarm on her watch.

The next morning Francesca planned to get up relatively early, have a good breakfast then make her way to the crash site. Settling down beneath the quilt and grateful for the comfort and warmth she felt after the cool air from the air-conditioning, she was fast asleep in no time.

Chapter 23

As Francesca settled down to sleep, Leroy was getting restless. He had been lying on the metal floor for over 3 hours and felt the chill of the steel that had cold soaked through his whole body. He stretched, cursed for not having brought along something to lie on. As he lay there the only thing that caught his eye was the sunlight straining to make an impression through the small windows scattered around the walls of the warehouse. With the sun gradually fading as it settled below the horizon, he watched the dust particles dance in the fading sunlight.

Suddenly Leroy jumped in fright as the sound of one of the large warehouse doors creaked and groaned under stress as it was opened. He felt his pulse begin to race. The gap widened and then stopped until it was wide enough for a car to drive through. After a short pause, a lone sedan appeared, a Lincoln Town Car, its windows blacked out. Driving slowly and cautiously it began to drive around the inside of the warehouse, its lights on full beam, seemed to search every nook and cranny like a predator circling its prey.

Finally, it stopped under the gantry. Brad and Ryder stepped out of the car. Brad had a small flashlight which he had turned on. Leroy silently slithered back into the office. As he did so the light from the flashlight lit up the gantry. Satisfied, that the area was empty, Brad and Ryder returned to the car and the searching lights from the Lincoln continued their journey. Leroy held his breath and moved with great care as he slithered back onto the gantry to take up his viewing position. Below, the big car continued its search around the rest of the warehouse. Its slow methodical search of the area finally complete it moved to the centre of the warehouse. It stopped, facing the entrance, with its lights on; it waited.

There seemed to be a tension, almost palpable circling the warehouse. The silence was everywhere. Leroy realised he had been holding his breath all that time. Trying to exhale without making a noise, he soon realised how stupid that was as the occupants of the car had not exited.

It seemed like an eternity until a noise of a fast-moving vehicle could be heard, getting closer. Suddenly the noise exploded in the enclosed area of the warehouse. A black menacing-looking SUV with 4 exhaust pipes bellowing out deafening decibels came into the warehouse at speed. Roaring past the Lincoln it circled the area, did a handbrake turn and ended up facing the town car. The smoke from the smouldering tyres drifted around the still stale air. Leroy could smell the rubber. Silence once again settled over the warehouse apart from the deep throbbing engine sound of the idling SUV.

Fumbling with the small cine camera and with shaking hands, Leroy turned on the device and started to film, hoping he had set up the camera correctly.

The first to show any signs of action came from the Lincoln. Ryder came out of the driver's side and stood by the door waiting. Brad exited the other door slowly and waited. Nothing happened for several minutes until the back door of the Lincoln opened. A tall thin man stepped out. He moved to the front of the car, stood and waited, highlighted by the lights of the SUV. The side sliding door of the SUV opened. A 300 lb Gorilla-sized man climbed out slowly from the side, the suspension groaned with relief as his size 16 feet took his full weight.

From the driver's door a normal-sized individual, tough looking and smartly dressed, exited slowly raising his hands to shade his eyes from the bright lights of the Lincoln town car. 'Dim your lights you cretin,' he shouted.

Brad smiled and leaned into the car and switched the lights from full beam to normal. As he did this the gorilla went to the boot of the SUV, getting out a small set of steps. He carried them around to the other side door of the SUV, positioned them underneath the door and stood back.

The door slid back automatically and a size 4 shiny polished black shoe appeared. The foot searched for the step. Finding it, that foot was joined by another and the legs attached to the feet appeared. A little under 4 ft the dwarf reached for the handles positioned inside either side of the door and lifted himself onto the steps. The Gorilla reached out to help but his efforts were brushed aside with an angry gesture by the dwarf. Dressed immaculately in a dark suit with a silk shirt and an emerald-coloured tie, the dwarf stepped down gingerly from the steps and walked towards the tall thin man.

Both Brad and Ryder stared in amazement finding it difficult not to laugh. The comparison between the two key players, one well over 6 feet and the other just over half that size caused Leroy to start a muffled laugh which he found difficult to control.

'Monty,' said the tall thin man speaking down to the dwarf, 'everything OK.'

The dwarf looked up, his neck stretched as far as it could be extended to see the face of the thin man, and said, 'As discussed, money in the boot.'

'Drugs in ours.'

'Pisses me off buying back my own fucking drugs,' said Monty.

Smirking, the thin man said, 'Way of the world. You either want them or I sell them to someone else.'

'Bastard, fucking bastard.' He turned to the gorilla. 'Get the money.'

The gorilla, turned slowly and resembling a waddling hippopotamus moved his enormous bulk to the boot of the SUV and took out a black hold-all. Taking it to the front of the SUV he placed it on the ground and kicked it towards the thin man with his foot. The thin man looked down and scrutinised the bag for several seconds then turned and nodded to Brad. Leaning into the town car Brad retrieved two large boxes, bound in red tape and sealed. Both had a reference number and a bar code on the side. He took them over to the gorilla who tore off the tape with his bare hands and took out a small bundle. Using a penknife he punctured the wrapping and took out a small amount of a white powder. He tasted it and nodded to the dwarf who turned to the thin man. 'OK, we have a deal.'

'Not so fast,' said the thin man. Turning towards Ryder he said, 'Random check on the money.'

Ryder opened the hold-all and rifled through the tightly bound bundles of money. He undid the wrapping on one of the bundles and then selected a note. This he examined carefully for several minutes before finally commenting, 'Looks fine.' His high-pitched voice sounding out of place, caused the gorilla to laugh.

'Boy, that's a squeaker. Whose a little choir boy then.'

Ryder flinched. Trying to control his temper he responded, 'at least I don't resemble a gorilla.'

'If I sat on you choir boy, do you think that squeak would pop out?' The gorilla laughed and was joined by the dwarf and his companion.

Years of abuse and mockery over his voice boiled over. Unable to control his instincts he quickly moved his hand to the shoulder holster and withdrew a Beretta model 92c. The model although rather bulky was lightweight made of aluminium, durable and could be set to automatic; Ryder's Beretta was set to automatic.

On the gantry, Leroy jumped at the sight of the gun. His motion was unfortunate; he dropped the camera. The sound moved at speed down from the gantry enveloping the group. Their reaction was the same, all turned to look up at the gantry. Leroy quickly removed the SD card from the camera and started to turn towards the stairs.

Ryder caught a glimpse of a shadow. Set on automatic the Beretta only required light pressure on the trigger for three bullets to leave the muzzle of the gun taking just 50 mm to reach the speed of sound. Accelerating to over 1500 metres per second, the first two bullets followed a similar upward trajectory. Both took out the window of the office destroying forever the legacy left by Henrietta.

The third bullet lost some of its momentum on its upward journey and followed a slightly different path from its companions. The first contact it made was with an iron down-pipe. Ricocheting off the pipe it lost much of its momentum but carried on its journey before glancing off a metal sign. Now deplete of much of its energy it found a final resting place, that being in Leroy's upper thigh.

Back on the floor of the warehouse, panic had set in. The dwarf shouted at the gorilla, 'Grab the drugs,' before he threw himself into the back of the SUV and cowered in the footwell. As the gorilla went for the boxes, both Ryder and Brad dived for the suitcase of money. The three met in a tangle of arms and legs as they fought for possession.

Common sense prevailed when the thin man shouted, 'Just take what we came for and get out of here.' Both sides retreated.

The gorilla threw the boxes into the boot of the SUV and climbed in. With a squeal of tyres, the nondescript driver accelerated hard narrowly missing the front of the Lincoln town car before it exited the warehouse speeding away into what now was a dark moonless night.

Having retrieved the money and back in the Lincoln town car the thin man shouted angrily at Ryder and Brad. 'You fucking idiots. You told me this place was secure. Find out who the fuck that was and bring them to me. You understand?'

'Yes Boss,' they both said in unison.

Leaving the car they both ran to the gantry. Weapons drawn and using the small flashlight held by Brad, they climbed the stairs warily searching the area as they climbed. Almost immediately they saw the stolen cine camera lying on the floor of the gantry. 'Shit, whoever it was, was filming the exchange,' said Ryder 'Yea really,' said Brad, sarcasm in his voice as he picked up the camera. 'Of course he was you idiot. Well, we have the camera so no harm done.'

'Look here,' said Ryder excitedly, 'I must have winged him,' pointing to the specks of blood on the floor. They tracked the blood down the stairs to the door. Outside they shone their torches around. Brad shouted as he saw the fleeting figure of Leroy hobbling a few hundred metres away.

Sauntering back to the car they updated the thin man after climbing back into the Lincoln.

Shouting at the two men, frustration and anger in his voice the thin man said, 'So why the fuck didn't you chase him, you morons. Christ almighty neither of you have a worthwhile brain cell between you. This bloody camera may have had some form of an external device for saving the film. So find this fucker or we're all done for.'

'He can't have gotten far limping like that,' Ryder remarked as he put his foot down accelerating hard out of the warehouse.

Chapter 24

The rain started falling lightly at first and then gradually increased to a torrential downpour. Leroy was drenched and in pain as he limped along the darkened street. No light came from the street lights. Their bulbs had been broken by youngsters, bored and showing off their throwing skills with rocks. The resulting success was displayed for all to see, with the smashed glass scattered on the ground.

Leroy jumped in fright as a scraggy half-starved cat, struggling rat in mouth, rushed out of a darkened avenue. Nervously he looked around. The streets were deserted and he limped on. The only light came from a small, run-down convenience store that displayed goods that were well past their sell-by dates.

Behind the counter, chewing gum as he thumbed through a porno magazine, an old white guy glanced up as Leroy limped past him into the store. Seeing no threat he returned to the curvaceous body shown on the page wishing he was still a young man with all the energy and testosterone to appreciate the picture.

Scanning the shelves, Leroy found what he was looking for. Taking a packet of condoms and some lubricant he limped towards the counter. Taking out a crumbled $10 bill, he left it on the counter and hurried out. 'Hey bud, you want some change,' the old guy shouted after Leroy. Laughing he said to himself, 'Boy, he must be desperate.'

Outside the store, Leroy looked around furtively. The pain in his leg was throbbing but a quick check revealed it was only a flesh wound. The blood had stopped dripping and started to congeal. His instinct was telling him that the pain was going to be worth it. If he could get this evidence to the right authorities he hoped he would be well rewarded. Better still he could make the deal before handing the SD card over whilst remaining anonymous. Feeling more confident he limped down the darkened street until he found a small alleyway. Ducking inside and well away from the entrance he took out one condom and discarded the rest.

He wrapped the SD card in some snot-ridden tissue from his pocket, put the contents into the condom and tied it off. Taking the cap off the lubricating jell he covered the condom in a generous amount and then put more on his fingers. Lowering his trousers and pants he lubricated his anus before he gingerly inserted the condom moving it around until it felt comfortable. Pulling up his trousers he went to move to the edge of the alleyway and froze. The black Lincoln town car he had seen earlier in the warehouse drove slowly by, the front passenger's window was open and a flashlight searched the side streets and the alleyways.

Inside the car, Brad shouted out, 'Found the little bastard.'

***

Strapped to a chair naked and covered in bruises, Leroy was only half conscious. He hardly felt the slap across the face and the burning sensation of the cigarette end as it burnt into the skin on his chest. Always considered a coward by anyone that had ever known him, they would have said he would easily break down under torture. But inside his confused mind, he had convinced himself that if he could just hold out there was a life-changing opportunity. The reward would make the pain and suffering worthwhile.

'You sure there was nothing in his clothes,' the thin man asked for the third time.

'Look Boss,' said Brad, 'his clothes are over there in a heap and we have torn them apart, there is no way he has hidden anything. Maybe you were wrong and there was no external device.'

'That's right,' came the feeble mutterings from Leroy's swollen mouth. 'No recording, honest.'

'OK,' said the thin man, 'destroy the camera.'

Ryder put the camera on the ground and using the butt of his gun smashed it to pieces.

'Now can I go, please?' the feeble voice of Leroy, barely audible croaked out.

The thin man stared at Leroy for a while. 'Can't risk it. Bag him, Brad.'

Brad grinned as he went to the boot of the Lincoln town car and took out a plastic bag. Not realising what was happening Leroy's head shot up as the plastic bag went over his head.

Leroy's last words were, 'I'll tell....' before they were extinguished.

Brad shaped the bag to the outline of Leroy's head expelling as much air as possible before he tightened it. Leroy struggled, thrashed around and his bladder emptied. The thin man and Ryder just looked on dispassionately.

The view they watched resembled someone trying to make a bubble out of chewing gum. The plastic ballooned and then subsided until eventually just the outline of the face and the teeth were visible like a death mask; which is exactly what it was. As the body went limp, Brad continued to hold onto the bag for a further minute until he was certain that Leroy was dead.

'Load him into the trunk. Tomorrow I want you to take him into the hills, away from any prying eyes and bury him,' said the thin man.

Brad and Ryder untied the body from the chair and together carried him to the trunk of the car and unceremoniously Leroy was thrown in. They failed to notice the end of the tied-off condom that protruded from Leroy's anus.

Chapter 25

Francesca woke with a start when the bleeping of her alarm interrupted her deep sleep. As she came to, she struggled to work out where she was. As she glanced around the bedroom the fuzziness in her head slowly began to clear. The incessant bleeping was switched off and Francesca lay in the comfort of the bed gathering her thoughts. Her emotions switched between excitement for the walk into the hills and the sights and sounds she would experience and the partly sealed-off area of the crash site.

After a refreshing shower Francesca, dressed in practical clothes for the walk, went into the kitchen. Her first job was to check her mobile that she had put on charge the previous evening. A message from Isabel wanting to know how the journey went, hoping she had arrived safely was answered with a short message and some smiling emojis.

Retrieving the grits from the fridge she tried to work out how to cook them. Made from whole dried white corn kernels they resembled sawdust. Taking a guess she mixed some with milk and water and boiled them for several minutes. The result, being much like porridge, was palatable when mixed with some sugar. Francesca decided that once she had consumed the eggs and the grits she would have had enough nutrients to keep her going for the walk. That, together with some sandwiches she had since made from the goody bag along with the cheese Agatha had left her, would see her through until dinner time. After the dishes were cleared away and she had been to brush her teeth she packed the sandwiches and 2 bottles of water into her rucksack. Francesca then put the site coordinates into the Goggle maps App she had on her phone, and set off, reminding herself again that she must drive on the right-hand side of the road.

***

As Francesca left the villa and made her way to the crash site, the Lincoln town car was leaving a secure garage. Brad and Ryder had discussed the site they would use to bury Leroy. They were certain that no one would be foolish enough to venture into the inhospitable area they would be in. They drove down the quiet highway until they came to a narrow track that led through the sparse woodland to a small clearing. They came to a stop and looked in surprise at the red Ford Fiesta parked in the clearing.

'Shit, what fucking idiot comes out to a place like this in the middle of nowhere,' said Brad with more than a hint of frustration.

'Well I'm not going anywhere else,' said Ryder looking around, scanning for the idiot who had come to this area. 'It's bad enough driving around with a naked body in the trunk as it is. Let's scout around to see who the bloody idiot is. If we can't see anyone we go ahead as planned.'

The route they planned to take was up a shallow slope which then flattened out to a barren scrubland with few features apart from the odd skeletal tree and dried-out bushes. The scrubland led to another small slope which then descended into further featureless terrain. It was this slope that Francesca had just traversed and started the descent to the other side as Brad and Ryder left the clearing and started to scout the area.

Ryder moaning said, 'Bloody no one. Maybe someone just dumped the car and buggered off. Right, let's get on with it. Can't believe we have to drag his sorry ass out here.'

'Fucking good job he's a skinny wretch. Can't weigh more than a hundred pounds,' added Brad.

Going to the trunk of the car they lifted out the body of Leroy, covered him in plastic sheeting and tied off the ends until he was a neatly rolled up bundle. Brad, being the strongest lifted the corpse onto his shoulder while Ryder collected two shovels.

Singing, 'Hi ho Hi ho,' Brad marched off up the shallow slope followed closely by Ryder.

***

Over a mile ahead, Francesca sat down for a rest. Although the weather was typical for the time of year in Texas, it was still in the lower 80s and Francesca was not acclimatised. She checked the route on her phone. 'Right, just under a mile to go.'

She took a quick drink from one of the bottles and continued the walk. Coming over the crest of a small hill she came to an abrupt stop. Ahead of her were the remains of red and white tape, some still attached to poles that marked the outer area of the crash site, some blowing in the light breeze. Francesca felt her heart begin to race and walked on for a few hundred yards more before she arrived at the chard crater in the ground. A few fragments of metal were visible in the bottom of the crater but otherwise, it was just a hole in the ground.

'Oh my Davy,' she sobbed almost uncontrollably, falling to her knees with her head in her hands. As she felt her emotions taking over control she suddenly felt an overwhelming sense of his presence. She looked up startled. 'Davy, Davy,' she cried out, 'I can feel you, I'm sure I can.' She waited but nothing happened, just a feeling of relaxation that suddenly overcame her. Now crying gently but regaining her composure, she felt as though he was beside her. She reached out but touched nothing. Gradually her crying ceased, she got to her feet and began a silent prayer.

Feeling as though she had paid tribute to her brother and bade a final farewell, Francesca looked around at the barren landscape, pictures taken and stored in her memory of where Davy had died. Turning around from the site she walked towards her car, with not even a backward glance at the site, determined to remember her brother as she last saw him, resplendent in his uniform.

***

Further down the path, Brad and Ryder had found a spot close to a small copse where the ground was not rock hard. Breathing heavily they had managed to dig a hole a few feet deep and now rested on the edge of the grave. Leroy, wrapped up in his plastic suit lay close by. 'Right, time to say goodbye to this bag of shit.' said Brad as he and Ryder each took an end of the plastic sheet.

As they were about to drop Leroy into the grave Francesca appeared over the small slope just yards away from the burial sight.

All three froze. Francesca took in the sight instantly and realised what she had stumbled on. 'Oh my God,' she said and turned to run.

Brad, reacted quickly, dropped Leroy on his head and ran after her, catching her easily after a few hundred yards. Francesca swung a fist at Brad, who laughed as it hit him on his many times broken nose. Not even flinching he grabbed Francesca as she struggled, kicking, and screaming making it difficult for Brad to get hold of her. Taking a swipe at her, his fist connected with the top of her head. Francesca staggered but still tried to fight. Brad hit her again, this time connecting with her temple. Francesca saw stars before she slumped to the ground, unconscious.

'Bloody hell,' shouted Ryder, 'thank god you got the bitch.' Brad smiled to himself as he picked up Francesca, carrying her over to the grave. 'She's out cold. Must be the car we saw. Where the hell has she been, the fucking idiot. We're going to have to bag her and then bury her as well. Hope no other idiots appear.' Laughing he said, 'That bloody grave's going to get crowded.'

After taking off her rucksack, he dropped Francesca's limp body next to Leroy's. As he searched through the rucksack he found her passport and purse. Opening up the passport he scanned it and then exclaimed, 'Christ almighty, this bitch is a Brit.'

'So what?' said Ryder as he took a plastic bag out of his pocket. 'We can still bag her,' he said holding up the bag, 'makes no difference.'

'Think about it,' he said his mind racing. 'She's probably a visitor from the UK which means if she goes missing there will be a massive search for her. Those Brits never give up on a missing person. What a fucking nightmare.'

'This was the boss's idea so he can bloody well come up with a plan. You call him.'

'You coward, you call the grumpy old bastard,' said Brad.

'Toss you for it,' said Ryder and produced a 10-cent coin. He tossed it in the air. Brad called, 'Heads'.

'You jammy bastard.' said Ryder. Getting out his phone he dialled a number on his call list and waited.

'What?' the voice sounded harsh and impatient.

Ryder hesitated, nervous as always of talking to the thin man.

'I'm not a bloody mind reader, what the fuck do you want?'
'We got a problem. Some bird saw us. We got her and were thinking....'

'Now you are talking rubbish, you guys thinking, give me a break. Just bag her and bury her with the scumbag. Now get on with it.' The phone went dead.

'Bloody hell,' shouted Ryder, 'why won't the old bastard ever listen.'

'Ring him again,' said Brad, 'I'm not going to the bloody chair for that cretin.'

Ryder called again. The phone was answered straight away.

'I told you to get on with it.'

'Look Boss this bird is a Brit, not some local piece of skirt we can bury and get away with. You know those cops over there.

They will turn over every bit of the earth to find an answer. She has a hire car so they would know she was in this area.'

There was silence. 'OK, good point. Take her to the old caves used by the smugglers years ago. Those caves are a minefield of smaller ones, dozens of twists and turns.' He stopped as if deep in thought. 'Take her deep in, together with all her stuff. Don't kill her just leave her there. If she's ever found it will be assumed she wandered in, got lost and perished.'

Sounding worried Brad answered back. 'Christ Boss those caves are a fucking nightmare. We've never been in there. How the hell are we going to get in and out of there without getting bloody lost ourselves?'

'Use your bloody brains,' said the voice on the phone. 'Use a large ball of string, two if necessary and use it to track yourselves in and back out. Make sure you go in as far as you can and don't, I repeat don't, mess with her, you know what I mean. No DNA.'

Chapter 26

After filling in the hole and sarcastically saying a prayer over the grave. Ryder and Brad together carried the still unconscious Francesca back to their car. Dropping her unceremoniously on the ground they rifled through her rucksack and found the keys to her car in a small pocket. 'You drive the rental, I'll take the Lincoln,' said Ryder.

Like a spoilt child, Brad began to object when they saw Francesca begin to stir.

'Give her a shot to knock her out for a few hours. Give us time to dump her in the cave and get out before she comes around,' said Brad trying to establish some form of leadership over the pair. Ryder glared at him then went to the Lincoln and took out a syringe and a small bottle of clear liquid from the glove compartment.

Ensuring no air was in the syringe, he extracted a full amount of the liquid from the bottle. As he went to inject Francesca she kicked him out and caught him on the ankle bone. Brad grabbed her as she fought like a lioness, biting, kicking and scratching.

'Keep hold of her,' shouted Ryder as Brad pinned her to the ground. 'Boy wouldn't mind a few hours in the sack with this bitch.'

Injecting the contents of the bottle into Francesca's arm he stepped back and waited. Gradually her struggles got weaker and weaker before she lapsed into semi-consciousness.

'She nearly broke my fucking ankle,' moaned Ryder bending down to rub the area where he had been kicked, 'that hurt.'

'Oh stop winging like a baby and help me get her into the boot. We then need to stop off at a convenience store and get some string, maybe two balls if we're going to take her deep into that hell hole,' said Brad, 'oh and some overalls and a torch'

Dumping Francesca into the trunk of the Lincoln and with Brad mumbling under his breath about having to drive the rental, the two cars departed.

***

The cave complex, the men were heading for, was one of many sculptured by nature over several thousands of years. Water entered, froze and melted, the cycle repeating itself eroding the limestone into a maze of caverns interconnected by both large and small tunnels. The Edwards plateau in Southern Texas was such a place.

Drug Barons in the early 20th century realised the potential of the site as a haven for storing and distributing their wares. The larger caverns housed the workers and the mules used for transportation. For many years the police, happy to receive a healthy contribution to their meagre pay, turned the proverbial blind eye until the FBI finally showed an interest. Workers, caught by the surprised raid fled deep into the caves, some never to see the light of day again. Their bones never recovered and the site was boarded up.

Occasionally local teenagers keen to prove their mettle would venture past the broken boarding, flashlight in hand only to stumble around before making a hasty exit.

***

Arriving at the entrance to the cave, Brad manoeuvred the hire car so it was partly hidden behind some dried-out bushes. When he got out of the car he turned back to survey his work. 'That should do. Looks like she parked it there, but isn't too obvious,' he said to himself.

Brad went over to the Lincoln and helped Ryder get the limp body of Francesca out of the trunk. Together they carried her down a narrow overgrown path which sloped down to the entrance to the cave. Dumping her at the entrance, Ryder went back to the car. Taking out a large shopping bag from the back seat he went back to Brad at the entrance to the cave. From his bag, he took out two large balls of string and looked around and found a large rock. Unravelling the first few coils of string he tied one end to the rock tugging it firmly, making sure it was attached securely.

Feeling satisfied he said, 'We'll take the other ball of string with us just in case we need more.' Taking out a large powerful flashlight from the bag, he switched it on, grateful that the light was strong enough, 'We should have brought two as I said,' moaned Brad.

'Oh shut up moaning. One's enough, waste of money buying two.'

Brad dragged the unconscious body of Francesca behind him down the slope, not bothered about all the scratches and cuts they had inflicted on her.

Taking a deep breath he said, 'Right, here we go. God, I hate this place. Gods hellhole the locals call it and for good reason. Once in there, it's like a fucking maze.'

At the entrance, Brad picked up Francesca and followed Ryder as they made their way through the entrance. The darkness enveloped them and even with the torch lighting the way there was a feeling of emptiness, loneliness and despair. 'How bloody creepy is this?' said Ryder as he made his way gingerly through the first cavern. Ahead he saw a choice of tunnels to follow. Choosing the right one and slowly letting out the string he ducked down under an overhead rock and entered a small cavern with no exit.

'Shit, backtrack,' he said bumping into Brad as he turned. 'Christ don't walk so bloody close,' he said as he felt a sense of panic begin to rise.

'I ain't going more than a few feet from you, not in this bloody place,' said Brad as he backtracked into the entrance tunnel, struggling to keep hold of Francesca.

Ryder took the left tunnel which opened out into a large cavern. The floor was uneven and rough causing Brad to stumble under the weight of Francesca. 'Can't we just dump her here, bag her and hope no one finds her,' he said, his voice showing the tension he felt.

'Just get on with it. We need to get her well into the caves to make sure she never gets out,' said Ryder giving a tug on the string to reassure himself.

At the end of the cavern, Ryder found an entrance to another small tunnel. As he shone the light down it he saw that that tunnel led to another cavern. Taking a deep breath he crawled through it and emerged into the cavern.

'This looks good,' he shouted back at Brad making himself jump as his voice echoed around the numerous caves.

Brad shouted back, his voice sounding tense and angry.

'How'd you expect me to get through there with this bitch.' 'I'll drag her from this end,' said Ryder bending down and crawling back to join Brad. With an exaggerated effort, he grabbed Francesca roughly by the head and dragged her through the tunnel tearing her clothes on the jagged rock causing even more cuts and grazes.

Ryder looked around the cavern and saw numerous larger tunnels. 'This ain't any good. If she gets this far she'll find her way out.'

'Not in the bloody dark she won't. Turn off your torch for a minute,' said Brad.

Turning off the torch they are immediately enveloped in complete darkness. Both feel a sense of panic. 'Christ that's scary,' Ryder said as he quickly turned the torch back on, the light bringing a sense of relief.

'Can't risk it, we've got to go in further,' said Ryder as he turned and made his way to the end of the Cavern.

For the next hour, they slowly made their way deeper and deeper into the cave complex. One complete ball of string had been used up and the second attached to the first. Finally, they reached a dead end.

'Right this is it,' said Ryder. 'Dump her here together with her rucksack and keys. Throw her phone over there,' pointing to the corner of the cavern. 'She'll never find it in this black hole. It'll look like she lost it. Now let's get out of this bloody hell hole.'

Dumping the limp body of Francesca unceremoniously on the ground, Brad stretched his arms and neck as he relieved the pressure of his aching muscles.

They backtracked, both holding onto the string for dear life until they emerged from the entrance into the light. 'Christ that was a fucking nightmare,' they both said in unison.

As they made their way up the slope to the Lincoln they both felt relieved, celebrating their efforts with a high five.

Chapter 27

"Francesca screamed".

The noise reverberated around the cave and back to her in bursts of eerie waves.

'Help, Help, please someone help me.' She sat in the darkness trying to compute where she was and what had happened. She put her hand to her face but although she knew it was there she couldn't see it. She began to feel herself slowly drifting into unconsciousness as the shock began to take effect. She shook her head and pinched herself hoping she was experiencing a nightmare dream, but the feeling was drastically real. Her head pounded, she ached all over and the numerous cuts and scratches on her legs and arms burned.

Wiping bugs from her face she tried desperately to compose herself. Moving her hands around she touched something that made her jump. Tentatively she touched the object again and breathed a sigh of relief as she realised it was her rucksack.

Grabbing it quickly, she hugged it to herself as if were a long-lost friend. She opened the top flap and felt inside hoping to find her phone. Instead, she found the rest of the sandwiches made earlier and the two small bottles of water.

She scrabbled around with her hands on the floor of the cave feeling numerous insects and the stickiness of some pungent substance but found nothing. Feeling completely lost she suddenly realised that she still had her smartwatch which showed 7.25 pm. 'Little comfort,' she thought.

Feeling stupid she remembered that her watch had a 'Find my phone' app that she had downloaded as she was notorious in the family for always losing her phone. She pressed the app and heard a bleep from behind her. Crawling towards the noise she pressed the app again and saw a faint flash of light and the familiar bleep. Clutching the phone she breathed a sigh of relief which was quickly extinguished when she saw no bars on the signal strength. Moving the phone around in desperation she quickly realised that there was no chance of a signal.

Francesca looked at the battery strength grateful that she had charged her phone when she had arrived at the villa. Despite using it to navigate to the crash site, the battery strength was just over 70%. Selecting the torch app she switched it on and shone the light around. She gasped in horror. The cave was no bigger than a small front room of a semi-detached house, with rough walls and an uneven floor, covered in bugs.

'My God they have left me in a cave,' then started to sob. 'They have left me to die in this cave, how could they.' She turned off the torch app, sat and cried, not knowing what to do.

A noise started deep in another cave. Not sure what it was she started to tremble. The noise was faint at first, like a train approaching through a tunnel. Gradually it got louder and then in her head, she heard a voice. 'Follow the bats, Follow the bats.'

'Davy,' she cried recognising his voice. Again the voice.'Follow the Bats.'

Then as she realised what the sound was, she switched on the torch and saw the exit to the tunnel ahead so grabbed her bag and crawled through it into another slightly larger cave with little headroom but still no sign of any bats. Scraping her knees and tearing her jeans on the uneven ground she crawled as fast as she could, using the torch in a panic to find an exit; there were two. 'Which one,' she cried in frustration and then caught a glimpse of movement off to her left. Scrambling as fast as she could she took the left exit coming out into a larger cave with enough headroom to stand. As she did this she glimpsed the tail end of what was the nightly exit of the bats. Moving as fast as she could she came to the last point she had seen them and realised with despair that she had no idea which way they had gone.

The cave she was now in was rounded with just enough headroom to stand and a floor that although ragged seemed to be free from bugs. She checked her phone signal but again nothing. Her battery strength was now down to 64% and the time was 7.32 pm.

'So the bats leave at 7.32 each evening but that means I'll have to wait 24 hours before I can follow them,' she said to herself, the despair in her voice gradually breaking down into a sob. She switched off her torch and sat down feeling the overpowering darkness surrounding her.

The voice again in her head, "Follow the bats." Francesca was shaken out of her sobbing. 'Davy, how can it be you,' she cried out in desperation.

The voice sounded distant, eery and broken, "Bats return." Francesca suddenly realised what a fool she had been. 'Of course, monitor where they have come from and when they return crawl against the flow. So, could be 12 hours approximately from now,' she said feeling more confident. 'But how much further that will take me, I have no idea.'

Francesca sat in the dark nibbling at one of the sandwiches she had retrieved from the rucksack. She took a sip of water from one of the bottles, realising that she would need to ration herself as she had no idea how long it would take to escape this terrible place. As she sat in the darkness, her thoughts turned black as she contemplated what the future may hold.

The worry and horror that she may not be able to find her way out at all, that she may even end up in one of these caves being her tomb. Trying to distract herself from the bleak thoughts she started to sing gently to herself. The Tom Jones classic coming into her mind, "Green Green Grass of Home". Using her own words she started to sing quietly at first and then gradually singing louder as she began to enjoy the accompaniment of the echoes.

"This old cave looks the same As I sit down feeling lame And there's no Davy or granny there to greet me Down the tunnel, I bet, there'll be more problems Bugs to beat and Bats to follow

It'll be good, to touch, the Green Green Grass of somewhere....."

She giggled to herself and began to think of other ways to pass the time as she thought of the old rhyme "One Man went to Mow". She wondered how many she would get to before the bats returned. She took a deep breath and started.

"One man went to mow, went to mow a meadow.

One man and his Dog Spot, bottle of pop, an old tin can and all the jolly lot, went to mow a meadow.

Two men went to mow, went......".

After an hour she had reached just 240 men going off to mow and realised the task was both boring, repetitive and a trifle soul-destroying, so she changed tack. She switched between men mowing and changed lyrics to her favourite songs. Thinking for a time she suddenly smiled. Right another song to slaughter she thought, "Can't hurry love" thinking it might brighten up her miserable time.

Thinking up the words as she sang, her voice sounded a little more joyful:

"I need freedom, freedom to ease my mind

I need to find, find someone to call for help

But Davy said you can't hurry bats

No, I'll just have to wait

He said bats don't come often It's just a game of wait and wait You can't hurry bats

No, you just have to wait

You've just gotta trust, give it time No matter how long it takes I'll bloody well wait."

She carried on giggling as she made up more words. After a while, she reverted to the men mowing and after another hour and another 250 men, she took a break. Her night vision had now become acute and the very vague outline of her cave became more distinct to her. She remembered talking to Davy about night flying. He told her that the pilots were encouraged to always keep one eye shut when they were in the crew room before walking out to their aircraft to help their night vision. Every time she used her torch she had done this and it seemed to work.

Francesca looked at her watch, 7.25 am. 'Right, let's get ready,' she said feeling extremely tired, her adrenalin began to rise.

She waited, but nothing. She checked her watch, 7.33 am. 'Surely I haven't missed them.' As she said that there was a faint noise from the far end of the cave. Turning on her torch and keeping one eye shut she moved the light around the cave which had numerous entrances and waited.

Suddenly the first bats appeared from one of the entrances and headed directly towards her. She ducked down and hurried against the flow of the bats. Some hit her and she felt droppings fall onto her head. She retched but kept her head down just occasionally looking up to ensure she was going in the right direction. As she reached the area where the bats appeared from she was forced to climb a slope, slipping, sliding and struggling against the thousands of bats. Reaching the top of the slope she used her torch to shine it ahead making a note of where they were coming from.

As the last of the bats flew over her she made her way to the point she had noted. Exiting through this tunnel she came out to yet another cave. Feeling despair flood over her she collapsed on the ground and began to sob. 'I thought that would be the end of it.'

Francesca settled down to the same routine as before trying to counter the boredom and terror she felt by making up songs and going through nursery rhymes. When the bats exited at 7.32 pm she was ready. Her phone showed just a 35% charge but she had to risk the torch app.

Going in the same direction as the bats was easier and so she made good progress going through 3 more various-sized tunnels before coming to a halt as the last of the bats left. 'I must be close now,' she cried as there appeared to be no sign of a final exit. Her battery charge was now just over 20% and the cave she was in had a high ceiling but was narrow like a gorge. With the torch off she felt her way along the side of the gorge and stopped suddenly when her foot trod on an object that cracked under her weight. She risked her torch app and shone the light at the ground and recoiled in horror. The outline of a skeleton was at her feet. Shining the torch around she saw another one not too far away. 'Oh my God,' she screamed, dropping the phone.

The torch went out and the now familiar total blackness surrounded her. Panic set in and she turned to run but tripped falling heavily. The fall saved her life. Jilted back into reality she realised she had lost her phone, her only possible lifeline to escape this madness.

Taking a deep breath then another she gradually began to feel herself calm down. Dropping down onto her hands and knees and ignoring the discomfort from the sharp pains, she felt around with her hands ignoring the bugs until relief flooded over her as she felt the familiar feel of her phone. She checked out the torch app and cried with relief when the small light shone brightly.

With her sandwiches finished and just a few mouthfuls of water left, Francesca was beginning to feel the first effects of hunger and dehydration. She had a moment of sheer exaltation as she searched through her rucksack for any crumbs that may have fallen from her sandwiches and found a small mint wrapped in paper. The feeling was one of excitement. She unwrapped the sweet, put it into her mouth and slowly savoured the moisture it created, the flavour of mint that burst out gave her a sugar rush out of all proportion to its size.

Reluctantly, she took the mint out and re-wrapped it realising that this small sweet now meant a small break from this deadly mind-sapping and frightening routine.

Despite feeling exhausted, sleep was near impossible. It was cold, the ground was rock hard, uneven and in some places full of insects. She had tried to lay down, even putting her head inside her rucksack to ward off the bugs but although she would drift off for a few minutes, she would quickly be awakened.

A creeping insect would decide to investigate the cavity of her nose or a sharp object would cause a shooting pain in her back. Her sleep deprivation began to cause her to have irrational thoughts and cause erratic behaviour. Her singing became louder which sounded more like a drunk trying to remember the words of his favourite song.

The return of the bats at 7.35 am caught Francesca completely by surprise. Surrounded by them she became confused not knowing which way to turn. Instead of crawling she stood and struggled being spun around in confusion until giddy. She fell heavily, her head striking the ground giving her a few moments of blessed unconsciousness.

Coming to and confused for a moment, she felt her head and found a large lump above her eye. 'Did I just have a moment of madness,' she said to herself as she rubbed her head and recalled her nonsensical singing. She switched on the torch and realised in the confusion with the return of the bats, which caught her by surprise, she had moved into another chamber. She was totally confused. There didn't seem to be anywhere for the bats to have entered, just a high wall which blocked her way. Shining the torch up to the ceiling of the cave she realised there was a large hole more than 150 ft wide and 60 ft high where the bats exited the cave.

Francesca sighed. 'There is no way I can climb that high, maybe this is the end. I have no food or water just a small half-sucked sweet.'

Sinking to the ground in despair, she felt a wave of helplessness overwhelm her. But as she went to switch off her torch, the light caught another entrance to a small tunnel.

Glancing at the battery level, she realised that soon the light from the torch, which had been her comfort, companion and a potential lifesaver in the darkness, would soon be extinct. As the light shone down the tunnel her eye caught sight of a small piece of material.

As she crawled further through the tunnel and risking the battery life, picked up the piece of material to examine it and realised it was blue and from what could be a pair of jeans. Backtracking through the tunnel she put the piece of material against her jeans, a perfect match. 'They dragged me this way through the tunnel,' she said.

As she sat with the realisation that she was on the right track, her world was suddenly plunged into darkness as the phone battery decided enough was enough and gave up.

The darkness made her jump. She felt a wave of panic as she realised her one source of light was gone and she was now completely blind. She felt for the outline of the tunnel but her nerve failed as her imagination played tricks with her mind.

'You will be stuck in a tunnel of darkness and die a slow agonising death' a voice in her head shouted at her. Terrified she crawled away and sat in the blackness sobbing. Suddenly she felt a presence beside her. A calmness came over her and a voice, gentle and soft whispered to her.

'This is your only chance, be brave.'

'Davy,' she cried out, but as she spoke the presence drifted away and she was once again left alone.

Summoning up all her courage she felt around the rock face until she found the opening to the tunnel. Breathing heavily she entered it and started to crawl again. Her mind was still playing tricks on her. Images of the skeletons she had seen flashed in her mind and she started to shake with fear. Slowly and gingerly she made progress feeling her way with her hands in front of her waving, searching for anything to touch, like a blind person; which in theory she was.

Suddenly she thought she was having a hallucination. 'Is that a tiny beam of light,' she said to herself. Ahead and to her left and a few hundred yards ahead, a weak beam of light appeared to cross her path almost at ground level. As she stared at it, it seemed to grow slightly brighter. But it was the motion upwards that fascinated Francesca. While the right side of the beam stayed on the ground, the left-hand side rose higher. The movement was agonisingly slow and the beam would dance, even change shape and colour. 'Of course, Sunrise,' shouted Francesca. 'The bats returned just before sunrise.'

With renewed energy, she crawled along the remaining length of the tunnel coming out into a large chamber. She hurried as best she could towards the beam of light, ignoring the pain that seemed to inhabit every part of her body.

Forgetting that the irises in her eyes were dilated to their maximum from two days of darkness, she stumbled out into the bright sunlight and screamed in pain as her eyes reacted to the light.

Falling to the ground and shielding her eyes, she waited. Slowly she allowed the light to come through her fingers.

Once stabilised she looked around her. The landscape was similar to what she had experienced on her walk to the crash site but no features stood out. As she glanced around her mouth dropped open in astonishment. There, partly hidden behind some dried-out bushes was her hire car.

'I don't believe it, this doesn't make any sense. They leave me all my belongings, even my car but expect me to die.'

Struggling to get to her feet, she began to feel the aftereffects of the adrenalin rush. Her whole body was ready to shut down. Lack of water, food and sleep and unimaginable stress was now taking its toll. She sank back down to her knees and for the first time looked at herself. Her jeans were torn and filthy and she could make out numerous cuts through her tears. Blood stains and a thick coating of some sticky substance, probably bat poo, she thought, completely covered her jeans and trainers and the rest of her body. Her jacket, once an item of clothing she had been proud of, was ruined, stained, torn and unrecognisable.

Anger took over. 'They have ruined my jacket,' she sobbed, 'my jacket.' The mere fact that a favourite item of clothing had such a stimulating effect on her was extraordinary. Francesca struggled to her feet, searched through her rucksack and found, in a small side pocket, the car keys. She pressed the button on the key fob, smiling when she saw the lights flash on the little car. Reaching it, after a painful walk on stiffened limbs she opened the door and climbed in. The first thing she did was to lower the vanity mirror which lit up from a small light.

She looked in the mirror unable to compute in her mind the individual that stared back at her. The blonde hair was blackened, matted and covered in guano. Her eyes had dark bags underneath with a purple swelling above. Her skin was parlour, dirty and covered in scratches. But the worry for Francesca was the defeat she saw in her own eyes. Always a top student, her green eyes had always sparkled, and been a focus for people she spoke to. Commented on as one of her redeeming features, but now, dull listless, lifeless.

Francesca turned on the engine and waited for the satnav to get a fix on a satellite. Once it did she searched through the menu to find recent entries and selected the villa. The landscape picture on the satnav did not cover the small town the villa was in and no roads or tracks were shown. Adjusting the picture to show a greater area, and rotating it to face North, the town appeared on the very edge of the screen and in a South East direction. The information on the display showed a distance of 18 miles and should take 32 mins. Francesca put the car into drive and, driving tentatively over the rough terrain searched for any form of track. She found what she deemed to be a rough wide path which pointed in roughly the right direction and after a few miles, shouted a gleeful, 'thank god,' as she came out onto a tarmac road.

Chapter 28

Reaching the villa Francesca parked the car in the driveway and sat for a while. Looking around she wanted to be able to enter the villa unseen, convinced that if she was seen by anyone in her current state, questions would be asked. Happy the area was clear she made the short dash to the front door grateful that it opened easily with the key. Once inside she made her way to the kitchen leaving a trail of dirty smelly clothes behind her as she tore them off, discarding them where they fell.

In the kitchen, she made straight for the sink and drinking water. Head under the tap she gulped down great mouthfuls of water wasting more than she swallowed until common sense took over. Opening up a cupboard she found a large glass, took it out, filled it with water and sat down on the floor and drank it as slowly as she could bear. Two further glasses and her body began to react, first by causing her to retch but then slowly to absorb and rejuvenate. Sitting naked on the kitchen floor her brain began to compute what had happened. How near death she had been, the callousness of the act of leaving her there to die a horrific death.

Tears began to flow and total exhaustion set in. Her body, still filthy and covered in dirt and filth started to seize up as the scratches and cuts began to fester. Making a supreme effort she crawled to the bedroom and through into the shower. Sitting on the base of the shower she reached up and turned on the hot water which, after an initial shock of cold, began to wash off the outer surface of the grime she was covered in. Slightly refreshed she found the soap and shampoo and for the next hour scrubbed herself until her skin was red and the scratches and cuts cleaned out.

She made her way painfully back to the kitchen and searched around for any first aid equipment grateful to find a small tube of antiseptic ointment and a box of plasters. When the worst of the cuts and scratches were covered she felt waves of tiredness begin to overcome her she grabbed a piece of bread from the fridge and ate it on her way to bed. Not bothering to dry her hair Francesca climbed in and within a few seconds was fast asleep.

***

In her cottage in England, Isabel was beginning to feel concerned. Since her Granddaughter had been in the USA she had only had one text to say she had arrived safely. It was now the fourth day where nothing had been heard. Isabel had sent numerous messages asking for an update and also called but had just had a message that the phone was off. 'Enough is enough,' she thought, 'something is not right.' Getting her phone she called the airline she had booked her flight with to the USA to join Francesca. After a short delay, the call was answered. Isabel requested the next available flight and was told there was one available the following morning. Happy that she had now some control over the situation, went immediately to her bedroom, packed a suitcase booked a taxi to the airport and then sent a message to Francesca. 'Arriving tomorrow Flight number B283, Gran.'

***

In the villa, Francesca was still in a deep sleep and had been for nearly 18 hours. When she did eventually wake, her first movement caused a wave of nausea as the pain from her various injuries woke her. Her stomach groaned a reminder that the only food she consumed in the past few days had been a few pieces of bread. Dressed in her spare clothes she glanced in the mirror smiling at the dishevelled hairstyle she had created. In the kitchen, she opened the fridge and saw the eggs and bread. 'That will do nicely,' Four fried eggs on 2 slices of toast later along with 2 cups of English tea, Francesca began to feel as if her body was on the first steps to recovery. Sat the breakfast table she suddenly remembered her phone. 'Oh no, Gran will be out of her mind with worry,'

She rummaged through her mud-splattered and filthy rucksack until she found her phone. Taking it to the kitchen sink she cleaned it carefully and then went to the bedroom found her charger and plugged it in. She waited impatiently for the battery level to show a few per cent before it could be opened noting with despair all the missed messages and calls from Isabel, the final message catching her attention.

'Oh my god, Gran's flight. Arriving tomorrow,' and said to herself, 'does that mean today.' She went to the house phone and dialled the municipal airport. The news shook her. 'Oh heck, she is arriving at 6 o'clock this afternoon, just an hour from now.' Rushing around as best she could she picked up the discarded clothes and threw them into the trash then looked around happy that the villa was not much different from when she had arrived. The only difference was herself. There was no way of disguising the terrible state she was in, something she could not hide from her Gran.

At the airport, the arrivals board announced Flight B282 was on time. Francesca was both excited and nervous. Excited to meet the woman she loved more than anyone else, someone she could trust with her life. Also nervous because when Isabel took one look at her she would know something serious had happened. She had already noticed the glances people had made in her direction and understood why. The lump on her head was turning various shades of purple, her eyes still had dark hollows below them and the cuts and scratches on her face and hands had started to scab over.

Caught by surprise she heard the familiar, loving voice of her gran, 'Francesca.' She spun round to find Isabel striding towards her towing a suitcase behind her. Isabel stopped when Francesca turned to face her. Dropping her suitcase she hurried towards Francesca, hugging her as they both burst into tears.

'Oh, my darling girl what on earth has happened?' asked Isabel as she put her hands on Francesca's shoulders holding her at arm's length and looking intently at the various bruises, scratches and cuts.

Francesca tried to sound more cheerful than she felt saying,

'Gran it's a long story and one best told over a bottle of wine.

We will have to stop off at a supermarket as there is nothing in the villa to eat or drink,' 'So what have you been living on, takeouts, fast foods,' queried Isabel, concern in her voice.

'I wish gran, oh how I wish.'

***

Back at the villa, groceries unpacked and a meal prepared Isabel was worried. Her normal gregarious Granddaughter was so much quieter than usual, lacking her normal wit and charm. After their meal they cleared away the dishes and settled down with a bottle of wine, Francesca recounted the full story, and Isabel listened in silence, feeling every part of her Granddaughter's pain.

When Francesca finally ended her story, Isabel hugged her scarcely able to believe what she had just heard. 'I suppose you haven't had a chance yet to go to the police,' asked Isabel. 'No, all I have done is cleaned myself up, slept for ages, eaten eggs on toast and rushed to get to you,' said Francesca. 'Maybe tomorrow morning.'

'Agreed, it is a bit too late now. But have you thought that if these people ever see you, they may try something else? After all, you witnessed what must have been a murder.'

'I haven't had a chance to think this through yet. Maybe I should change the car. It would be recognised if I drive it around town.'

'Good idea,' said Isabel. 'First thing in the morning and then to the police station. Now let's finish this rather good bottle of wine. I need to go to bed. Never have been any good handling jet lag.'

***

The rental company exchanged the red Ford for a dark blue Chevrolet. Francesca was still feeling delicate with her various cuts and scratches stiffening up, so Isabel drove. She quickly settled into driving on the opposite side of the road impressing Francesca. 'How come Gran you are so confident driving over here,' she asked.

'Before I met and married your Granddad I spent two years

touring the States. I joined a chapter of the Hells Angels.' 'Say that again,' gasped Francesca. 'You joined the Hells Angels.'

'Yes, I know you will find it difficult to comprehend but I was quite wild as a young woman,' Isabel said laughing. 'I had my own Harley Davidson and went with the crowd. Looking back I was quite a rebel, smoked pot, had lots of sex.'

'Gran, do I need to hear this? I've always thought of you as this rather matronly figure who has led a dull and law-abiding life. Now I hear you were a free spirit, probably one of those flower girls I read about who believed in free love, back in the 60s.'

'Late 70's actually, but yes that is what I was. Managed to visit every state apart from Alaska which is still on my bucket list.'

'How come I never knew all this?' asked Francesca looking at her Gran in a new light.

'No reason. Never talked much about my life before I married, it was as if it didn't matter,' answered Isabel. 'Once I met your

Granddad I truly believe my life started. I calmed down. I loved him so much.'

Silence followed and tears began to trickle slowly down Isabel's cheeks. 'I have now lost my Grandson and so nearly lost you too. We could give up and go home but I feel that would be the easy way out. What these men did to you is unforgivable. I think we should go to the police and see this through.'

Francesca sat silently in the car. After a while, she looked at Isabel wiping her tears away. 'I agree Gran. I still don't understand how anyone can leave someone to die in such a horrific way. If they wanted me dead why not just kill me.'

'My thoughts on that. I believe they wanted to cover their tracks. If found, the thought would be that you wandered into that cave, got lost and died. You would have had your rucksack, car keys and phone with you so would assume it was just an accident.'

'Yes, that scenario crossed my mind. It's the only situation that makes sense. So next stop the police, agreed!'

'Agreed.'

Chapter 29

The municipal police department building, a rather austerelooking structure was situated on the northern edge of the poorer part of town. The Department was split into two buildings, the larger of the two housed a small jailhouse and the booking-in area and the smaller one to the rear, primarily administration. Both buildings were nothing to look at. Square with little imagination given to making the buildings have any ascetic pleasure to the eye. Built with white bricks that were showing the passage of time and looking rather grimy, the whole building complex needed a power wash. The impression was of a building guarding a long-lost past, a past of better times. A large sign over the main building 'To protect and serve" needed a good coat of paint.

The main road through the town ran directly past the complex. The entrance to the larger of the two buildings was directly from the roadway. Situated to one side was a small restricted parking area for the police and staff, but visitors had to find any space on the road that they could. The area breathed poverty and a serious lack of investment. A burned-out car and the few men who hung around looked menacing which gave the impression of an area best to be avoided.

The satnav took the women directly to the area and although Isabel nearly drove past the building, neither believed it could be a police department.

Francesca saw the sign "To protect and serve" in time. After driving around, Isabel eventually found a parking space a few hundred metres from the entrance.

'Right, here we are. Doesn't look a very imposing place for a Police Headquarters,' commented Isabel. 'How are you feeling?'

'Nervous, I suppose I haven't got my confidence back after the ordeal and not sure they will believe my story, especially now I've seen the state of the building.'

Isabel, with a glint of steel in her green eyes, said, 'They must do, especially as you know where a body is buried. Just try not to burst into tears although I wouldn't blame you if you did.' Getting out of the car she added, 'not over keen on this area. Looks run down and needs a good clean up.'

Isabel did a double-check to make sure the car was locked and then clasped Francesca's hand squeezing it. They hurried down the street to the entrance of the Sheriff's office. As they entered through large double doors they found the inside to the same standards as the outside. A long narrow hallway was crowded with what appeared to be the lower levels of the food chain. The noise in the hallway was deafening as people argued with each other and the few police that were there in uniform were busy trying to stop fights from breaking out.

The hallway had 4 benches screwed down and was on the opposite side to a reinforced glass partition behind which sat a bald-haired, overweight police sergeant. The walls were covered in posters, most of them explaining the types of sentences one could expect for a variety of misdemeanours, and most of those had graffiti-type comments written over them.

Under stress and showing the signs through stained armpits and a brow that he constantly mopped, the police sergeant was arguing with a 'Lady'. The term could be applied rather liberally as her clothes told a different story. Short skirt over black holed stockings, a short brightly coloured jacket over a blouse that had a deep plunging neckline. Her heavy makeup covered her once young pretty face now showing all the signs of ageing and a hard life. She chewed gum noisily and blew out expertly shaped bubbles as she grinned, seductively at the sergeant.

Showing no real interest, the sergeant, sounding bored said, 'I am sure you were just walking down the street innocently and had no intention of soliciting but it does seem a bit of a coincidence that you offered our undercover cop a blow job for $25. Remind me, Kalinda, how many times have you been up before the judge?'

Kalinda stopped chewing for a moment, leaving her mouth half open showing a piercing in her tongue. 'Look here Serg,' she said leaning against the counter and fiddling with the pen attached to the counter by a sturdy piece of chain. 'Just a few times and the old boy always got a freebie when I saw him. So how about I make your short and curls even curlier?'

'Yea yea, heard it all before,' said the Sergeant getting agitated. 'Now go and take a seat. I will process you and call you when one of the detectives is ready to see you.'

'Don't you have to caution me or something,' said Kalinda warming to the discomfort she was causing the Sergeant.

'You know the procedure. I have all your details on file. Now if you just want to get away with a caution this time, I suggest you get some fresh gum and chew that for the next hour or until you are called forward.'

Kalinda gave Francesca the eye as she walked over to the benches. 'Hope you have more luck than me, honey. Probably can't get it up anyway.' She expertly spat out her gum into a trash can a few feet away and took a seat.

Francesca slightly taken aback looked at Isabel and whispered, 'The sooner we get out of this place the better.'

At the counter, the Sergeant wiped away sweat from his forehead as he filled out a form. Francesca and Isabel waited patiently. Eventually, Isabel gave a polite cough hoping the Sergeant would notice them but he ignored them continuing his form-filling. Finishing he looked up.

'Yes,' he said with all the charm of a man seemingly devoid of any further pleasure in life.

'We wish to report a possible murder and kidnapping,' said

Francesca, sounding less confident than she felt.

'Really,' said the Sergeant sounding as if a story like this was a daily occurrence. 'Take a seat and I'll have a detective take down your story.' He went back to filling out forms leaving the two women somewhat perplexed.

'I'm not sure you heard my Granddaughter correctly,' added Isabel, 'she witnessed a possible murder and was kidnapped and left to die.'

'Look I heard you lady, and as I said I'll get someone to see you as soon as I can. Now take a seat and wait.'

Reluctantly the two women walked over to the benches.

Isabel managed to find a gap between an old-looking tramp whose smell made her feel like vomiting and a young girl who sobbed continuously. Francesca squeezed in next to Kalinda on the edge of another bench. She looked at the large analogue clock on the wall above the benches, 10.15 am she noted.

An hour went by, and the discomfort from the hard wooden benches began to tell on Isabel. She shuffled around as best she could to ease the pain in her back and buttocks but every time she moved the old tramp groaned and exited a smell that made her gag.

'Enough is enough,' she thought. Standing up she approached the Sergeants desk. 'Sergeant, can you give me any idea how long I will have to wait? We have already been here an hour and nothing has happened.'

'Look, madam. I told you I will get you to see a detective as soon as one is available. So you will just have to sit back down and be patient.'

Reluctantly she turned back to her bench just as Kalinda was called forward. Quickly taking her chance Isabel went and sat down next to Francesca. 'This place belongs in a museum, disorganised, dirty and so uncomfortable, my backside has never felt so sore,' said Isabel.

Francesca laughed and then suddenly froze. She grabbed Isabel's hand squeezing it tight. 'Ouch, that's one hell of a grip,' said Isabel.

She looked at Francesca who had gone deathly white.

'What's up honey, you look as if you've seen a ghost,' 'I just have,' said Francesca, pointing at the backs of two men who had just entered the hallway, one talking on a small flip mobile phone, as they walked down the corridor. 'Those two men who have just walked past are the two men who left me to die.'

As Francesca started to shake, Isabel put her arms around her and cuddled her. 'Are you sure?' she asked.

Francesca answered, still shaking. 'How could I not be sure? It's definitely them.'

Isabel stood up and went over to the Sergeant's desk. 'Not you again. Look it won't be much longer, two of our detectives have just got back. One of them will be seeing you shortly and you can tell your fairy story to him,' he said.

Pointing at the two men walking down the corridor, Isabel asked, 'So who are those detectives?'

'Detectives Brad Montgomery and Ryder Jenkins, why are you so interested?'

Isabel ignored the question and turned away and grabbing Francesca by the arm as they made for the door.

As they went to leave they heard the Sergeant shout at them. 'I thought you wanted to see one of these detectives. I just told you they were .....,' His final words were lost as the two women left the building.

***

Back in the villa, Francesca sat on the sofa stunned by what she had just found out. Isabel walked in from the kitchen carrying two glasses of white wine. She sat down beside her Granddaughter giving her a glass. 'This may help, although I have a feeling we are going to have to finish the bottle between us before we can begin to relax even a little.'

'I can't believe it, the police were responsible. I have always put policemen and police women on a pedestal. I would have trusted them with my life,' said Francesca.

Taking a sip from her wine Isabel thought for a while and then said, 'I know. But honey we now have to decide what to do. We can just go home and try to forget the whole horrible episode or plan some form of retribution.'

'Retribution Gran. How on earth can we get revenge in what is to us, a foreign country, up against the police and no one to turn to for help,' argued Francesca.

'Well let's think what we have going for us.' Hesitating, Isabel took a long drink from her wine glass and then put it down firmly on the small table speaking with conviction. 'They believe you are dead. You know where the body is buried and we, above all, have the element of complete surprise.'

She stood, picked up her wine glass paced around the room in deep thought. 'If we think this through carefully I believe we can get the evidence we need to prove that these so-called police detectives are guilty of murder and kidnapping.'

Francesca stood and joined her Gran, glass in hand. 'Yes I agree but it will be very risky.'

Isabel spoke with passion saying, 'I think we would live to regret it if we just went home now and let them get away with it.'

Francesca sat back down and sipped her wine in silence. Deep in thought, she twirled the wine around in her glass. 'I think you're right. We have never been ones for dodging issues and I'm not going to start now. You always taught me to face my challenges, fight for what you believe is right,' she hesitated. 'Let's get planning.'

Chapter 30

The town had a large mall to the south which contained several well-known retailers. Francesca parked the Chevrolet near the main entrance. Exiting the car the two women made their way through the main entrance to the mall and headed straight for the nearest coffee shop.

Isabel ordered two flat whites and joined Francesca who had found seats near the entrance. 'Thanks, Gran,' she said as she stirred a couple of sugars into her coffee.

Seated together Isabel took out a piece of paper from her bag. 'Right here is the shopping list. Not sure about the paint though. Are you positive you can get it?'

'Gran, don't forget I work in the research department for my company. This paint is special but not on the market at present. I have texted my colleague in Oxford who will contact our sister company in Detroit.'

Francesca got out her smartphone and searched through Google. 'It's the special torch which we will also need,' remarked Francesca as she continued to search and eventually found what she had been looking for. She showed a picture to Isabel.

'Wow they are different,' remarked Isabel as she looked at the circular black torches with small LED-like bulbs in them and a wrist strap attached. 'So how big are they?'

'They fit into the palm and with the wrist straps, there isn't much chance of losing them.'

'Perfect.'

'So as I mentioned, I also requested these two infra-red torches.' She put her phone away. 'They have promised to ship both the paint and torches to us straight away. They should be here tomorrow.'

'OK, the rest of the equipment should be easy to get including the mace spray. You can buy that quite easily over here. I just hope I get a chance to use it on one of those two bastards.'

'Gran, such language. I am learning new things every day about you. I have never heard you swear before.'

'Well, it's enough to make any Grandma swear.'

'Now Gran I am not sure about hiring a motorbike. I mean no disrespect but you are getting on a bit and ...' said Francesca before Isabel interrupted.

'My darling girl, I rode motorbikes for years and I still have my license. It makes sense and fits in with our plan so well. Easy to hide near the cave, has far more flexibility over the terrain and is quicker than a car. It's a no brainier.'

***

Francesca and Isabel left the Mall carrying a large bag each.

'Well that was successful, now it's just the motorbike,' said Isabel grinning as she put the bags in the trunk and got into the driver's seat.

Getting out her phone Francesca typed in Motorbike sales in the search bar. 'There are two Motorbike shops, if that's what you call them, on the outskirts of town,' Scrolling through their websites she read through their details. 'The closest one is called Jakes. He claims to have the best deals in town. Over 50 bikes to choose from. Let's try that one first. Someone is going to get a shock when an ageing Grandma comes in shopping for a Hot rod,' she laughed.

Giggling Isabel said, 'OK smart Alex, so I am an ageing Grandma and will act as one but don't underestimate the older generation. We may have slowed down but we have both experience and cunning on our side.'

Francesca gave out the directions to Jakes. As they parked in the forecourt, Isabel sat for a while surveying the bikes neatly lined up. 'They have quite a mixture here, Harleys, Yamaha, Honda. Boy does this bring me back,' she said. 'Right let's do a deal.'

They left the car and as they walked towards the entrance Isabel slowed down and started to stoop a little.

'Gran, what are you doing?'

'Just preparing for some negotiating,' she said with a sly smile.

As they entered the showroom, a young man dressed in a smart white shirt with a bola tie, blue jeans and cowboy boots, jumped up enthusiastically from behind a desk. He stretched out his hand in greeting which Isabel took giving his hand a weak handshake.

'Howdy folks, how can I help?' the salesman said with enthusiasm.

'Well,' said Isabel sounding unusually old as she made her voice croaky. 'We want to tour your lovely state and we are here for just a week so were hoping we could hire one of your bikes.'

The salesman taken aback and sounding embarrassed said, 'Well I'm afraid we don't hire out our bikes, and surely, with no disrespect Ma'am but wouldn't it be best to tour in your car.'

'No young man, you see I will be returning to the United Kingdom in a few weeks and will never return to your beautiful country again. I spent two wonderful years in my youth touring on a motorbike and just wanted to recapture some of those incredible memories.' She wiped away an imaginary tear. 'I know I look old but I am still capable of riding any of these machines, she pointed around the showroom. I only want one for just a week. I am quite prepared to pay for the insurance and a generous hire rate,' she added looking directly at the salesman who became transfixed as her green eyes bored into him.

Francesca, finding it difficult not to laugh turned away and went over to a new Yamaha looking over it as if she knew what she was doing.

'Do you have a license,' asked the salesman.

Isabel took out her UK driver's licence and showed it to the salesman who looked at it bemused as it was different from anything he had seen before. Becoming uncomfortable with the prospect of leasing one of his bikes to an old lady, he asked, 'That seems in order, but may I ask how old you are,'

'No, I'm sorry young man you may not, and as you know you cannot deny me the right to lease one of your machines on age alone. Now, I know you would hate to break the law so why don't you let me demonstrate that I am more than capable of riding, let's say the Harley over there,' she said as she pointed to a brand new Harley Davidson.

The salesman gulped. 'Madam that is one of our most expensive machines, it has...'

'I know,' said Isabel, 'It's a Max 1250 T Power train with ABS, adjustable performance suspension, LED lights, and cruise control, shall I go on?'

Standing open-mouthed the salesman was lost for words. 'Look, young man, let me prove to you that I am not a de-creped old lady. Why don't you get the keys, a couple of helmets and I'll take you for a ride,' she said as the act of ageing suddenly seemed to disappear as the true Isabel emerged.

'I'll have to ask my dad first,' said the young man looking and sounding confused.

'How old is your Dad?' she asked.

'Early 60s,' he answered, 'why do you ask?' 'Just say to him, always a Hells Angel.'

Turning towards the office he walked like a man who knew he had met his match.

Francesca came over to Isabel. 'Gran, what on earth was that all about and the old lady act?'

'Honey I have found through my years of experience it is always a good idea to unbalance your opponent. I once read a book by a Russian, Igor Ryzov called "The Kremlin School of Negotiation" where the key message was to always put your opponent into a zone of uncertainty. So I thought I would give it a go. Seemed to work.'

'Well, it certainly did that. That poor young salesman, he didn't stand a chance. He was totally confused.'

'I know, but if we had just asked directly I don't know if they would have let us have one for just a week. In this way he is confused and I have been able to muddy the waters, and more importantly, I thoroughly enjoyed myself. Here he comes now.'

Walking with less confidence than he had shown initially, the young salesman approached Isabel and said, 'I have managed to convince my dad to let you have a test drive, but he insists on being the passenger.'

From out of an office at the back of the showroom, a short, rather plumb greyed-haired man emerged and walked over to Isabel. He was carrying two helmets. 'Hi, I'm Jake the owner.' He winked at Isabel giving a knowing nod. 'I understand you want to hire one of my bikes for a week. We don't normally do this but I must admit you have rather sold yourself to my son, Matthew here, and business is slow so let's see what you've got.'

Francesca had been invited into a small but clean waiting area where the walls were adorned with pictures of motorcycles going back years. Sipping a rather insipid cup of coffee in a paper cup she walked around the room looking at the pictures. Three of them had Jake sitting astride various bikes; one of them showed him proudly holding a trophy. The bikes were barely recognisable as they were covered in mud. The inscription underneath one of the pictures read 'Jake Munro 1995 all-state champion.'

'All state champion for what,' she muttered to herself.

She turned as Matthew entered the waiting area. 'Everything OK,' he asked.

'Fine,' answered Francesca, 'but what was your dad All State champion for?' pointing at the picture.

'Yea, he always said the picture doesn't tell the whole story.

He was All-State for Motor cross, the first one that had been held and before it became really popular.'

'So he has been riding and selling bikes for years,' said Francesca.

'Long before I was born. Knows all there is to know. Must admit to being surprised he decided to give your gran a ride. He doesn't normally do that. Maybe it was something to do with her comment about the Hells Angels,'

'Could be,' added Francesca, 'although how my Gran was connected with them I have no idea.'

'Seemed to have an impact on my Dad,' said Matthew. 'They are similar ages so I suppose there might be some story there.'

'Maybe, although for the life of me, I can't work it out.'

They both looked out of the waiting area as they heard the roar of the Harley return. Sweeping expertly into the parking area and coming to a smooth stop, Isabel turned off the engine and put down the stand as she and Jake climbed off. Francesca grinned as she watched Gran and Jake give each other a high five.

As Isabel removed her helmet she grinned over at Jake. 'Now that brought back a host of memories,' she said.

'Well lady, you definitely can handle a motorbike,' said Jake grinning from ear to ear. 'How did you know I was with the Hells.'

'I didn't, just a lucky guess. Your sign said established 1983 so if you were the owner since then and a bike enthusiast, stands to reason you may have been with them at some stage in your life. Many bike enthusiasts were,' said Isabel. 'Just a shame they developed such a bad reputation. When I was with them we just toured, had fun and kept out of trouble for the main part.'

'Yea, the same. Wonderful times,' said Jake still grinning. 'Let me get you a coffee and we can sit down and negotiate a deal. I suppose you will want leathers and a helmet.'

'Certainly and also for my Granddaughter.'

'OK but it's going to cost you,' he added laughing. 'Hells Angels or not this is still business.'

'Of course,' replied Francesca. 'I'm sure you will make mincemeat of a poor ageing widow,' she added using a croaky old voice. Both laughed as they walked back into the showroom, chatting.

Francesca watched her Gran with fascination. 'That woman never ceases to amaze me,' she said quietly to herself. 'Hope her plan works?'

Chapter 31

Arriving back at the villa, Francesca parked the car and smiled as she saw a Yamaha already parked in the driveway with her grandmother nowhere to be seen. The bike was from the company's sport touring range, a Nikon GT in silver and black and Francesca looked at it wondering how her Gran was able to ride such a bike.

She collected the shopping bags from the boot of the car, locked them and made her way into the villa to be greeted by Isabel with a big smile on her face. 'Thought you had got lost.'

Laughing Francesca said, 'How many speed limits did you break.'

'Maybe a few,' replied Isabel grinning as she started to take off her leathers. 'I've managed to negotiate a set of leathers and a helmet for you too.'

'Is this part of your master plan?'

'Yes,' said Isabel still smiling as she moved into the kitchen and filled the kettle. 'Tea and how about a cheese, ham and pickle sandwich?'

'Oh that would be perfect, I'm starving,' said Francesca unpacking the two shopping bags. 'All we need now is the paint and the two torches I mentioned. I hope they will be here tomorrow.'

'Wonderful,' Isabel said as she made the tea and sandwiches. She carried them into the lounge and placed them on the small table by the settee before she settled down beside Francesca. Looking at her Granddaughter she said, 'What?' as she noticed Francesca staring at her questioningly.

'Gran, I thought I knew you but I'm not so sure I do now. This afternoon,' she hesitated, 'Hells Angels, riding a Harley like a pro and now that bike outside that looks as if it's for a young guy to go touring on.' She stopped, taking a sip of her tea. 'And that negotiating stunt you did, which incidentally had me in stitches. You're my Gran, not some wild woman with a history to make your hair curl.'

Isabel smiled at her Granddaughter. 'My darling, maybe it's time you knew a little about me. I haven't always been the model citizen people seem to think I have been. Not the mother and grandmother who has no past. That is one of the difficulties as you get older.' She picked up her cup and after taking a drink stared into it, deep in thought.

After a while, she said, 'People only see what they want to see, they forget that we all have a past, some like mine full of excitement, adventure and,' she hesitated, 'romance.'

'Gran, I assume the romance is just with Granddad,' said Francesca.

Isabel smiled. 'Your assumption is quite wrong, Fran. Let me tell you about my life before I met your Granddad.'

Isabel took a bite from her sandwich and after a few moments deep in thought continued. 'First, let me tell you a little about my mother. She was a twin which is probably where the connection to you and Davy came from. She and her sister lived in Southern Ireland not far from Dublin. Their lives were harsh. Up every morning before 4 am and into the peat fields cutting peat for the fire before walking 3 miles to school. They had little to eat and the clothes they wore were the only ones they had. So you see you come from hardy stock.'

'Ireland, I had no idea,' said Francesca settling into a comfortable position, knees up under her chin, tea in hand. 'I have a feeling I'm about to have a family history lesson.'

'Yes, I have a feeling this story is well overdue. So Agnes, my mother and her twin Mary decided to run away from home. They were only 14, can you imagine?' Isabel paused. 'Nothing but the clothes they stood up in and a few morsels of bread they had managed to procure. They made their way to the docks, walking over 12 miles and waited until they identified a boat going to London, crept on board in the middle of the night and stowed away in one of the lifeboats.'

'That must have taken some nerve,' interjected Francesca. 'No doubt. When they arrived at the London Docks they were caught as they tried to leave and taken to the local magistrates court after spending 2 days in a child's detention centre. My mum said although they were as such prisoners, they were fed, "Never had so much food" she would say. They had decided to lie to the court and not mention Ireland pretending they had just crept on board for some fun. The Magistrate didn't believe their story thinking they were a couple of stowaways and ordered they be returned to Ireland on the next available ship.'

Isabel looked at Francesca who was completely absorbed in the story.

'As they were being taken to the ship on an old open wagon drawn by a poor worn-out old horse, they jumped over the side and ran. The man in charge didn't even bother to shout, just let them run probably feeling sorry for them as stories of poverty in Ireland were always in the news. So there they were, in the Capital City with nowhere to stay, no money, no food, just the clothes they lived in.'

'So what happened? asked Francesca sounding disbelieving. 'You have seen the film 'Oliver', well their lives were not much different from that. They joined a group of runaways, lived rough, stole what they could, and never got caught. They developed a reputation as the Irish Twins, who stole with a smile and a laugh. The police were never really interested as they mainly stole to survive and people realised it.'

'So they were like two artful Dodgers, lovable rouges just finding a way to survive,' said Francesca.

'That's about it. They survived living rough, getting away from the law for two years until,' Isabel paused. 'Until what?' asked Francesca sounding anxious.

'Until my mother bumped into my father. She was in a marketplace by herself when she turned around and collided with him. She said it was the strangest feeling she had ever had, literally love at first sight for both of them despite, as my mother said, she looked like a scarecrow. That said she was a very pretty girl. Anyway from there things progressed, they were married, and had me but then the War came along and well, I lost my Father.' Isabel stopped talking and wiped away tears that began to flow down her cheeks.

Isabel leant towards Francesca and they hugged both in tears.

'When I lost my mum a few years later, I was on my own, late teens, with no prospects and to be honest, rather lost. So I decided if my mum could be adventurous, so could I. Booking a flight to the USA and a temporary visa, I left. No plans. When I arrived with little money, I got various jobs from waitressing, fruit picking in California and even hosting at Disney World. When my work visa was coming to an end, I decided I wasn't ready to go home but knew I would be in trouble if caught. I had no social security number, which is used all the time in the USA for any form of accounting so I had to be creative. Fortunately, there were plenty of illegal workers in the USA mainly from Mexico and I found there was no shortage of work, cash in hand for a well-spoken Brit.'

'So where did the Hells Angels come into the story,' asked Francesca sounding a little impatient.

'Just coming to that,' Isabel said laughing at Francesca's impatience. 'I was working as a waitress in a small restaurant in Florida when three Hells Angels walked in. I knew of their reputation so was expecting some trouble but the opposite happened. Admittedly they looked rough with their leathers covered in graffiti-type slogans, badges etc., but they were polite and great fun. They left a heavy tip and one of them, Jimmy Blackman, he was called, asked me if I would join him and the rest of his group for a party at a trailer park a mile out of town. When I told him I had no transport he said he would pick me up. He arrived on a Harley, I climbed on for my first ride on a motorbike and I was hooked.'

'Hooked, really,' said Francesca sounding amazed. 'From just one ride.'

'I know, but as soon as we took off I felt exhilarated by the speed and power of the machine. The complete freedom, wind in my hair and all that. Sounds corny but that's how I felt. After the party, which was really an introduction for me to the world of smoking hash, telling outrageous stories and laughing as I have never laughed before, I joined the group. There were 15 of us. Eleven men and 4 young women. We dressed like wild warriors, drove wherever we wanted, stayed in trashy accommodation, did any job for cash in hand and lived and loved as if there was no tomorrow.'

'When you say loved as if there was no tomorrow, do you mean, like free love,' said Francesca in disbelief.

Isabel smiled and held out her hand, taking Francesca's. 'Yes honey, it was a wild time but looking back I have no regrets. I worked hard whenever I could, saved and soon bought my first bike, a Honda CB750. Oh, how I loved that bike. I kept that bike for over a year.'

'So how long were you in the States for?'

'Well, now comes the crunch to the story, I fell pregnant.' 'My God,' said Francesca putting both hands to her mouth in shock. 'Can I ask,' she said hesitating, 'did you know who the father was?'

Isabel laughed, 'Yes my darling I did, I wasn't that promiscuous. A couple of flings but mainly Jimmy. He was a hard nut but that was just a show. He was a softy at heart. I never told him believe it or not.'

'You never told him he was to be a father,' exclaimed Francesca.

'That's right. As soon as I found out I was pregnant I left the group. I had no medical insurance, no social security number. I was an illegal immigrant.'

'So what on earth did you do?' said Francesca getting tied up in the story.

'I headed for home. I was in New Mexico when I found out and knew I couldn't fly out from the States as there was a strong possibility I would have been arrested for overstaying my visa, so I crossed the border into Mexico. That proved easy and then flew back to the UK from there.'

Francesca got up from the settee and walked around as if absorbing the story. 'So that means my Granddad was not my Granddad,' she said tearfully.

'Sometimes young lady you have to show a little patience and wait until the end of the story.'

'You mean there's more,' said Francesca sounding upset. 'I have had you on a pedestal all my life. The perfect Gran, respected, loved by everyone. The pillar of the community.'

'Darling you have to remember, everyone has a past. Old people were young once. Had adventures, made mistakes, took wrong turns, loved the wrong people and no, Jimmy was not your Granddad.'

There was silence. Isabel stood up and took Francesca in her arms. 'Your Granddad, even though you never met him, was your Granddad. I lost the baby shortly after returning to this country. I couldn't go back to the States as I would never have been let in, so stayed in this country and started a new life.'

Francesca held on to her Gran who could feel the sobbing through her granddaughter's body. 'When I thought that the man I had believed to be my Granddad, the one I had come to love just through the stories you have told me then thought he wasn't my Granddad, I felt an immense sense of betrayal. I'm sorry I should have let you finish the story.'

'Well, I have now. You know the rest. I went to a colleague to study art and fell in love with the not so good looking but utterly charming tutor who although several years older

swept me off my feet as the saying goes. We got married had your father, and set up a successful business until he...' Isabel hesitated as if trying to find the right words, 'passed away.' 'Oh Gran,' said Francesca, 'no more surprises I hope.'

'Just the ones we are going to plan for those two, excuse my language, bastards who left you to die in those caves. We will make them sorry they ever decided to mess with me and my Granddaughter.'

Chapter 32

Back in the kitchen Isabel washed the dishes and then with her green eyes blazing with grim determination, looked through the purchased items: two large balls of string, two minerstype helmets with lights attached, two mace sprays, a set of scissors, a large paintbrush, an A1 blank scrapbook, a selection of coloured pens and the last item, a single short Baseball bat. Laying out the scrapbook on the kitchen table with Francesca by her side, Isabel opened up the plastic container holding the pens and selected a black and a red one. 'First, we need to know, as best we can the route the bats take. So, I know this will be difficult, but can you mark out any route in the caves that you can remember,' said Isabel.

Francesca took up the red pen and sat silently thinking. Starting in the corner of the scrapbook and with her eyes closed she slowly drew a line, stopping occasionally to refocus before continuing. Isabel also sat silently watching her granddaughter as the pen moved slowly across the page in a zig-zag motion until she stopped and opened her eyes.

'Not sure if that is much use,' she said looking at the line on the page.

'It's a start. Now can you add in any details about the various caves you went through, small, large, tunnels etc...' said Isabel handing Francesca the black pen.

'That's fairly straightforward. That journey out of the caves will be engrained in my memory forever,' said Francesca as she started to draw outlines of the caves around the route of the bats she had drawn.

'Interesting,' said Isabel as she looked at the drawing made by Francesca. 'It looks as if the route the bats take is not that straightforward which makes it a bit more difficult if we want to use them as a distraction.'

'A distraction! You plan to use the bats, but how?'

'Honey we know exactly what time the bats leave in the evening and we will ensure we are there at that time with the two so-called policemen. If everything goes to plan, which it rarely does, the bats will be our ticket out of the caves and the beginning of the policeman's time of darkness.'

'Not sure I fully understand Gran,' commented Francesca. 'Right let's start from the beginning. Once we have enticed the policemen into the cave where I will be......

Isabel concluded her plan to Francesca who nodded in approval.

'You sure Gran, you will be taking one hell of a risk.'

'I know,' said Isabel 'but with a little luck and plenty of nerve we could get away with it. Are you sure you heard them planning to use a string when they first took you?'

'Positive, I was drifting into unconsciousness after they drugged me and I heard one of them use the word string. So I assume they had been planning to use the string as a guide through the tunnels.'

'Well let's hope you are right because it means they do not necessarily know the caves. Now try on the helmet and the leathers.'

Francesca took the leathers that Isabel had hired and tried them on. 'Perfect fit,' she said before putting on the helmet and checking the lights. 'How I wish I had this when I was in the caves. This together with the leathers are perfect for crawling and stumbling around in that hell hole.'

'Hopefully, they won't be as well prepared. It will also stop us from getting cut and bruised like you were. Now are you sure you will be OK to venture back into the caves as soon as the paint and torches arrive?'

'There is no turning back now Gran. Retribution is in the air.'

***

A post van pulled up outside the villa early the next morning and a young energetic black man ran up the driveway carrying a parcel. Ringing the doorbell it was quickly answered by Francesca. 'Parcel for Miss Francesca Fordham,' he said with a big grin.

'That's me,' said Francesca. The young man handed over the parcel and then a form, 'Would you please sign for it Ma'am.' Francesca took the form, signed it and as she handed it back noticed the young man staring at her. 'Is everything OK,' she said.

'So sorry for staring Ma'am but you look as if you have been through a tough time, I hope you are OK.'

Francesca put her hands to her face realising that she hadn't had a chance to put on any makeup to cover the scratches and bruises. 'Yes,' she said trying to smile, 'I had a minor accident on my bike, came a cropper.'

'A cropper, what's a cropper?'

'Oh, just an English expression. Means I fell off my bike.

Thank you for your concern.'

'OK Ma'am, have a great day and hope you don't have any more croppers.' He turned waving cheerily as he made his way back to his van.

Back inside the villa Isabel was in the kitchen preparing breakfast. 'Full English,' she shouted to Francesca who was busy opening the parcel.

'That will be great,' said Francesca who smiled as she took out the paint and two small torches confident that they were the correct ones. 'These are the right ones, Gran,' she shouted through to the Kitchen. 'By the way, remind me to make sure I put makeup on first thing in the morning will you? I forgot what a sight I look without it. Don't want to draw attention to myself.'

'OK, will do. Right as soon as we have finished breakfast, we can get our leathers on and then,' Isabel hesitated and smiled at Francesca, 'stage one of our plan can be put into operation. Now what do the kids do,' she put her hand in the air, 'High five,' she laughed as Francesca raised her hand and high fives her gran.

***

The Yamaha, ridden by Isabel with Francesca hanging on behind her, drove at speed and expertly through the traffic on the highway until Francesca taped Isabel on the shoulder and pointed to a track coming up on the right. Isabel slowed down, indicated and smoothly leant the bike over, which caused Francesca to hang on with her eyes shut. 'Just relax Honey,' Isabel shouted back at Francesca, 'this is my territory.'

Arriving at the entrance to the cave, Isabel and Francesca climbed off the bike and Isabel put the stand down. They both removed their helmets and Francesca opened up the two panniers on the back of the bike and removed a bag from each. In each bag were the items from their shopping expedition. Taking out the miner's helmets, she gave one to Isabel. Putting them on and adjusting the straps for comfort they then checked the lights. Satisfied they were working, Isabel took out the two balls of string while Francesca took out the paint, the brushes and the small torches.

Finding a large rock near the entrance to the cave, Isabel tied one end of the string to it starting to pan out the rest. Francesca joined her and together they made their way down the small slope to the cave entrance. 'How are you feeling,?' asked Isabel.

'Nervous. This brings back horrific memories,' said Francesca shuddering and hugging herself.

'Well this time we have the right equipment, I'm by your side and we have a plan.'

'I know Gran,' said Francesca taking a deep breath. 'Right let's get on with it.'

Entering the cave they both switched on the helmet lights and looked around. 'This is the easy bit,' said Francesca as she lead the way through the first large cavern heading for the small tunnel she remembered. 'This is where we have to crawl.' She pointed up to the cavern ceiling, 'That's where the bats leave the caves.'

They both got down on their hands and knees and began to crawl through the tunnel. When they reached the end, they stood up and looked around. 'Right Gran, this is where we will mark our exit point.' She took out the paint and with the brush painted a small mark on the ground near the entrance to the tunnel. 'Right lamps off,' she said.

As they turned off the lamps, Isabel gasped at the total darkness.'

'My God,' she said, 'I knew it would be dark but this is unbelievable. No wonder you were so terrified.'

'If it hadn't been for that small light app on my phone, I don't think I would have ever got out,' said Francesca. 'I just hope the police haven't got the same one. That said when we saw them at the sheriff's office the one on the phone was using an old flip one, probably police issue, so hopefully just a basic one.'

'Right let's see if this paint idea of yours works,' said Isabel. Francesca took one of the small infrared torches out of her pocket. Strapping the wrist strap to her wrist she switched it on. Initially, nothing was seen until she pointed it at the paint on the ground giving off a faint yellow glow.

'Brilliant,' said Isabel, 'this is going to work.'

Switching on the helmet lamp she took out the paper with the drawing made by Francesca of the route of the bats. Studying it and looking around she pointed to an entrance to another cavern. 'Is that the route the bats take?'

'That's the one,' said Francesca pleased that the map was working out as a rough guide.

For the next 40 minutes, they tracked their way through the cave complex marking out each of the key points for the journey back with the paint and for the way in and using the string as a backup. Suddenly Francesca stopped and looked around. 'This is where they left me,' emotion evident in her voice.

'Let's find a more suitable place. We need to set up a place directly in the bat's path and one where we can surprise those bastards.'

They searched around until they found a small cave off of a larger one. 'This is perfect,' said Francesca as she bent down to examine the Guano on the floor of the cave. 'This is definitely on their route. Are you sure you will be OK here by yourself Gran, in the pitch black just waiting.'

'I will be able to have the light on until I see you approaching, hopefully with those bastards behind you,' said Isabel studying the layout of the small cave. 'Then when you switch your light off I will do the same. The surprise must be aggressive and sudden, with no hesitation. Once we have smashed their lights we leave, but the timing is everything.'

'Yes, I know,' said Francesca. 'The bats leaving should cause all the confusion we need.'

'Now all we have to do is go back to the beginning and go through the route one more time. This time taking a careful note of how long it takes us, then knowing what time the bats leave we can work out what time we plan to meet those...'said Isabel.

'I know,' interjected Francesca. 'Bastards,' they both said together and laughed.

The couple made the run back through the caves twice more until they were confident of the route and the timings.

Isabel looked at her watch. 'That averages out at 36 mins, so with the bats due out at sunset which tomorrow night is 7.38 pm we need to be ready by 7 o'clock.'

'Agreed, the bats only take a few minutes to travel from their roost to the outside so our timing hopefully should work,' 'Yes, not an exact science but close enough to help us cause the confusion we need, I noticed you were limping slightly the last time we went through the route, you OK?' asked Isabel.

'It's the old hip problem, Gran. Had it all my life as you know, but it does get tired and I have been crawling up and down those caves but hopefully, it should be alright by tomorrow.'

'I hope so, we can't have you struggling tomorrow. Right, let's get back to the villa. Phase two of the plan now needs to be instigated.'

'Hold on a sec, I have an idea.' Francesca took out her phone taking pictures of the entrance to the cave. 'I'll get this developed and we can add it to the letter, gives us a bit more clout when they read it. See if you can spot anywhere on the way back where we can have the pictures developed.'

'Good thinking. Would it be worth taking one of the burial place as well,' added Isabel.

'I don't think so. I will just add the map coordinates so they know I have the evidence.' 'Yes, that should be enough.'

***

On the way back to the villa Isabel pulled into the entranceway to a small convenience store standing by itself on the side of the highway. The sign by the entrance advertised photo development. As they stopped, Francesca got off the bike and shouted through the helmet to Isabel, 'Nice spot Gran.'

Leaving her helmet on Francesca entered the store. Looking around the rather run-down, worn-out looking displays she spotted a CEWE photo station at the far side of the store. She walked over to it and took out her phone, opened the back and took out the SIM card. Looking over the instructions on the photo station she inserted the card and selected the photos she wanted. Beginning to feel rather hot under the helmet she started to take it off as the system printed out her photos. Suddenly her phone rang. Looking at the screen now with her helmet off, she saw it was her 'Gran.

'Missing me all .....' Before she could say another word, her Gran interjected.

'Listen, keep your helmet on,' Isabel said with urgency.

As she heard her Gran call, the shop doorbell rang. Francesca looked towards the entrance and froze. Two men entered the store with a swagger, both grinning.

Francesca recognised them instantly. Brad and Ryder made their way over to the counter. Quickly Francesca put her helmet back on and turned back to the photo station.

The storekeeper, a small portly individual with a goatee beard, horn-rimmed glasses and greasy hair looked up and swallowed hard. Sweat began to show on his brow and trembling with fright he looked visibly worried and frightened as the two police officers approached him.

'Well if it isn't that time of the month again, Lenny,' said Ryder picking up several items from the countertop and dropping them on the floor. 'You know the routine, CCTV off.'

The Storekeeper went over to the CCTV system and after putting in the relevant code shut it down.

Brad looked around and saw Francesca. Assuming that it was a man dressed in leather with a helmet on standing at the photo station said to Ryder, 'Better get that bloke out of here.' Ryder glanced at the leather-clad individual. 'No worries, won't hear a thing with that stupid helmet on.' He turned back to the shopkeeper. 'Right Lenny me lad time to pay up.'

Standing at the photo station Francesca looked up and could see the three men at the counter reflected in a large mirror hung up above the displays; a way for the storekeeper to keep an eye on customers from behind his counter. She watched as Lenny opened the till and took out a wad of notes. He counted them out and handed them over to Ryder.

Laughing Ryder said, 'Now that wasn't too difficult was it Lenny me boy. Just guarantees you are kept safe until next month.'

'Look guys, you need to give me a break. This store doesn't make much and most of it goes to you. Give us a break man,' said Lenny almost in tears.

'Oh my bleeding heart,' said Brad as he leant over the counter and grabbed Lenny by his coat. 'Stop fucking whinging or the price for this first-class protection we give you, goes up. You understand?'

He pushed Lenny who fell backwards taking with him a metal sign advertising a popular drink, which crashed to the floor. Francesca jumped as she heard the noise and looked up at the mirror seeing the two police officers look over at her. She pretended to be concentrating on the photo screen and after a short while collected her photos, turned and walked quickly out of the store. The two detectives turned back to Lenny who was busy putting the sign back up.

Giving Lenny a friendly slap around the face. 'Until next month Lenny. Don't let us down,' said Ryder.

As they reached the shop door, they looked through the glass and saw the Yamaha moving at speed down the highway.

Chapter 33

Back in the villa, Francesca and Isabel stripped off the leathers and sat down tired from the exertions. 'Tea,' said Isabel.

'After that fright, I have a feeling we need more than tea Gran. Good job you recognised them.'

'Bit of luck. As the car drew up alongside I recognised the shorter one by his nose, real pugilist one. Was just hoping you didn't take off your helmet, that really would have caused us some problems.'

'I don't think you could see me in the store but I had just taken my helmet off and thanks to you put it back on pretty quick. I can't believe those guys are not only murderers but also extortionists.'

'I wouldn't be surprised if they have several small stores under their so-called protection. Makes me even more determined to ensure these guys are put away for a very long time.'

'Definitely Gran, but not before we have had our retribution,' said Francesca emphasising the last word.

'So let's forget about tea,' said Isabel. 'Remember when we went shopping we bought a rather nice couple of bottles of red wine. I think before we go to phase two tomorrow we get a little bit tipsy. What do you say?'

Francesca laughed. 'You know Gran sometimes you come up with some really good ideas, but that is one of your better ones. I'll get the glasses.'

Settled down with a glass of wine in hand, they discussed phase two. 'I think it's too big a risk for either of us going into the Sheriff's office,' said Francesca. 'The sergeant who we spoke to before may be on duty and would remember us if we gave him the letter. I think we need to muddy the waters as much s possible.'

'Agreed,' added Isabel. 'I'm sure we can find somebody to take the letter in for a few dollars.'

'Right, we have their names, we have the paper and pens, no envelope but we can fold it over so the next job before I fall over from this rather delicious wine is to write the letter,' said Francesca giggling. 'Boy, this wine has gone straight to my head,'

Smiling Isabel said, 'Leave the letter writing to me, but I think I will write it in the morning when hopefully we will have clear but slightly tender heads. Cheers.'

They chinked glasses then after finishing both bottles of wine made their way, slightly unsteadily, to their bedrooms.

***

The rental car driven by Isabel parked in a street adjacent to the Sheriff's office. Sat quietly inside the car, Francesca and Isabel kept a lookout for a likely candidate to help them out.

Riding a skateboard, a young man not yet in his teens, rode expertly around the corner towards the parked car.

'He'll do,' said Isabel. Francesca wound down her window and as the young man approached held out her hand with a $10 bill waved enticingly. The young man slowed down and grabbed it but Francesca pulled her hand away,

'Tempted young man,' she said, as he slowed to a stop. 'What's your game, Lady, nearly had me off my board, waving that note in front of me like that,' he said with a heavy Texan accent.

'You didn't seem to have any problem as far as I could see. Now, how would you like to earn this $10 bill and another $10 if you carry out the task as given.'

'What's the catch, nothing illegal, ain't into that.'

'No catch. I just want you to deliver this letter to the Sergeant behind the desk in the Sheriff's office. Just put it on his desk and walk out. That easy.'

'So if it's that easy, why can't you or the other lady do it,' said the young man as he looked inside the car towards Isabel. 'Personal reasons. Ex-boyfriend trouble, now do you want to earn the money or not?'

The young man hesitated then nodded his head. 'OK, but the first sign of trouble and I'm off, understood.'

'Understood,' said Francesca. She reached into her handbag and took out the letter. 'To be clear, don't say anything, just leave it on the Sergeant's desk, turn round and walk out.'

'OK, OK. Got it.' He took the letter and getting back on his skateboard turned around, and made his way towards the Sheriff's office.

***

Walking into the Sheriff's office, skateboard under his arm and with more confidence than he felt, the young man pushed his way through the throng of people; prostitutes, rough looking individuals and men who dressed like women. 'Boy am I earning this $20' he said to himself. Before he reached the Sergeant's desk he waited in a queue of people who all seemed to have a problem talking normally. Raised voices demanding immediate attention, others shouting abuse, the whole scene was from a badly made movie. Not wanting to stay any longer than necessary, the young man pushed his way to the front of the queue. Ignoring the protests he slid the letter underneath the perspex protection shield that separated the Sergeant from the hostilities all too common in this part of town.

As he turned to go he heard the Sergeant shout, 'Hey you kid, you can't just dump this letter without an explanation.' 'Do you want me to nab him,' came the shout from an old man who had just entered the building.' But the young man ducked under the outstretched arms and before the old man could react, was on his skateboard accelerating away from the building.

At the car he stopped, panting heavily. 'Bloody hell lady, that's the first and last time I ever want to go into that place, it's mayhem.'

'Thank you, young man,' said Francesca, handing over another $10. 'You have saved me a great deal of trouble.' Taking the note from Francesca, he grinned and waved as he pushed off on his skateboard.

'Now back to the villa and this time I think tea would be better on the agenda. Still feeling slightly under the weather from last night's wine tasting,' said Isabel.

'Don't you mean wine drinking Gran, a bottle each is my limit?'

'Yes, but it was fun,' laughed Isabel.

***

Inside the Sheriff's office, the chaos gradually calmed down and some form of order was established. The Sergeant wiped the sweat from his brow and shouted down the corridor to a young constable, 'Hey Bernie, get us a coffee, make it strong, I bloody well need it.'

Bernie, a recruit who only just managed to pass both his physical and his entrance exams hurried off to the canteen. At the minimum height for entry and always struggling with weight problems, he suffered from a lack of self-confidence due to a receding hairline and teeth that were desperately in need of straightening.

Returning shortly afterwards with the coffee, he put it on the Sergeant's desk.

'There you go Serg, anything else?' 'No thanks, Bernie.'

As Bernie made to leave he noticed the letter on the desk. 'Hey Serg, this note is addressed to Detectives Montgomery and Jenkins, shall I take it to their office?'

The Sergeant looked at the note and remembered the young lad who had left it there. 'I suppose so, I planned to throw it in the bin, to dam busy. Left here earlier by some lad who scampered away pretty dam quick.'

The young constable picked up the note and walked down the corridor towards the open office area shared by the detectives.

Glancing down at the note he saw that it hadn't been sealed, just folded over. Tempted to see what the note said, he went into the Gents. As he started to open it a young good looking Detective came out of one of the cubicles catching him in the act. 'Peeking into someone else's correspondence are you young Bernie.'

He took the note from the embarrassed recruit and saw who it was addressed to. 'Right, I will deliver this. Not too impressed with you young man. You are meant to set an example not be dishonest yourself. I'll overlook it this time but be warned.'

The Detective took the note and walked through the open planned office. 'Hey Shiny, was that you coming out of the loo with a young constable, didn't take you for a shirt lifter,' laughed an older Detective. There was a chorus of laughter.

'Wrong as usual Glen. Just giving the young man a few words of wisdom, something that you would know nothing about,' answered back Shiny, smiling. 'In your case, wisdom doesn't seem to have come with old age. Seems to have passed you by.' He walked on to more laughter from the other detectives.

Making his way to the end of the open planned office he came to a small separate office with the names on the door of Detective Brad Montgomery and Detective Ryder Jenkins. Seeing no one inside he entered, noting the shambles of empty coffee cups, open files and a desk full of odd bits of paper. Shaking his head in disgust he looked around for somewhere to leave the note.

As he did so Ryder and Brad walked in. 'What the fuck are you doing snooping around our office, Shiny. We're the senior detectives round here and if you want to enter our office you bloody well wait to be invited, got it,' shouted Ryder, his high-pitched voice seeming to hit higher notes as his anger increased.

Shiny looked at the two officers. Smiling, he handed over the note to Ryder and went to walk away but was blocked by Brad. 'You little shit, you need to know your place. You fast-track bastards know nothing about real police work.'

'I'm sure you are right Detective Montgomery. I have a lot to learn from you two, especially how to keep a tidy office.' He looked back at the shambles in the office and smiled. 'A lot to learn.'

As Shiny made his way back to his desk, Brad threw the note into the trash can.

'Hey what are you doing, that may be a note from Katrin,' said Ryder going to the bin and retrieving the note.

Laughing and giving a snipping gesture with his fingers Brad said, 'Boy I hope your missus doesn't find out, she'll nip your balls off in the middle of the night for sure.'

Opening the note Ryder whispered to Brad, 'Keep your voice down.'

'She loves me, she loves me not,' taunted Brad. 'Man, you'll do anything for a blow job.'

'Shut the fuck up and close the door,' said Ryder taking the note to his desk and sitting down. 'Shit, shit,' he shouted as he handed the note to Brad.

Reading the note aloud Brad began to pale.

"Dear Scumbags, extortionists, kidnappers and finally murderers

I hope this note finds you in shock. You will probably remember me, the young woman left to die in the cave. I have attached a picture of the cave entrance in case you have forgotten.

So scumbags, yes I survived. I'm fighting fit and about to ensure you pay heavily for your crimes. Two options. One, I contact the FBI giving them the coordinates of the burial site, and information on my time in the cave. I have so much forensic evidence from my clothes, rucksack etc. to convince any jury of your guilt. I have also bagged all the evidence and addressed it to the FBI office in Austin to be delivered if I don't return in 24 hours. Correct me if I'm wrong but I believe they still have the death penalty in Texas. I hope I'm invited.

Option two. You meet me at the cave entrance tonight at precisely 7 pm with $50k."

Ryder and Brad ashen, fell silent. As Brad sat down, Bernie knocked on their door. 'Coffee,' he asked. In unison, they both shouted, 'fuck off.'

The office area goes quiet as the staff looked towards the offices of the two detectives. As Bernie retreated, Brad got up and walked aggressively to the office door, stared at the other staff members and shouted, 'What the fuck are you lot looking at. Get back to work you lazy fuckers.' He slammed the door causing the glass panels, surrounding the door, to shake.

Brad went back into the office and sat down next to Ryder.

'Bitch,' is all Ryder could think of saying.

'Well, that's very helpful. Here we are facing the bloody electric chair and all you can think of saying is 'Bitch.'

'Alright, what the fuck do you suggest?' said Ryder angrily.

'We meet up at the caves, waste the bitch and this time take her dead body into the depths of that bloody cave so far in no one will ever find her.'

'Alright, as soon as we see her, and provided there is no one else around we take her out. Guns this time, no messing.'

'No guns until we have got the information we need out of her. If she has a plan that the evidence will be posted if something happens to her, we need to know.'

They both sat in silence for a while and then re-read the letter. '$50k, bloody cheek. Not a chance you miserable bitch,' said Brad as he screwed up the paper and threw it into the bin. 'You bloody idiot, we need to burn the fucking paper,' said Ryder getting up from his chair and going over to the bin. 'Someone gets hold of that and we will be for the chair.' Getting out his lighter, he set fire to the piece of paper, the ashes floated into the bin.

As the smoke from the burning letter began to circulate through the office there was a heavy knock on the door and Shiny walked in. 'Hey, guys be bloody careful, smoke from that fire you've just started could have set off the sprinkler system.'

Losing his temper Brad jumped up from behind his desk and moved aggressively towards Shiny, grabbed hold of him by the jacket lapels, 'Mind you're own fucking business.'

'This is my business, you moron. I'm the health and safety representative for this building and you have just broken a golden rule. No open flames in the building' said Shiny.

Looking Brad squarely in the eyes he placed his thumbs on the back of Brad's hands with his fingers underneath. Using pressure, he slowly bent Brad's hands sideways causing him to wince and release the jacket lapels with a pained expression on his face. 'Don't you ever lay a hand on me again? Next time I'll break both your hands.' Shiny turned and walked out leaving Brad rubbing his hands.

Chapter 34

Isabel and Francesca arrived at the entrance to the caves early. Leaving the Yamaha well hidden in the undergrowth, together with their helmets, Francesca took all their equipment out of the panniers. Putting on the miner's helmet and sounding nervous she said, 'Check the lights.'

'They are fine, I put fresh batteries in last night as you know Honey.' She gave Francesca a reassuring cuddle and turned on her light.

Francesca did the same and smiled, 'Sorry Gran feeling rather tense.'

'Understandable. Now let's check all the equipment we need and get ready. We have over half an hour, sufficient time for me to get into position and you to take a very deep breath and remain calm.'

Together they checked through the equipment they had taken with them. Isabel picked up her short baseball bat and the mace spray giving it a quick squirt which produced a satisfying spray, pungent even in the open air. Francesca did the same then checked out the infra-red lamps and handed one over to Isabel.

Giving Francesca a final cuddle, Isabel made her way into the cave. Using the infrared lamp and the lights from her miner's lamp, she made her way confidently through various tunnels until she reached her planned ambush point. Settling down and turning off the light, she took several deep breaths and waited.

Outside the cave, Francesca stood close to the entrance feeling nervous. The light was beginning to fade slightly and the air getting cooler. She checked her watch for the umpteenth time looking intently down the track wondering if their plan would fall at the first hurdle. 'Nearly 7 pm,' she said talking to herself, 'doesn't look as if they are coming,' her voice sounding a mix of relief and disappointment.

As she turned to go into the cave to find her Gran she caught a glint of a light out of the corner of her eye and turned quickly. Looking down the track she saw a black Lincoln making its way towards the caves, its lights bouncing as the car rocked over the uneven ground.

***

Inside the car, Brad scanned the area around the cave entrance. 'There she is. Bloody hell she is in leathers with a miners helmet.'

Ryder, slowed the car, coming to a halt over 50 metres from where Francesca was standing.

'Right let's play it cool. As we planned, we pretend we have the cash and at the first chance grab her. OK,' said Ryder.

Getting out of the car the two detectives went to the front and stood waiting. Ryder was holding a bag. Shouting, 'Here's your cash Bitch. Now where is the evidence.' He threw the bag a few metres ahead of him.

Nothing happened, Francesca just stood there.

'Look bitch, we have kept our side of the bargain, there's your cash now stick to your side of the deal,' added Brad getting annoyed.

Still, Francesca just stood there, not moving.

'I've had enough of this,' said Brad and started to walk towards Francesca. 'Right you whore you asked for this.'

As if by magic Francesca vanished into the cave. 'Shit,' shouted Brad. Running back to the car and yelling at Ryder, 'We need to get the bloody string and the torch.'

Ryder opened the boot and took both out. 'Christ we need to catch that bitch before she gets too deep into the caves.'

Rushing down to the entrance Brad grabbed the string from Ryder and hastily tied it to the large rock they had used previously. Switching on the only torch they had, together they hurried into the cave entrance.

Shinning the torch around the light captured Francesca entering the narrow tunnel. 'There,' shouted Ryder pointing the light at the tunnel. Both running they collided as they try to enter the tunnel together.

'Look, Moron, I've got the fucking light so I lead.' Brad backed off as Ryder crawled into the tunnel cursing as his knees scraped the hard uneven ground and he felt his trousers begin to tear. 'Shit should have put on those overalls,' he complained.

'Shut the fuck up and get a bloody move on,' shouted Brad.

'When we catch the Bitch I'm not hanging back this time. Once I get her to talk I'm having my way with her, bugger all that stuff and nonsense the Boss croaks on about. We bury her where no one will ever find her,'

'Yes OK, but me first,' said Ryder.

**

Ahead, Francesca glanced back to make sure she was being followed. As she climbed out of the tunnel she caught her foot on a small protrusion causing her to stumble; she felt a sharp pain in her hip. 'Oh no, not now,' she cried.

Limping on as fast as she could and feeling the pain build, she felt her hip seizing and begin to drag. 'Christ what a time for it to play up.' Hurrying as best she could, she glanced back again, now nervous as she realised they were gaining on her.

Behind Francesca, Ryder realised the gap was closing. Excitedly he said, 'Looks as if we will catch the Bitch. Look she's injured and limping. I don't know what her plan was but it's backfiring big time.'

Francesca realised that although close to the meeting point with Isabel, she wasn't going to make it. She shouted, 'Gran I need help.' Her voice echoed around the caves becoming barely audible as Ryder stopped to listen and tried to make out what she had said.

Further down the route, Isabel heard the cry and immediately made her way back down the tunnels. 'All the best laid plans and all that,' she murmured to herself. Using the infrared lamp to guide her she moved effortlessly towards her Granddaughter.

Ahead she heard a commotion and saw a light flashing around. 'They have caught her,' she said to herself as she gripped hold of the baseball bat in her right hand and the mace spray in her left.

Ryder and Brad were joyous. They had hold of Francesca who was struggling and shouting.

'Let go of me you animals,' she screamed at them but her struggles were easily controlled by the two detectives.

'Now you stupid Bitch, where have you kept all the evidence,' shouted Brad as he smacked her heavily around the face avoiding the helmet. 'The sooner you tell us the sooner we'll let you go.'

Francesca collapsed to the ground stunned by the blow. Reaching down Brad grabbed hold of Francesca's leather collar and hauled her to her feet.

'If I tell you anything that will be the end of me, and you know it,' said Francesca as she wiped the small trickle of blood running down her face from a cut above her eye.

'Give me the torch,' Brad yelled at Ryder who handed it over. Brad shone it into Francesca's eyes. 'Pretty little thing aren't you, even with those cuts and bruises. But lady by the time we have finished with you those small marks will be the least of your worries. Ryder get over here, we need to get these leathers off her.'

Creeping into the area where the two detectives had caught Francesca, Isabel with the light on her miner's helmet off, stood up unnoticed. As Ryder moved towards Brad she sprayed the mace directly into his eyes.

Ryder stopped, stunned and shocked by what he felt. 'What the fuck was that?' he shouted as he moved his hands up to his face rubbing his eyes.

As he did so the oil from a variety of plants including the chilli peppers in the mace, began to burn. 'Shit my eyes, my eyes,' he screamed and then even louder as the baseball bat collided with his shin, causing him to collapse to the ground, his shin bone suffering a hairline fracture.

Brad, taken completely by surprise, let go of Francesca who fell to the ground. Turning to see why Ryder had screamed like a baby, he shouted, 'What the fuck are you screaming about?' He moved the torch around, the light illuminating Ryder rolling about on the ground.

Brad looked around in panic. 'What the fuck's going on?' A movement in the shadow caught his eye. He turned towards the movement and then suddenly felt a burning sensation as the mace spray found the perfect target; his eyes. 'What the fuck,' he yelled dropping the torch in panic as he moved his hands to his eyes.

'Get the torch,' shouted Isabel. Francesca still stunned from the blow shook her head to clear it and made a grab for the torch.

Brad, eyes streaming fell to his knees and scrabbled around seeing through the tears, the light of the torch. He found the torch at the same time as Francesca and swung his fist wildly connecting with the back of her helmet. He felt a bone break in his hand and cried out in pain. With his free hand, he grabbed Francesca, wrapping an arm around her neck. Dragging her to her feet, he moved the torch around illuminating Isabel just a few metres away. 'Christ another one,' he shouted as he tightened his grip around Francesca's neck. 'One more step Lady and this young neck will snap then it will just be me and you.'

Isabel glanced down at her watch. 'Hold on honey just another few seconds.'

'What the fuck are you talking about. Look you bitch we came here to make a deal and that's all we're interested in. Tell us where the evidence is and we can all walk out of here.' 'I don't think so for two reasons. First, your partner here isn't walking anywhere and secondly,' Isabel hesitated as she heard the sound she had been waiting for, 'We have another weapon.'

As the first of the bats arrived their sonar tracking ensured they would avoid the group, Brad looked around confused. 'Is that your weapon,' he laughed, a few insects flying around.' Suddenly the cave filled with thousands of bats making their way through the tunnels of the cave. Brad let go of Francesca, as he moved his hands to protect his face from the bats, eyes still streaming. 'Christ get them away from me,' he screamed. Isabel ducked down below the mainstream of bats and grabbed the torch. She smashed it on the hard ground but the light stayed on. She felt the casing and realised it was rubber. Thinking quickly she undid the front of the torch exposing the small bulb. 'That should do it,' she said triumphantly as she broke it on the ground.

The cave was blanked in complete darkness. Francesca moved the infrared torch around until she found the paint marks. 'You OK Gran?'

'Yep, I can see the paint, let's go.'

The two women made their way quickly through the darkness and following the paint marks, stayed low to keep below the bats. Behind them, they heard the moaning from Ryder and the shouts of anger from Brad.

'Find the string,' said Isabel.

Francesca scrambled around feeling on the ground until she found the string laid out by the two detectives. 'Got it,' she said as she took out the scissors, cut the string and rolled it up as they made their way out of the caves.

'Let them try and find their way out now,' said Isabel. 'We'll let them stew for a couple of days before we tell anyone. That should be enough to make them realise what they did to you.'

***

As the last of the bats left the cave, Brad, who was sitting down in the darkness, protecting his head, breathed a sigh of relief. 'Thank god for that, now let's get out of this hell hole. Where the fuck are you?' he said as he realised the torch had gone.

'Over here,' came a weak groan from Ryder.

'Where the fuck is over here, I can't see a fucking thing.' 'I can't move, she broke my bloody leg.'

Brad got out his flip phone hopeful for a signal. The small bars showed none and the light from the phone was so dim as to be any use. He crawled around until he found Ryder. 'Come on. I'll help you out. Those bitches don't realise we had the string to follow to get us out of here. Right, stand up and grab hold of my jacket.'

Ryder struggled to his feet realising that he could put a little weight on his injured leg. 'Not as bad as I thought,' he said relieved. 'Once we get out of here we'll make sure those two bitches regret ever coming to this country.'

Brad, still holding onto the string which was wrapped around his injured hand and with Ryder holding onto his jacket, began to follow it. He moved slowly feeling his way in complete darkness, hands out in front of him like a blind man, which in

230

reality he was. Stumbling occasionally and continually cursing he reached the point where Francesca had cut the string.

Brad stopped, his mind unable to compute that the string had ended. 'Oh Christ no, Christ no, those fucking bitches have cut the string.'

Chapter 35

T he lights from the Yamaha lit up the driveway to the villa as Isabel brought the machine to a stop. The two women sat there for a few minutes, both with their thoughts.

'Right let's get changed and maybe another bottle of wine and what do you say to a takeaway,' said Isabel as she climbed off the bike and lowered the stand.

Francesca removed her helmet and shook her head to fluff up her hair. The cut above her eye had begun to show the first signs of a bruise. 'I vote for a Pizza, a very spicy one.'

'I'll go along with that. I've seen a handout in the kitchen,' said Isabel as the two made their way up the short drive to the villa.

As they entered the villa they both took off the leathers which were covered in dirt. 'So nice to get out of those leathers. Crawling around in that Bat poo was not the most pleasant of experiences,' laughed Isabel. 'We will have to sponge these down before we return them to our friendly Hells Angels.'

'We could do that in the morning before we carry out the next phase of our plan. You know Gran this is beginning to get rather exciting,' said Francesca as she gathered her leathers and took them to the sink.

Isabel followed and together they sponged them down and hung them up to dry on a corner of the door. Isabel fetched a large towel and put it on the floor underneath the leathers that began to drip.

'That should do for the moment, now let's organise the Pizza and go over the day's activities. That cut needs attending too. Wish I had got to you sooner,'

'Just glad you got there at all. Boy Gran, you were a titan. Do you think you broke that Detective's leg?'

'I don't think so, although I did give it one heck of a wack. Quite enjoyed myself. Boy was I grateful when the bats arrived. That was the only part of the plan that worked perfectly,' said Isabel reflectively.

'I owe my life to the bats again. Good job they stick to a pretty rigid timetable,' added Francesca. 'Now let's get some dinner ordered.'

Isabel looked through the handout advertising Pizza deliveries. 'Spicy chicken with jalapeños.' 'Perfect,' said Francesca.

Isabel rang through the order and fetched a bottle of red wine from the kitchen cabinet pouring out two glasses and together they settled down on the settee. 'So here we go again, dejavu, only this time I'm limiting myself to a couple of glasses,' said Isabel. 'Have been feeling a little under the weather after that full bottle last night.'

'Not that it showed in your performance though Gran. You were awesome.'

'Teamwork my lovely. We both did extremely well. Now the next part of the plan. I have been thinking. I believe this time one of us ought to deliver the next letter by hand. We need them to find out where we live.'

'Why?

'So we can have some control over the information we give and check out the honesty of the Detective they send to see us.'

'What happens if they don't find us?' said Francesca.

'Oh, they will. We will park on the main road in full view of the CCTV they have covering the whole road around the Sheriff's office.'

'Hope that doesn't mean we will have a dozen heavily armed macho characters arrive at dawn to break down the door and drag us screaming out of our bedrooms, dressed only in our night attire,' said Francesca smiling. The two women looked at one another for several seconds and burst out laughing.

'Might not be so bad,' added Isabel nearly spilling her drink as they both collapsed in fits of laughter.

Their laughter was interrupted by the doorbell ringing. 'Hope that's them,' said Francesca still smiling as she got up to answer the door.

'Pizza delivery,' said a young-faced white lad looking as if he hadn't started shaving yet.

Francesca paid the young lad and gave him a generous tip. 'Great lady, thanks,' he said as he walked back down the drive to his moped.

Back inside the pizza was divided up and eaten with relish. 'You will need to write out the letter this time. You have the coordinates and a description of the place where they buried the body,' said Isabel sounding croaked as she felt the burning sensation of the Jalapeños. 'Boy this is good,' she added barely audible as she struggled to speak.

'OK,' added Francesca with tears running down her face. 'These chillies are something else,' she said sounding as though she was speaking with a hoarse whisper. 'I think I'll get us a glass of milk.'

She returned with the milk and with paper and a pen. They both drank the milk feeling their voice boxes begin to return to normal.

'That is beginning to feel better,' said Isabel her voice slowly returning to normal. 'Now we need to install some urgency into them reading the letter and taking action. The place seems to be full of corruption so it's going to be vital that we trust whoever we give the information to.'

'We could put URGENT on the front, follow it up with a phone call and mention we have evidence we will be sending to the FBI. If that doesn't get their attention then we will go directly to the FBI. They have an office in Austin, which isn't too far away and wouldn't take us too long on that machine of yours with you driving,' remarked Francesca with a big grin on her face.

'Thanks for that,' said Isabel laughing. 'But I agree, we need to ensure they take the letter seriously. Pity we haven't got a picture of the burial site. I suppose we could drive up there and take one.'

'Let's think about that only if they don't take any notice of the letter. Remember we need to get this sorted out in the next two days or we are going to be in trouble for leaving those two detectives in the caves for too long. Two days should be enough especially as they won't have any food or water.'

'Good point, we don't want to be had up for murder. Right, you write out the letter whilst I finish the wine and you can have the final piece of pizza,' laughed Isabel.

'Not so fast Mrs Fordham, just you share out that wine and with regards to the pizza, I don't think my mouth can take any more.'

***

Isabel parked the Chevrolet on the road close to the Sheriff's office.

'Right, here we go,' said Francesca as she prepared to leave the car, letter in hand. 'At least no one will recognise me this time.'

Exiting the car and after checking the road was clear, remembering that the traffic was on the other side of the road, crossed over and entered the Sheriff's building. She looked around in despair at the commotion. 'Not much changed,' she thought to herself as she made her way through the bodies of people towards the Sergeant's desk and the queue. She felt as though she could be in there for hours. So she made her way to the office area. Despite the No entry notice she opened the glass door and walked in causing several heads to turn.

'Hey lady you can't come in here,' said Bernie as he got up from his desk and walked over to her. Without saying a word she handed over the letter then turned around and walked out through the mob of people.

Bernie stood for a few seconds holding the letter. 'Not another one,' he said. His mind suddenly remembered the embarrassment of the dressing down from Shiny as he was caught opening the previous letter. 'Better play it safe this time,' he said, turning back into the office area, searching out Shiny.

He noticed him on the phone so waited, fidgeting as he felt the urge to open the letter feeling it could be something to break up the monotony of endless streams of paperwork.

'Bernie, snap out of your daydream,' said Shiny as he put down the phone. 'What's up?'

'Another letter, similar to the last one only this one is marked urgent.'

He handed over the letter towards Shiny. 'Just put it on the desk,' he said, 'you never know we may have to check it out for fingerprints.' He got out a set of plastic gloves, put them on and then carefully opened up the letter.

Bernie watched Shiny intently. His intelligent, handsome face betrayed nothing as he read through it. He looked up at Bernie and asked, 'Who gave you this letter?'

'Some broad just walked in put it in my hand and walked out,' he answered taken aback by the intensity of the question from Shiny.

'How long ago?'

'Just a few....' The word minute faded out as Shiny got up from his desk and ran down the office.

Shouting behind him to Bernie, 'Follow me.' He hurried through the door of the office area and then pushed his way through the crowded outer area. He reached the street and looked around then realised he had no idea what he was looking for. As Bernie joined him out of breath, Shiny asked, 'What did this person look like?'

'Real stunner, blonde hair, amazing green eyes but quite a few scratches and bruises on her face.'

Shiny looked around but failed to notice the Green Chevrolet as it passed in front of him. Scanning the roads he looked for the blonde but saw no one resembling the description given by Bernie. 'Dam,' he said. 'Right, go back inside and make sure the CCTV covering this area is impounded.' 'What did the letter say?' asked Bernie.

'Just do as I say now,' answered Shiny, urgency in his voice.

'I'll explain later.'

Inside the Chevrolet, Francesca saw the young good looking man rush out of the Sheriff's office, frantically looking around. He was followed by a shorter man breathing heavily. 'Looks as if the bait has been taken. Just hope the young good looking guy is the one that tracks us down to interrogate me.'

'Tart,' laughed Isabel as they sped away from the area.

***

Back at his desk Shiny re-read the letter. Getting out a largescale map of the local area he checked out the coordinates given by Francesca. He nodded to himself when he recognised the area. 'I hope this isn't some practical joke,' he mumbled to himself.

'CCTV impounded', said Bernie. 'I asked the IT guys to track the woman as she left the building. Boy would sure like to meet up with her again. Strange that such a looker should have those marks, even her makeup didn't cover them very well.'

238

'Great, now get a couple of other members from the team together, a couple of shovels and tell the forensic guys to be on call.'

'Really, so what's going on?' asked Bernie sounding confused.

Shiny grabbed his coat and made his way through the office area, followed closely by Bernie, he answered, 'We might just have a murder case on our hands.'

Chapter 36

The police car driven by Shiny was followed by two vans with the inscription of Police Vehicle, emblazoned on the side. Parking in the same area used previously by Ryder and Brad, Shiny stopped the car and switched off the engine. Leaning over to the back seat of the car he reached for the large-scale map that he had carefully folded to cover the area of the coordinates given in the letter.

Getting out of the car and looking around, he quickly identified the direction Ryder and Brad must have taken. 'Right Bernie,' he said as Bernie joined him, 'let's see if this letter bears any resemblance to the truth.'

Behind him, the van's rear doors opened and 4 policemen from each van climbed to join their drivers. All were dressed in overalls and carried two shovels between them.

Addressing the group, Shiny said, 'Guys, we have had a tipoff of an unlawful burial therefore it's likely that a murder took place. I have been given the coordinates but they may cover a reasonably sized area. So when we get there I want you to carry out a square search, look for any recently disturbed areas. Any questions?'

All the police shook their heads.

'Right let's go.'

With a map in hand and a handheld compass, Shiny lead the group away from the parked cars and through to the sparse undergrowth towards the given coordinates.

Carefully following the compass heading and continually checking the map, Shiny eventually reached the point he had marked on the map. As he looked around the area it appeared undisturbed. 'Right,' he said, 'start the search.'

The men moved off and started their detailed search of the area. After several minutes there was a shout from a team member. 'Over here, looks as if this area has been disturbed recently.'

Shiny and Bernie hurried over and examined the ground. 'This looks a likely spot,' observed Bernie as he towed the ground with his foot seeing the earth crumble.

Shiny turned to the rest of the group. 'Guys, rope off this area and then in pairs start to dig, being as careful as you can.'

Two men took their shovels and started to dig. The rest all stood around and waited.

After several minutes there was a shout from one of the diggers. 'Detective looks as if there is something here. Pretty sure it's a body covered in a plastic sheet.'

'OK, stop digging. Bernie, call forensics and tell them we have a body.'

***

Back at the Sheriff's office, Shiny and Bernie searched through the CCTV and identified Francesca as she made her way through the crowds at the building entrance.

'There,' shouted Bernie excitedly as he pointed at the screen, 'the blonde, that's her.'

'Keep following her on the screen,' said Shiny.

The CCTV ended at the entrance to the building which showed Francesca leaving.

'Next tape,' Shiny said as Bernie quickly switched to the CCTV covering the outside of the building. They waited impatiently as Bernie scrolled through the new tape until he came to the point where they knew Francesca had left the office block.

Scanning slowly, Bernie looked carefully at the tape. 'There is so much going on, it was difficult to pick out individuals,' he said.

'There,' shouted Shiny, 'stop the tape.'

Bernie froze the tape and nodded, 'Yes, that's her.' 'Now track her, slowly.'

Bernie moved the screen a few frames at a time. 'She got into a green Chevrolet, 'he said.

'Dam,' said Shiny. 'I remember that car. It passed right in front of me after we left the building. Can you get the number plate?'

Bernie froze the screen and then focused on the number plate. 'Got it,' he said triumphantly, 'looks like it's a rental from the tag by the number. Should be easy enough to track.' 'That's provided they gave an honest answer to the rental company. Right, looks like a local company operating from the airport. Time for a visit.'

***

At the airport, Shiny and Bernie parked up and headed towards the Rental company. The office was well-lit, the walls painted in a pale blue with pictures of vintage cars hung on them. As they entered, the two detectives were greeted by a young, pretty auburn-haired woman. Smartly dressed in a dark blue suit, with a white blouse and a name tag of Anne on the jacket. 'Good afternoon gentlemen, how can I help?' said Anne smiling at Shiny as he produced his warrant card and showed it to her. Anne examined it and looked towards Bernie. 'May I see yours as well,' she asked politely.

Bernie got out his warrant card reluctantly, and opened it up with what he had hoped was a flourish but left Anne unimpressed.

'Ma'am, we are here on official business. We are trying to trace the person who rented a green Chevrolet within, we believe, the last week or so,' said Shiny as he smiled at Anne. 'We have a number of those being rented, our most popular model. Can you give me any more details?' said Anne, returning a smile.

Bernie, felt left out as Anne talked to Shiny. Interrupting he said, rather aggressively as he gave the number. 'Here is the licence plate number, so I'm sure it won't be too difficult to trace.'

Entering the licence plate number into her computer and giving the occasional smile to Shiny, she quickly found the details of the rental. 'Here we go. Oh, I remember this one. The young women initially rented a Ford Fiesta but then returned it after about 4 days, looking the worse for wear.'

'What the car or the woman?' said Bernie.

'The woman,' said Anne with a sigh as if the answer was obvious. 'She was accompanied by an older woman, I think it may have been her Grandmother. Anyway, they wanted to change the car, no reason really, so I gave them a Chevrolet.'

'A green one,' asked Bernie.

The woman raised her eyes to the sky. 'Yes, a green one.' 'So can you please give us her details?' said Shiny.

Anne smiled at him again. 'Of course,' she said as she quickly and efficiently typed away on her computer. A printer on her desk next to the computer began to whirl and produced a single A4 page. Anne checked it over and handed it to Shiny. 'There was one unusual thing I do remember. Her driver's licence was not from this country. It was from the UK. Difficult to work out at first as they are so different from ours. I took a scan of it. Let me find it.'

She spent a few more seconds on her computer before smiling and said, 'Got it.' She printed out a copy of the licence and handed it over to Shiny.

He looked at it saying, 'I see what you mean. I wonder what on earth someone from the UK was doing in our neck of the woods. Not exactly a major tourist attraction. Then changing her car after a few days, as you said and looking rather the worse for ware.' He paused. 'How do you mean the worse for ware exactly?'

'Well although she had makeup on, you could tell she had lots of cuts and bruises on her face.' She smiled at Shiny again adding, 'She was really pretty. Long blonde hair and amazing green eyes, the same as the other woman which is why I assumed it was her Grandmother, although it might have been her Mother. She was a very attractive older woman.'

'Thank you so much, Anne, you have been most helpful,' said Shiny.

Anne stood up and held out her hand to Shiny. Shaking hands she said with a smile 'Anytime you need a car just give me a call,' handing him her business card.

'Thanks,' interrupted Bernie, 'but we have our police car,' waving the keys to the car in the air. 'We will be in touch if we need any more help,' he said sounding resentful of the attention she had given to Shiny.

As they walked out he said, 'How come all the women flash their eyes and smile at you and ignore me.'

Shiny smiled at Bernie. 'I have no idea Bernie, no idea at all.'

Chapter 37

Francesca looked out of the window of the villa. 'Do you believe the police will come Gran?'

'I hope so. We left them enough clues for them to find us.' 'But do you think they will believe us? Maybe we should have staked out the burial site, made sure they went there and found it.'

'I think you are overthinking this one Fran. They took the note seriously. You saw that young man, the handsome one as you mentioned, run out of the building. He had the note in his hand so that means they will be investigating. They have no option.'

Francesca moved away from the window and joined her Gran on the sofa.

'This waiting is so frustrating. I fancy a coffee, how about you?'

'Please,' answered Isabel. Francesca went to the kitchen and as she filled the kettle she heard the doorbell ring. Isabel looked out of the window. 'You're wait is over Fran. There is a police car outside and at the door is you're handsome detective with another policeman.'

Francesca hurried from the kitchen and stopped. Glancing in a tall mirror by the door she made sure her hair was in place and took a deep breath. Opening the door she looked directly at the young detective and noted, once again, how good-looking he was. Dark hair, blue eyes with eyelashes even Francesca envied, set in a chiselled face with slight stubble.

'Good afternoon Ma'am, I'm sorry to bother you but I believe you may be able to help us with an enquiry we are conducting,' he said as he showed his warrant card.

Bernie, mouth open, as he stared at Francesca and showed his as well.

'May we come in?' said Shiny.

'Not a chance,' said Francesca.

Shiny taken aback by the hostility he heard in her voice said, 'I'm sorry but we are conducting an investigation into a very serious crime and believe you may be a material witness. I could get a warrant.....'

Before he could continue Francesca interrupted, 'OK. I will see you when you have a warrant.' She went to close the door but Shiny stopped her.

'Ma'am I don't understand why you won't help us. It is my understanding that you left us a letter.' He produced the letter and showed it to Francesca. 'It implies that you witnessed the burial of a body.'

'So I assume you found the body at the location I gave but that doesn't mean I can trust you,' said Francesca.

'Lady, we are the police, if you can't trust us who can you trust,' interrupted Bernie.

Francesca stared from Shiny to Bernie and looked Shiny directly in the eye and using a forceful tone that implied there was to be no argument said, 'Give me your phone.'

'I'm not giving you my phone,' he said defensively.

'No phone no entry,' said Francesca and shut the door.

Listening in the lounge Isabel was laughing. 'Boy, you are playing hardball.'

'Just wait Gran, that doorbell will ring any second.'

After a few seconds, the doorbell rang. Francesca stood and waited for a short time. She opened the door. 'You still here, I thought you would be off applying for a warrant.'

'Look Lady, I don't want to argue with you but this is a very serious investigation,' said Shiny. 'I would greatly appreciate your help.'

'I am more than willing to help but first I want your phone.'
'Why? asked Shiny.

'I need to make sure I can trust you.'

'We have already said, we are the police. We have shown you our warrant cards,' said Bernie sounding frustrated.

'Trust two guys who come to my front door, flourishing a couple of so-called warrant cards at me and ask to come into this villa. Not going to happen unless I look at your phone.'

Shiny shook his head in confusion. As he looked at Francesca he got out his flip phone and handed it over to her.

'Not that cheap one issued to you. Your private one and don't tell me a young guy like you doesn't have a modern phone.'

'Are you for real?' asked Shiny, 'you want to look through my private phone.'

'Yes and please unlock it.'

Realising he was up against a very determined young Lady, he smiled and took out his I-phone. Using his fingerprint to open it he handed it over to Francesca.

As she scrolled through the contacts she asked, 'Who is Sonia?'

'My older sister,' answered Shiny.

'Perfect,' said Francesca selecting the number then transferred it across to her phone. Selecting it she called Sonia.

The call was answered. 'Good afternoon, Sonia speaking.' 'Good afternoon Sonia, my name is Francesca and I have to organise a party for several police officers who have done exceptional service to the community and I was wondering if you could give me a quick rundown on your brother, especially his integrity.'

'Oh my gosh, how exciting. Where do I start? Well, he is my little brother...'

Francesca listened intently for a few minutes and once she has heard enough, ended the call.'Who is Caitlyn?

'Accounts manager. She handles all my claims,' said Shiny sounding frustrated.

'Perfect,' said Francesca as she transferred that number across to her phone and dialled.

'Accounts, Caitlyn speaking.'

'Caitlyn good afternoon, my name is Francesca and I am from a dating agency. We have Detective Johnson on our books and need to ensure he is a credible individual. I would appreciate an endorsement as to his honesty and integrity.'

'Shiny, using a dating agency, wow, with his looks I'm amazed. But in answer to your questions, yes he is honest, and he has impeccable integrity. His accounts claims are always on time, receipts etc. Nicknamed Shiny because of his character and honesty. Just wish all the other detectives were as efficient and honest.'

'Thank you so much, that is all I need.' Francesca ended the call.

'Dating agency,' said Shiny, 'you realise I will never live that one down. Now have you gained enough evidence to let me in?'

Smiling and holding out her hand she gave back the phone and shook Shiny by the hand. 'You will see why I was rather paranoid about talking to you when I explain what has happened.'

Isabel stood up as the two police officers entered the lounge. 'So, you two gentlemen have met my rather feisty Granddaughter. I'm sure when you have heard her story you will understand why she has been so cautious.'

Shiny shook Isabel's hand. 'Pleased to meet you Ma'am, and this is my colleague Bernie.'

'Nice to meet you, Ma'am,' said Bernie shaking Isabel's hand.

'Can we use christen names? The Ma'am bit makes me feel my age. I'm Isabel and my Granddaughter is Francesca.'

'I'm Shiny.'

'Good that makes life a little more sociable. Would you gentlemen like coffee?'

'No thank you,' they both said in unison.

'OK please take a seat and be prepared to be shocked and disturbed,' said Isabel warming to the prospect of Francesca telling her story.

Francesca sat in one of the armchairs, crossed-legged and began. 'I came out here to visit the crash site.....' She continued her story up to the part where she escaped from the caves. Both Shiny and Bernie sat in silence.

'There is a lot more to the story but I will leave that for tomorrow,' she added finally.

'I don't understand, why can't you tell us the rest of it?' said Shiny who felt frustrated at only being told half a story. 'You gave us the coordinates to the burial site and then walked out of the office, why didn't you report this?'

'I tried but your Sergeant wasn't the most helpful of individuals. Gave us the impression that our story was just that, a story.'

'Would you be able to recognise the two men again?' 'Oh yes. Without a doubt.'

'Look there are numerous questions that need to be answered. I suggest you come down to the station and make a formal statement and look through some photos of local criminals.'

'No,' said Francesca forcibly, 'as I said, all will be revealed tomorrow.'

'You know you are obstructing an ongoing enquiry,' said Bernie trying to sound official, 'you could be held in contempt of court.'

'I don't think so Bernie,' interjected Isabel smiling. 'You can see my poor Granddaughter has been under intense strain, haven't you dear?'

Francesca nodded and smiled back. Continuing Isabel added, 'I think she needs to rest until tomorrow afternoon when I'm sure she will be fully recovered and willing to tell you the rest of the story and then answer any of your questions.'

'Yes Gran, I do feel really tired,' added Francesca putting a hand to her head in a dramatic pose. 'I think I will go and lie down.'

She got up, winked at the two detectives and said, 'See you tomorrow guys.'

***

Back in the office, Shiny sat down and started to prepare his report, when his mobile rang. 'Shiny, it's Morrison'

'Morrison, how is the world of the dead, not much action I assume,' Shiny added laughing.

'Very funny. Just got the body in that your guys found in the grave and have started the post-mortem. Thought you ought to have one of your underlings come over and be initiated into our gruesome world.'

'I was waiting to hear if you had found anything before I came over, but we do have a newish recruit, Bernie. He will need to get used to your grisly ways. I'll send him over. Thanks.'

'Bernie,' shouted Shiny, 'over to the Path Lab. Introduce yourself to Dr Morrison and stay there until the post-mortem of our body is complete. Call me if anything of interest is found.'

'Shiny, I don't have a very strong stomach, can't you go?' said Bernie rather feebly.

'Not a chance. I have to get this final part of the report off to the boss. You know what he's like if he isn't kept up to date. Just take deep breaths and try not to faint.'

At his computer, Shiny noticed that the first report he had submitted after finding the body, had not been read by Ryder or Brad. The protocol in this office was for Shiny to send everything through them. That would then be discussed at the morning meeting with the Boss, a Senior Detective, and work allocated accordingly. Realising this meant that their Boss had no idea they had found a body or that they had witnesses. He thought to himself, 'No wonder no one has been around asking me what's going on.'

He finished his report stating all the details about the finding of the body and the witnesses. Shiny then sent the completed report through to Brad and Ryder but also copied in the Senior Detective. 'Can't complain now. The Boss is totally in the loop.'

***

In the path lab, Bernie struggled to keep his lunch down. The smell and the sight of a corpse with the intestines and skull opened up was more than he could stand. He rushed out of the room and was violently sick into the toilet. He wiped his mouth and took a deep breath as he returned, reluctantly, to hear Dr Morrison say, 'Interesting.'

'What's that Doc?' said Bernie who tried to sound as normal as possible.

The Doctor was examining the plastic covering that Leroy was found in. The plastic had been covered in a very fine powder and he gently stroked away the powder with a soft brush. 'It looks

253

like a partial print. Whoever buried this poor devil wore gloves but may have taken them off at the last minute possibly to get a better grip when he was thrown in the hole. I don't think it will stand up in court but it may give a lead.'

'That's great doc. Have you established how he died?' asked Bernie.

'Oh no doubt about that, he was bagged. There is evidence of plastic in his mouth and around his teeth as he desperately tried to bite his way out. I'll get this partial print through to the forensic department and see what they come up with.'

'Many thanks, Doc,' said Bernie as he turned to leave, pleased to be getting out of the place.

As he reached the door, he heard a noise like someone passing wind. 'Don't worry Bernie, just the gasses inside the body escaping,' laughed the doctor as Bernie held his nose. 'Good job it's just wind coming out,' said Bernie as he glanced back. 'What's that?' he said looking down at the end of the condom that had been forced out of Leroy's anus by the gas.

The doctor opened the dead man's legs and carefully pulled out the condom. 'Good spot young man. This is not an area we would normally have examined.' He carefully opened up the condom and pulled out the small flash card. 'Well, would you look at that, a flash card? Now why would anyone put one of those up their ass,' he laughed. 'Would you like to take it through to the IT guys? You spotted it so you can take all the credit.'

Bernie looked at it as if it was an alien object but then realised the credibility he would get for spotting it. Taking a pair of plastic gloves offered to him by the Doctor he put them on and took the card. 'Many thanks, Doc,' he said as he carefully handled the card and left the path lab.

***

Back at the office, Shiny was at his desk where Bernie described to him what he had been told by the Doctor. 'The victim was bagged and there is a partial print on the plastic sheeting but not a great deal of use in court. The big find that, I spotted, was when the corpse farted,' he laughed, 'would you believe it, was a condom sticking out of his ass. Inside it was,' he paused dramatically, and then produced the flash card, 'this.'

'So what the hell is it doing in your grubby little mitt? This could be crucial evidence. You need to get it to the IT guys immediately. We don't have the technology to open this up here.'

Crestfallen Bernie went to walk away but brightened up when Shiny shouted after him for the whole office to hear. 'Great job Bernie, really well done.'

Shiny added the information he had been given by Bernie to his report. He then circulated it to the distribution list that now included the Senior Detective. Still concerned that he had not seen or heard from Brad or Ryder or received any instructions on how to proceed he decided to carry on until he received any new instructions. Getting up from his desk to make a coffee he saw an email alert.

Opening up the message he read it twice not sure he fully believed it the first time. "Do not proceed any further with this investigation. This is a direct order. I will personally take charge."

Stunned by the message from the Senior Detective, Shiny sat back down and wondered what on earth was going on. 'Better tell the IT guys,' he said to himself.

Using the internal phone he rang the IT department. 'Hi Shiny,' came the immediate answer to the call, 'if you are asking about the flash drive, we have already been contacted by the Boss telling us not to open it and to hand it over to him or Brad or Ryder, but nobody else. What the hell's going on?' Shiny thought for a while. 'I have no idea but nothing has been said about making a copy. Can you burn one off and keep it in the evidence lock up? Just a copy, so we can view it at some stage if we need to.'

'Be it on your head Shiny, but will do.'

Chapter 38

The Dwarf, Monty, looked at his phone as a message appeared. "Exchange was compromised. One witness, a female to be eliminated. Possible companion. Address and description to follow."

'Shit,' he shouted, waking the gorilla from his peaceful slumber, feet up on a table snoring like a warthog.

'What's up boss?' he stammered as he came to with a start. 'Gus, get your lazy good for nothing ass up. Looks like we have some wet work. Tell Al to get the van ready, fuelled up and you get tooled up.'

Monty sat and waited. His mobile pinged and the address came up. He read the description of the woman. 'Shouldn't be too difficult to recognise. Good looking broad by the sound of it.'

A short time later, Al, his driver appeared. 'Everything's ready.'

'OK,' said Monty. 'I've got the address, we will leave just as it's getting dark.' He described the target and got out his iPad and Googled the address.

Seeing the image of the villa, they discussed the best way to enter the building noting the open area to the rear of the property. 'Nothing to stop us parking up nearby, making our way round to the back and getting in through those sliding doors. Silenced weapon, she won't be found for a few days. She may have a companion, if so we do her too. Any questions?'

Both Gus and Al shook their heads.

**

In the villa, Francesca and Isabel were sitting reading. 'I'm feeling a little bit guilty making those two detectives stay in the caves for a further day,' said Francesca.

'Don't feel guilty, they will have only been in there for two days. Remember they left you in there to die. At least we will be sending in people to rescue them. I dare say they will be traumatised when they are found but a few dozen years in a state penitentiary acting as a bitch to some hairy gang boss will soon make them feel more alive.'

'Gran, I thought I knew you so well but these last few days have been quite a revelation.'

'All to the good I hope,' laughed Isabel.

'Certainly that. What say we go out for dinner tonight? Get a bit dressed up before we have to confess all to the two detectives tomorrow.'

'Great idea but can we go in our scuffs? We have to give the bike back in the morning so I would love to have a final burn. Find some dive that has lots of loud music and sells great food.'

'In other words a final trip down memory lane,' said Francesca with a smile.

'Spot on, what do you think?'

'Great idea. Let's get these leathers on one more time.'

***

On the road leading to the villa, the powerful SUV driven by Al cruised around slowly in search of the correct address. 'That's the one,' he said as he drew up a short distance away. 'Lights are on so hopefully she is home.'

As they prepared to leave the vehicle, Francesca and Isabel walked out of the front door, both in their leathers carrying their helmets.

'Fuck, if that's them in leathers looks as if they are on their way out,' said Al.

Leaning forward and nearly toppling off of his booster seat strapped into the rear, Monty looked through the front windscreen. 'That's her. Don't know who the other bitch is. Right change of plan. The first opportunity we get we drive alongside and waste them both.'

Isabel relished the ride. Joining the dual carriage-way, that circumvented the town she set the cruise control at 50 mph just below the speed limit of 55 mph. The evening was a typical Texas one for that time of year; warm, clear skies with the slightest breeze. There was little traffic to worry about, just the occasional pickup, a Winnebago towing a small family car and behind her, the lights of a vehicle travelling at speed and closing fast. Isabel was on the inside lane expecting the vehicle to overtake her.

When the vehicle slowed down and maintained a hundred yards behind, Isabel felt the faintest of alarm bells ring.

Inside the SUV, Al held his distance behind the Yamaha until he was sure there were no other vehicles around. 'Here we go Gus,' he shouted back as he accelerated and moved to the outside lane.

As the SUV closed on the Yamaha, Gus slid back the inside door and positioned himself in the footwell as best his oversized bulk would allow. He made sure the safety catch was off on the semi-automatic. He then waited until Al had drawn up alongside the bike and took aim.

Isabel's alarm bells were now at full volume. As the SUV drew up alongside and stabilised she braked hard. The first bullet that left the automatic impacted on the side of Isabel's helmet knocking her head sideways. Struggling to maintain control of the bike she ground to a halt on the grass verge, dazed but conscious.

'Gran, gran,' screamed Francesca, 'are you OK.'

'Yes,' is all Isabel said as her head began to clear. She looked up and saw the SUV had screeched to a stop 50 yards ahead, with the smell of burning rubber in the air and long tyre marks on the tarmac.

There was silence. Gus leaned out of the SUV and looked back surprised to see the two women still alive sitting on the bike. 'Missed the bitches,' he said.

'Well don't just sit there like a dummy, finish the job before anyone comes along,' screamed the Dwarf, agitatedly fidgeting on his small booster seat.

Gus began the laborious task to move his giant frame out of the SUV so he was in a better position.

Still on the bike Isabel looked ahead and saw a huge-sized hulk struggling to climb out of the vehicle, gun in hand. 'Hold on,' she shouted back to Francesca. She switched on the lights to full beam and pressed the horn as she opened the throttle fully.

Gus finally extricated himself from the vehicle and turned towards the target. Suddenly he was blinded by the lights and disorientated by both the roar of the Yamaha and the scream from its horn. He froze.

Covering the short distance to the SUV, the Yamaha hit over 40 mph. Gus, turned sideways to avoid the bike unprepared for the pain that his body was about to feel as the bike hit his giant frame. The impact from the three parts of the Yamaha's handlebars did untold damage.

The first of the impacts was the review mirror on the lefthand side that snapped off after breaking three of his ribs. Isabel counteracted the shock of the impact by pulling down hard on the opposite handlebar. The second impact, a fraction of a second later, was the brake lever. Solid metal with a shaped end, it tore into Gus's side, opening it up. The third impact did the most damage. The handlebar ripped open the hole made by the brake lever, which gouged deep into his stomach area and left an exit for the intestines.

Isabel struggled to maintain control as the impact threw the bike sideways. The bike left the road careering across the grass verge in a drunken fashion with Francesca hanging on tight to Isabel for all she was worth. Finally, Isabel regained control and brought the bike to a halt. Both women looked back to see the giant sitting half in and half out of the SUV looking down at his stomach.

Inside the SUV the dwarf screamed, 'Get him out of here,' as he tried to kick at the back of the giant, but his small legs were too far away to reach. 'Get out Al and pull him out, then get us the fuck out of here.' Struggling to release his seat belt in a panic, he eventually succeeded and fell off the booster seat. As he picked himself up he pushed against the back of the giant, still to no effect.

The two women saw Al get out of the SUV and start to pull Gus out of the vehicle. Francesca unzipped her leathers and took out her I phone. After turning the phone on she selected the video app. Filming the activities she zoomed in on Al trying to pull Gus out of the vehicle and then at the number plate. As Gus slowly tumbled out of the vehicle she saw the dwarf glance out of the vehicle directly at her.

'Let's go,' she shouted at Isabel who opened up the throttle and accelerated down the Dual carriageway. As she glanced in her remaining rearview mirror, Isabel saw the SUV do a Uturn across the central reservation and accelerated away in the opposite direction.

Gus lay on the ground. He looked down and for the first time in his life saw his intestines as they slipped out of his stomach area. Struggling to hold them in, he began to realise he was fighting a losing battle. Slippery and coiled like snakes they seemed to have a life of their own. Despite his efforts, they slowly seeped out together with pints of crimson red blood. He began to feel a wave of tiredness gradually start to overcome him as blood pooled around where he sat. As he slipped into unconsciousness he regretted the day he had ever met the Dwarf.

***

Gus had had a difficult childhood. Outgrowing his clothes at a rate his parents couldn't keep up with, weight gained on almost a daily basis and the butt of ribbing by his so-called school chums, he had been a miserable child. By the time he was 18, he had finally stabilised at 300 lbs. Employment was near impossible. His slow lumbering gait, illiteracy and lack of mental agility were not good selling points to a future employer. So when by chance he met the Dwarf, who was scouting for employees, at a refuse for down and outs, he was flattered for possibly the first time in his life to be offered, what Monty described as, gainful employment. The employment being to act as a deterrent and bodyguard.

Monty on the other hand had had a privileged childhood. Born to rich parents who indulged his every wish, he did however hold a deep-seated grudge against them. In his young twisted mind, his dwarfism was their fault. Despite their reassurances that it was due to a genetic mutation, he convinced himself that it was something they must have done. Was it the food or drink his mother had eaten or drunk during pregnancy, drugs she had taken or lack of care for the embryo she carried inside her? Whatever the reason he was certain it was her and his father's fault.

As he grew older his resentment grew to an irrational level. His devious and vengeful mind started to plan revenge. Seeing the large pathetic figure of Gus one day in the refuse he decided he would be the perfect bodyguard. The comparison between the two, although to an outsider looked ludicrous, worked well for Monty. Gus was easily managed, Monty paid him well and when he suggested to Gus that he wanted him to carry out a rather unusual task, Gus was only too pleased to help.

Monty's parents always enjoyed a Sunday afternoon carvery at the local pub. As regulars, they had always arrived early to ensure they managed to get the very best of the meats on display. Afterwards, they would enjoy a few drinks by the fire in the lounge area before walking slowly back half a mile to their sumptuous 6-bedroom house in a private cul-de-sac.

Nearing the end of the walk, the couple always took a shortcut through a seldom used narrow path, just 200 yards long, boarded in by tall fences. Both were in a relaxed mood and took little notice of the very large individual, head down and dressed in a hoodie, who was walking towards them in the opposite direction. After he passed them they knew little of their deaths. Both were grabbed from behind and their heads banged together which such force that their skulls cracked. Death was instantaneous.

The bodies were not found for over 24 hours. No evidence, no CCTV and a verdict of unknown cause was left open. Monty and Gus's partnership was cemented.

Chapter 39

In the SUV Monty was close to having a fit. 'I told you to follow them, you imbecile. They have to be taken out, they are witnesses, now turn this vehicle around and do as you're bloody well told. I pay you remember.'

Al ignored the ranting and got out his phone. Whilst driving, he dialled his girlfriend. 'Honey, get the Go bag and meet me on the Highway just after the intersection at Crones Croft. Make sure you bring the passports and make it as quick as you can.'

He ended the call and said to the Dwarf. 'Look here you fucking little turd. I'm finished working for you. You're a nasty little mean bastard and fucking stupid with it. Those women videoed us. This vehicle description and registration will now be the focus of every State policeman. We have nearly half a million dollars worth of drugs in the back. If we're stopped we will be inside for 20 years.'

'So you're girlfriend will pick us up and we take the drugs and lie low. Is that the plan?' said the dwarf hopefully. 'Not quite, but close.'

***

Four miles along the highway, Isabel pulled into a shopping precinct and looked for a phone booth. The shops in the precinct were mostly well-known brands with a few smaller stores. All were shut and in darkness. The only lights were from a restaurant with several people sitting inside. She spotted a phone booth close to the restaurant, so drew up alongside and shouted back to Francesca. 'Call it in. That poor bastard could be slowly dying by the roadside.'

Dismounting the bike, Francesca removed her helmet and hurried to the booth. After dialling 911 she told the operator of the location of the body and gave a brief description of what had happened. She cut off the call as soon as the operator asked for her name and quickly returned to the bike. Francesca looked at Isabel and started to cry. Isabel took her in her arms and felt Francesca shaking.

'That's the adrenaline, Fran. Let's get a coffee with plenty of sugar and discuss what happened and why.'

Although the restaurant was busy serving dinner, there were two empty tables. Entering and causing heads to turn as they walked in dressed in leathers, they made their way to one of the tables. The waitress gave them menus but Isabel made it clear they just wanted coffee.

Looking slightly resentful with the possibility of losing a tip, the waitress returned filling two cups with hot black coffee.

'Just what we needed,' said Isabel. Having put her helmet on the chair beside her, she gasped as she just noticed the long deep groove across the front of the helmet where a bullet had glanced off. 'Talk about lucky,' she said as she shook her head, running her finger down the groove.

***

Al pulled the SUV into a shaded area off the highway and close to the intersection where he planned to meet his girlfriend.

'So where is she?' said the dwarf looking around agitatedly. 'She will be here, stop panicking.'

After a few minutes a blue pickup, old but in good condition pulled up alongside the

SUV. Al said, 'Stay inside until we have everything sorted out.'

'Why can't I get out?'

'Because you are rather distinctive, to say the least. Now I'm running this, so just shut the fuck up and do as I say.'

Getting out of the SUV, Al greeted his girlfriend and together they went to the back of the van. After opening the doors they transferred bundles of drugs into the back of the pickup. When over half had been transferred Al whispered to his girlfriend who nodded and got into the passenger seat of the pickup. Al closed the rear doors of the SUV and walked around to the driver's door, leaned in and took out the keys. He threw them to Monty.

'There you go big boy, all yours. I've taken my half. Have fun.'

Before Monty could reply Al had closed the driver's door and made his way to the pickup. As they drove away he honked the horn as a farewell salute.

Monty looked at the keys in stunned silence. He had never driven the SUV before let alone any car. He knew the basics, gear lever, accelerator pedal etc. but his height had always precluded him from driving as he couldn't reach the pedals. He felt panicked and screamed in frustration.

Struggling forward between the front seats he sat in the driver's seat and thought, 'I can do this. I fucking have to.' Stretching to reach the ignition switch he put the key in and turned. Smiling as he heard the engine start. 'Piece of piss,' he said to himself. He took the gear lever in his small podgy hand, selected drive and felt the SUV begin to move slowly forward. He waited expecting the vehicle to accelerate but it just crept along in first gear. As he looked over the steering wheel he could just about see the way ahead as he steered onto the highway.

Blaring horns greeted him as two vehicles swerved to avoid him. 'Oh fuck off, you idiots,' he shouted back. He sat for a while hoping the vehicle would pick up speed but it trundled along at under 10 MPH. He knew where the accelerator pedal was but despite looking down, stretching his leg as far as possible, he couldn't reach it.

Realising his predicament of a slow-moving vehicle, probably already on the police radar and the chance of being stopped anyway for crawling along, he took a deep breath. Sliding down under the steering wheel he tried to keep it straight at the same trying to reach the accelerator pedal. Reaching it he pushed it as hard as he could and felt the big vehicle respond. 'Great,' he shouted gleefully but as he struggled to get back onto the seat he felt the vehicle had begun to decelerate; he panicked. Pressing every button he could find he inadvertently pressed the cruise control. The vehicle stabilised. Not knowing what had happened but not bothered he concentrated on steering the vehicle which had drifted to the outside lane.

He regained control and returned to the inner lane. Taking a deep breath he looked around the instrument panel. He was doing 42 mph, not bad he thought. Ahead the dual carriageway ran straight for several miles but then came to an end. The road narrowed into a single lane. On either side was a mixture of scrubland and trees planted in what appeared to be a haphazard fashion.

The bend ahead was a slow right-handed one that gradually tightened slightly before straightening. It had been constructed to avoid a steep bank, at the bottom of which was an old disused oil derrick. It was the only remnant of a much larger group of derricks that years before had been a profitable oil drilling site.

Monty held onto the steering wheel as hard as he could as he began to steer the big SUV around the first part of the bend. But as the angle tightened he began to feel a loss of control. The vehicle was going faster than he had wanted it to. The bend in the road should have been no problem for the SUV. However, the dwarf had steered into it too early and realised his mistake had turned in the other direction. The zigzagging motion of the vehicle began to grow as the dwarf overcorrected, the lights illuminated first one side of the road and then the other.

Unable to slow down, again panic set in and the corrections became more exaggerated until the SUV was on two wheels. The dwarf screamed as the vehicle left the road on its side and crashed head-on into one of the few trees around bouncing off before descending the slope. As the vehicle came to an abrupt stop, the dwarf was thrown forward under the steering wheel and jammed into the footwell.

The dwarf lay stunned and unable to move. At first, the smell that reached him confused him. He could see a faint mist around him reflected in the headlights bouncing off the old oil derrick. 'Fuck,' he said, 'that's the bloody cocaine gone.'

Shaking his head to clear it he struggled to climb out from behind the steering wheel. He stopped. The smell wasn't cocaine, it was petrol and the faint mist, not from the cocaine but from fuel vapour. The soft roar that started from the engine area quickly caught the vapours that surrounded him. Two vehicles on the road above witnessed the fireball but no one heard the agonising scream.

***

Sipping at their coffee in the restaurant and having looked at the video Francesca had taken, Isabel said, 'I trusted that young Detective, but I find it difficult to believe he lied to us. Could it be possible someone else found out?'

'But he was the only one we gave all the details to, well him and Bernie.'

'The question is do we trust him? Maybe we should test him.'
'How?' said Francesca.

'I suggest we send him the video, a photo of the helmet and tell him that copies of them will be sent together with our thoughts to his sister, the accounting lady and finally to the FBI in Austin.'

'OK, and we insist he comes alone.'

'One of us stays out of sight to record the meeting. It isn't likely he would try anything with other people around. I'll meet him inside and you do the recording. Better me because

if he tries anything you will still be around,' said Isabel.

Francesca thought about it for a while. 'It would still be a big risk.'

'The only other option would be to go straight to the FBI. We could do that if this doesn't work.'

***

Sat in his one-bedroom flat in a modern high rise, Shiny was comfortable. He was lying on his lounger with a beer in his hand and was watching the final episode of Breaking Bad. He groaned when he heard his phone ping. 'I'm off duty,' he said to himself as he leaned across to retrieve his phone from the small coffee table.

Opening a message that had popped up on his screen, he saw it contained a video and a photo. He looked at the video first and sat up quickly feeling a rush of adrenaline. 'My God,' he said as he realised that what was being shown could be a murder. He then looked at the helmet picture and tried to work out its significance. After having read the text message, he stood up quickly spilling beer on his beige carpet. 'Shit,' he said as he ignored the stain and re-read the message.

***

In the restaurant, Francesca's mobile pinged. Looking at her phone she told Isabel, 'The message was from Shiny stating. "I had absolutely nothing to do with the attempt on your lives. Give me details of where you are. I will come alone."

Francesca replied. "My Gran will meet you. I will be close by. We are at the Richmond restaurant. You will need to find it."

Shiny looked the restaurant up on Google and made a note of the postcode. He rushed to his car, started the engine and entered the details into his Satnav. '20 minutes,' he noted and sent a message to Francesca telling her when he would be there.

Along the dual carriageway, he saw flashing lights ahead and a police officer stood on the inside lane, signalling him to slow down. Stopping alongside, Shiny lowered his window and recognised the young man. 'What's happened?' he asked believing he already knew from the video.

'Evening Sir. Giant of a man, stomach ripped open and just left on the side of the road.' 'Is he dead?'

'No, alive but only just. We had trouble getting him into the ambulance. He must weigh 300 lbs.' As he said that, the ambulance lights flashed, left the area and headed at speed down the carriageway.

**

Parked near the restaurant, Shiny sat for a while as he looked around. Although the precinct was quiet only a few cars could be seen, he was cautious. The experience the two women had just experienced had set him thinking of how an attempt had been made on their lives. It concerned him greatly that within his police force, there was an element of corruption. The report he had circulated only went to a handful of people, the majority senior to him, including Ryder and Brad. He had never understood how they had risen to the ranks of senior detectives. Their cavalier attitude to even the most mundane of tasks had irked him. Slovenly and disrespectful to the rest of the staff, they seemed to be above the law.

The more he thought about the attempt on the lives of Francesca and Isabel, the more he concluded that Ryder and Brad must be implicated somehow. That said where had they been for the past 24 hours? He knew they were a law unto themselves but they were seldom out of their office and when they were, they were always together.

Putting aside his concerns he left his car and headed to the restaurant. He was prepared to be given a hard time by Isabel. He had liked her the first time he had met her and instantly realised she was a woman not to be messed with.

As he entered the restaurant he immediately spotted her at a table on her own. He scanned the area but did not see Francesca. Taking a seat opposite Isabel he felt the impenetrable gaze from her green eyes. On the table was a small recording device that she had switched on. Trying to take some form of control over the situation as he felt himself begin to feel uncomfortable, he said, 'You need my permission to record any conversation.'

The only answer he got back was,' Tough.'

The silence between them lasted several seconds before Shiny felt the pressure and opened the conversation. He felt surprisingly nervous. 'I understand there has been a problem,' immediately he regretted his poor choice of words.

'A problem,' said Isabel as she leant forward to whisper. 'Look down by your feet,'

Looking down Shiny saw Isabel's helmet had a large groove across the front. 'That groove was caused by a bullet fired from a vehicle that drove alongside us in an attempt to kill us. So yes, I believe there was a problem.'

'Mrs Fordham, I can't tell you how concerned I am, but please be assured I had nothing to do with that incident.'

'So how do you explain the fact that these men knew our address, and I can only assume, followed us from there? My Granddaughter is a material witness to what must have been a murder and the victim of a kidnapping and attempted murder, details, all of which were given to you,' said Isabel, her voice raised slightly but under control even though her eyes blazed with anger.

'I am required to submit a report as you probably understand. That report would have included all of the information you had given to me, together with details of your address etc… I can only assume that someone on that distribution list used that information.'

'Do you have any idea who it might have been,' asked Isabel, sounding a little less angry.

'Yes, I do but am not at liberty to say.'

'Bullshit detective, you owe us an explanation. Don't forget we have only given you half the story.'

Shiny sat feeling agitated. 'It is more than my job's worth to speculate but completely off the record there are two detectives, whom I suspect had some involvement.'

'I presume you mean Detectives Montgomery and Jenkins.' Completely stunned, Shiny was at a loss for words. Isabel waved her hand and Francesca appeared from the corner of the restaurant where she had been sitting unobserved. She joined them, sat down and noticed the shocked expression on Shiny's face.

'I presume Gran, you have just given our young, rather naïve detective some important information.'

'Yes,' said Isabel. 'I mentioned the names of two detectives and he appears to have been struck dumb.'

'How on earth did you know about two of our detectives,' asked Shiny who had regained some of his composure.

'Let me ask you a question first, detective,' said Francesca.

'When did you last see them?'

Struggling to think, Shiny eventually answered, 'I'm not sure a day or so ago but that wasn't unusual, they come and go as they please as they are a law unto themselves.'

'Would it surprise you to know that you would not have seen them or have any idea of their whereabouts,' Francesca looked at her watch which showed just after 8 pm, 'for a little over 24 hours give or take a few minutes, and I may add you will not see them for another 24 hours.

'Now listen young Lady, if you are holding Detectives as some form of hostage, have you any idea how serious that offence would be.'

Francesca and Isabel looked at one another and smiled. They both got up to leave, leaving Shiny in an agitated state. 'Ladies I have no option but to arrest you both on suspicion of withholding crucial evidence,' he shouted across the restaurant, causing heads to turn in his direction.

As he shouted across at the two women, they both turned and held out their hands. 'I hope you have two sets of handcuffs detective, but as you appear to be off duty I'm not sure you would even have one pair,' said Isabel smiling.

'Look this is embarrassing,' remarked Shiny to Francesca and Isabel who stood there, hands out. He turned to the occupants of the restaurant. 'It's OK folks, please just get on with your meal, everything is under control.' He ushered the two women outside and pointed to his car. 'Please, can we have a sensible conversation in my car?'

They sat in the back seat of his car with Shiny in the front, he turned and smiled, in an attempt to regain the initiative.'

Ladies, I understand the trauma you have both been through...' Before he could say another word Isabel interjected.

'Can you?' she asked. 'How many times have you been kidnapped, left to die in a cave, and then nearly died from a gangland-style execution.' There was total silence in the car.

'Alright,' said Francesca, who smiled at her Gran. 'Look we have to trust you Detective but for tonight we need protection. That is why we were happy for you to arrest us and then hold us in protective custody. If you do that, then in the morning we will tell you the rest of the story. But protective custody must mean exactly that. I would suggest we drive to Austin to the FBI office and stay there for the night. We don't trust the company you keep back in your Sheriff's department.'

'No,' said Shiny, 'I have a better idea. Just follow me.'

Chapter 40

'Well if it isn't my kid brother,' said Sonia, an attractive young woman with long glossy dark hair, hanging loose over her shoulders. Her smile seemed to light up her whole face. Turning her head she called back into the house. 'Girls it's your Uncle.'

Out of nowhere two young girls, Isla, 5 and Emily, 4 followed by a large brindle-coloured Boxer, Max, appeared in the hallway.

There was a rush towards Shiny with the Boxer first to jump up at Shiny leaving a white froth of drawl over his jacket. 'Hello old fellow,' he said as he wrestled with the dog, 'and how are my two beautiful nieces,' as they managed to push past Max and jumped up to give their Uncle a loving hug.

'If I get the poo bags can we play the poo bag game?' asked Isla sounding older than her years. 'Poo bag, poo bag,' joined Emily excitedly.

'Later girls, now let your uncle and his guests in first, please,' said Sonia as she ushered the girls inside allowing Francesca and Isabel to be introduced by Shiny.

'Yes,' said Sonia as she smiled at Francesca, 'we had a brief conversation on the phone. If I remember you were trying to get information out of me about my brother.'

'Sorry about that,' said Francesca looking a trifle embarrassed. 'Maybe when you hear why, you will forgive that little indiscretion.'

'Of course, now let's get you inside and maybe find you some temporary clothes so you don't have to sit in those leathers all evening.'

'Why not,' said Shiny laughing, 'I think they both look rather sex...'

Before he could finish the word, his two nieces appeared, holding a few poo bags each. Looking up into his face, they both smiled sweetly, handing him the bags.

'OK you monkeys, Poo bag time. 30 seconds now. Go.' There are screams from the girls as they raced away to hide. Inside a very comfortable, homely and well-decorated lounge, Francesca and Isabel settled themselves down on a large 4-seater settee. The exhaustion from the evening's activities began to show.

'I understand you have had a terrible evening,' said Sonia. 'My brother gave me a brief outline of what happened. So you will stay with us until he has sorted out the problem.'

Her voice was suddenly drowned out by screams from the two girls and the barking of the dog. Both Isabel and Francesca jumped at the noise. 'What on earth?' said Francesca sounding worried.

Sonia smiled. 'No need to worry. My kid brother, always the instigator, is playing the girl's favourite game. He chases them around the house brandishing a bag containing pretend poo. It will last another few minutes of him trying to catch them. If he does he pretends to wash their hair in it. Crazy but they love the game.'

Francesca smiled, her confidence in Shiny growing. 'Sounds as if the girls adore him.'

'Without question. Now I assume by what I've been told you probably haven't eaten. I have some cold chicken and salad and maybe a glass of wine to steady the nerves?'

'That would be perfect but are you sure we are not intruding,' asked Isabel.

'Not at all. My husband, Mike, is at a conference in Dallas so your company will be most welcome. The girls can sleep together. I assume you wouldn't mind sharing a bed and my brother can sleep on the couch. You just sit there and I'll get you some food and a well-earned drink.'

Sonia returned from the kitchen with two trays full of food and an unopened bottle of wine under her arm. Sitting on the settee with the trays of food on their laps, Isabel and Francesca finally began to relax.

Opening the bottle of wine and pouring them all a generous glass, Sonia smiled at them both. 'Here's to the two of you finally being able to enjoy the rest of your visit. Good health.' 'We will drink to that. Cheers,' said Isabel as the three of them raised their glasses.

The screaming had stopped and the two happy, smiling girls came rushing into the lounge, followed by a rather sweaty, red-faced-looking Shiny. 'We won,' shouted Isla sounding triumphant with Emily jumping around.

'Well you may have won but it's now time for bed. You know the routine and I'm sure you can persuade Uncle Poo Bags here to read you a story.'

'Can I do that?' asked Francesca.

'Can she, please Mummy?' asked Isla full of enthusiasm.

'Of course,' replied Sonia as Isla grabbed one of Francesca's hands and Emily the other leading her up to their bedrooms.

Sonia looked at Shiny as he watched the three depart. She smiled at her brother, 'Care to help me with the dishes?'

'Yes of course I will.'

'Let me do that,' said Isabel.

'Not a chance. Just sit there and enjoy the wine, it won't take us long.' She ushered Shiny into the kitchen.

Standing at the sink Sonia washed the dishes and Shiny dried them, Sonia looked at her younger brother. 'Pretty girl, have you managed to get anywhere with her yet?'

Shiny went a slight shade of pink. 'Typical of you Sis. I've only known her for a few hours and besides this is a murder investigation and she is a key witness.'

'So I ask again have you got anywhere yet? She is really pretty and I saw the way you looked at her. Make a move kiddo. Girls as sharp and as pretty as her don't stay on the market for long.'

Shiny smiled and nodded. 'I must admit she is somewhat of an attraction, and from the story, she told me about her escape from the cave, quite a tough cookie too.'

'I must admit she would make a great Sister in Law,' laughed Sonia, 'and add a bit of class to the family'.

***

Sat in the kitchen the next morning at a small dining table, Sonia, Francesca and Isabel enjoyed a late breakfast of eggs, bacon and pancakes.

'It always seems strange that once the girls are off to school and play school, the quiet takes a bit of getting used to. Well at least for the first two minutes then I sit down and thoroughly enjoy the peace,' said Sonia laughing.

'They are a delight,' added Isabel, 'and your brother seems to adore them,'

'Absolutely, he winds them up with the most outrageous games like the Poo bag game which you witnessed.'

'I assume he isn't married or has a serious girlfriend,' said Francesca trying to mask the question behind the coffee she was drinking. Isabel and Sonia looked at one another and laughed.

'Thinking of applying for the job,' said Sonia.

Francesca blushed as she saw the two women watching her.

'Well .. no just making conversation.'

'Really,' said Isabel, 'bit of a catch wouldn't you say Sonia?' 'I must admit he would be. He has had a few girlfriends but they haven't lasted long. All were pretty but not much else.'

She looked at Isabel and winked. 'He is quite a clever fellow and should go far in the police force but he needs someone by his side who can be his equal. Someone maybe with a first-class honours degree from Oxford,' she said bursting out in laughter, joined by Isabel.

'How did you know that?' said Francesca.

'Oh you know honey how us women like to gossip,' said Isabel who was interrupted by Sonia's mobile buzzing.

'Excuse me,' she said as she stood up from the table and moved away as she listened to what the caller was saying. Answering she said. 'That's good news. Love you.'

Returning to the table and joining Francesca and Isabel she said. 'Well, I suggest we enjoy another cup of coffee and then you two ladies can safely make your way back to your villa.' 'What about the guys in the SUV?' asked Francesca.

'They found the SUV burnt out this morning with one body in it, the dwarf you saw,' said Sonia. 'They are certain the driver, who they know as a small-time criminal and not the murdering kind, got away. My brother wants to meet you at your place at noon. He said so you can finish your story.'

Chapter 41

S hiny, sat with Bernie who took notes. Francesca relayed the execution of the plan they had made to trap Ryder and Brad in the cave. 'As we haven't seen them for nearly two days, I presume they must still be in there,' said Shiny shaking his head in amazement.

'You took an almighty risk. Why didn't you just report it to us?' said Bernie hoping to make an impression with Francesca who he had difficulty taking his eyes off.

'Now if I may say,' said Isabel, 'that is not a question I expected. Do you remember how cautious my Granddaughter was when you first came to the villa? She wouldn't let you in. We had lost all faith in the police.'

'Yes, sorry,' said Bernie looking embarrassed.

'No need to be,' said Francesca smiling at Bernie, 'you didn't know the full story.'

'So what do we need to get into the cave and search it thoroughly?' asked Shiny.

'We have the infrared torches that can lead us to the area we left them. You will still need string and strong flashlights,' said

Francesca, 'and I would suggest some medical backup as they may be slightly traumatised.'

'I will arrange for a team of paramedics. I also have several staff members I can call on to help. I will meet you back here at 2 pm and we will follow you to the site.'

'Just one more thing. Tell all the people involved to wear some form of protective clothing. It can get awfully messy,' added Isabel.

***

Francesca drove the green Chevrolet with Isabel in the passenger seat. Both were wearing their leathers, freshened up earlier, having decided they were the best form of protection for the caves. Behind them was a small convoy. In a police vehicle were Shiny and Bernie followed by an ambulance with two paramedics. In an unmarked black van were 4 police officers.

Arriving at the entrance to the cave, the vehicles parked up. Isabel was the first out of their vehicle walking over to the Lincoln still parked where it had been left. She felt the bonnet. Joined by Shiny and Francesca, she said, 'Just checking it hasn't been used. So they are still here.'

'Right gather around everyone please,' shouted Shiny. The police officers and the Paramedics joined him. 'You will be wondering what on earth we are doing out here; why you were asked to wear overalls and bring flashlights. Well, today we go looking for two police officers who we believe are lost in these caves. If you are asking yourselves how this could happen and why there aren't dozens of people out here searching, well all those questions will be answered after we find them. Be under no illusions. These two officers, if found will be instantly arrested. I will charge them with several federal offences.' He looked around noticing several astonished faces.

'If any of you suffer from claustrophobia then please wait outside the caves. Your job will be to act as a liaison with those searching. We will be led by Francesca and Isabel.' He turned and introduced the two women. 'They have an intimate knowledge of these caves.' He turned to Francesca. 'Is there anything you would like to add Francesca?'

'Yes, just one point. The route into the cave is marked by infra-red paint that can only be picked up with one of these torches,' she held up a torch. 'When I need to use it I will ask you to switch off your flashlights. It will plunge all of you and the caves into complete darkness so just wait until I signal for the flashlights to go back on again. Also, we will need one of you to be responsible for the string.'

Bernie put up his hand. 'I'll do that Francesca,' he offered. 'Thanks, Bernie, please make sure it is tied securely to the bolder you will find near the entrance. The string is used just as a backup to map out our route and to help anyone to leave if they have a panic attack. Any questions?'

A paramedic put up his hand. 'Can I ask how long they have been in the cave, did they have any water, food etc? I will need to know if they need to be sedated. Will we need to take in stretchers?'

'Many thanks, Kevin,' said Shiny. 'I do not believe they had any water or food with them and we are not sure of their condition. We believe they have been in there for a little under 48 hours. So please take everything you need for the worst-case scenario'.

***

Francesca stood outside the entrance to the cave dressed in her leathers and her miner's helmet and waited for the team to organise themselves behind her. Bernie pleased that he had an important job, was busy tying the string around the boulder.

'Ready Francesca,' he shouted.

She smiled at him saying, 'Good job Bernie. Right everyone if you are ready follow me.'

Behind Francesca, as she entered the cave, Isabel and Shiny followed closely. Shiny had a large flashlight that lit the area and Francesca easily recognised the first part of the route.

As the team progressed through the various caves and caverns, Francesca would call out for lights off as she made certain they were following the correct route. After over 30 minutes she stopped the team whilst she looked around. 'This is where the route ends.'

Shiny gathered the team around him. 'Right guys, in teams of two spread out to search the tunnels.' Turning to Bernie he said, 'Cut off long pieces of string and give to each team.'

Bernie took out a knife and measured out 3 long pieces of string giving them to Shiny 'Thanks, Bernie.' He gave one to each team. 'Francesca will stay here with Isabel and hold the ends of the string. When you unroll it out try not to pull it too hard. If you feel three tugs make your way back immediately, understood?' There were nods from the group.

Francesca gathered the ends of the string and tied them together and held onto them. The three teams made their way in different directions, the light from their flashlights dancing around the caves, until they were out of sight.

***

Francesca and Isabel sat down in the corner of the cave, the string held tight. The only light they had was from the small bulbs in their helmets.

'Beginning to feel like home now,' said Francesca, giving out an unconvincing laugh

'Hopefully the very last time,' said Isabel.

Suddenly there was a scream from one of the tunnels and the string was nearly pulled out of Francesca's hand. She held on tight as Isabel found the strand under tension and followed it. After several tunnels she saw flashing lights ahead, snaking around randomly. She entered the tunnel and stopped, shocked by what she saw. One of the policemen was lying unconscious on the ground, a large rock, stained in blood next to him. The other policeman was struggling with a man. The man, dishevelled, his trousers soaked in urine and resembling one of the undead, was screaming incoherently.

Isabel picked up the rock and waited until the man had his back to her then calmly stepped forward and hit him, measuring the strength of the blow to ensure not to cause him too much harm. The man dropped to the ground. The policeman fell back collapsing to the ground with exhaustion. 'Have you any handcuffs?' Isabel asked. The policeman nodded gesturing to his side pocket. She got out the handcuffs then rolled the man over trying not to gag from the smell of him, and cuffed his hands behind him.

'Well done Ma'am,' said the police officer. 'He came out of nowhere screaming like a maniac. He hit my mate with a rock. Can you check him over?

Isabel went over to the policeman. 'He is in a pretty bad way. I wouldn't be surprised if he has a fractured skull. Let's make our way back to the centre point and get the others to join us. The paramedics need to stabilise him.'

As she said that there was a groan from the man she had hit. He shook his head and looked around. He stared at Isabel his eyes ablaze, his lips curled back over his teeth. He screamed obscenities struggling to get to his feet but was restrained by the other policeman. Isabel tapped him again with the rock, just hard enough for the man to fall dazed.

'I'll get the others. Stay here.' She backtracked to Francesca. Three tugs on the string brought the others back to them. Isabel explained what had happened and two paramedics hurried off following the string through the tunnel.

'Well that's one of them,' said Isabel. 'First time I have seen someone completely mad. He will need years of therapy I would guess.'

***

The man, identified as Detective Ryder Jenkins, had been subdued by injection from the paramedics that would ensure he was unconscious for a few hours. In the meantime, the police officer still unconscious, was now on a stretcher being taken back to the ambulance. Four men carried the stretcher leaving just 2 police officers together with, Shiny, Bernie, the two women and Ryder.

Ryder was carried back to the nominated centre by the two police officers. When they arrived they dumped his body on the ground both breathing heavily.

Shiny was concerned. 'That was not something planned for. As soon as the paramedics are out of here they will be calling for support. So I suggest we carry Detective Jenkins as far as we can until we are relieved, and then return and start a search for Detective Montgomery.'

'Agreed,' said Isabel, 'between the six of us we should be able to manage.'

Shiny smiled, 'I thought you would be part of the team,' 'Of course. Right Francesca and I will take the first shift, your two police officers look about done in.'

Struggling, the four carried the inert body of Ryder through the first of the tunnels. When it came time to change over, Francesca and Isabel gave their positions to the two police officers. 'Can we take a short break?' asked Bernie, trying to maintain a macho image but struggling.

'Good idea,' said Shiny. '5-minute break.'

The four settled down in a small cavern. 'We should have bought some water,' said one of the police officers.'

'Yes, we should .....,' Isabel was about to say when she stopped. 'Everyone, silence.'

They all went quiet and then the sound came. A soft gentle sobbing.

'It's Brad,' said Shiny. 'I can hear him.'

They moved the flashlights around the cavern. Sat curled up in a foetal position in the shadows and swaying backwards and forwards was Brad. Isabel went over to him and as she shone the light on him, he started to crawl away hiding his eyes from the light.

'I don't think he will be any trouble. He is completely traumatised,' said Isabel.

Shiny went over and looked at the pathetic figure curled up in a ball. 'Why don't we take Ryder out and if you are OK, maybe you and Francesca stay here. I will then call for support and then come back.'

'Yes, I'm OK with that,' said Isabel and Francesca nodded.

***

When Shiny returned with two new officers and a paramedic they found Francesca and Isabel talking softly to Brad. He was still curled up rocking backwards and forwards. One of the paramedics gave him a sedative and when he was unconscious they loaded him onto a stretcher and made their way out.

In the daylight outside the caves Francesca and Isabel were sitting on the ground sipping water from bottles given to them by the paramedics. 'That will be the last time I ever go into a cave, ever,' said Francesca.

'Oh, I don't know. A place to find peace, no phone messages to answer, no exhaust fumes to breathe in,' said Isabel as they both laugh.

Shiny joined them, sitting down next to Francesca. 'I can't believe you spent nearly 3 days alone in that cave with no water or food. Surely it was a miracle you managed to escape.'

'Not really. I just followed the bats out as I told you. Without them, I would never have got out of there. Now I'm going to sit here until,' Francesca said looking at her watch, 'until just after 7.30 when the bats will leave. I want to say thank you to them one last time.'

'Would you mind if I sit here with you?' asked Shiny, his voice sounding slightly emotional, 'I would like to thank them as well.'

Isabel got up and placed a hand on her granddaughter's shoulder. 'I will see you back at the villa. I am sure this young man can escort you home safely.'

Chapter 42

Bernie waited impatiently for the two phones to be charged. They were cheap flip phones issued to all police officers. These two belonged to Ryder and Brad. With no indicator as to the battery level, Bernie decided after 20 minutes that they would be charged enough to find out the information that Shiny wanted.

He gave the phones to Shiny, who checked the last calls that were made. 'The number on Ryder's phone, the last one he had dialled,' said Shiny, pointing to the phone's small screen, 'just says private.' Sat down behind his desk he took a pen from a cup holder and a notepad, then dialled the number.

'Where the hell have you been, you skiving bastard? You and that useless partner of yours have been out for 2 fucking days. So what the fuck have you been up to and it had better please me,' said the voice on the other end of the phone.

Shiny sat in silence. 'So, what the fuck have you got to say for yourself,' the voice asked, sounding angry and frustrated. Shiny was cautious. He recognised the voice and decided to tread carefully. 'Sir, this is Shiny. We have found Ryder and Brad and

I have just been checking Ryder's phone to see who he had been contacting. They are both in a bad way and currently in hospital.'

There was silence on the phone. 'Sir,'

'Well, of course, he had contacted me, I'm his boss and why the hell haven't you kept me updated.' 'We have only just....'

'I don't want any excuses. Just get them both back to work. There's probably nothing wrong with them and I want you off this case. You have failed to keep me updated as I made clear to you a few days ago. I have taken over this investigation,' he shouted and cut the call off.

Shiny was stunned. He sat there for a while, hoping what he was thinking could not be true but knowing it was. Using his phone, he rang the Chief of Police back.

'I thought I told you Detective;,, you are off this case...'

Interrupting, Shiny took a deep breath and said forcefully. 'Sir I understand, and I will stop my investigation but both Detectives will be in Hospital for some time and I would....'

'Those two useless pieces of shit will be skiving for weeks making the most of it. To be honest I don't give two monkeys about them. As I told you before, I have taken over this investigation and if I need your help, I'll fucking well ask for it. Is that clear enough for you?'

'Just one question so I can finish my report. Did you find anything on the SD card we found on the dead man?'

'You can forget about that. I checked it out and it was corrupted. Bodily fluids. Now I have work to do,' said the Senior Detective and as before ended the call.

'Corrupted through bodily fluids, my Ass. That's very funny. He had no idea it was found inside a condom,' commented Shiny to no one in particular.

Bernie came over from his desk. 'What happened on the call from Ryder's phone.'

'Not much was only answered by the Chief of Police.' 'No! You are kidding.'

'Surprised me too although I suppose it makes sense that Ryder would be calling him. It was just his reaction. Defensive. Then he told me that the SD card was corrupt. It was inside a condom for god's sake so it couldn't have been.'

'Didn't you ask the IT guys to make a copy?' said Bernie. 'Yes,' said Shiny, 'I hope that one hasn't been corrupted by being up someone's bottom,' he laughed.

***

Shiny and Bernie sat in the IT department drinking coffee. A friendly, cheerful civilian named Stokes, who was attached to the police department and an IT specialist, was in the evidence room. He came back with a small plastic folder which contained an SD card.

'Here is the copy you requested. The original one given to Captain Wilcox seemed to be fine. Not sure how he thought it was corrupted but if it was, we may have been able to find something on it.'

'So, is this copy OK?' asked Shiny.

'I have no idea. We just de-encrypted the original, made a copy and stored it,' said Stokes.

'So no one has any idea what's actually on the card,' said Bernie warming to the investigation.

'Spot on Bernie. We will be the first to see it. So, let's load it up and see what delights it holds.' He placed the SD card into a smartphone and selected video then waited for the card to load. He pressed play and the three of them stared at the screen as an image of a Japanese Lady gesturing to the surrounding buildings and speaking in her native tongue filled the screen. 'Boy this is a fun movie,' said Stokes, 'hope it doesn't move onto Porn. If so Bernie would have to close his eyes.'

'That's the Alamo, in San Antonio,' said Shiny. As the film progressed it moved onto local scenes most of them featuring either a Japanese man or woman who pointed to something of interest to them. The scenes suddenly change. A flurry of disjointed views as if the holder of the camera had lost control when suddenly a face appeared.

'Freeze that,' said Shiny. They all stared at the picture of the man. 'That's the guy in the morgue. I would guess he stole the camera from the Japanese couple and was trying to work out how to use it. OK move it on.'

The next frames showed the inside of an empty warehouse with the focus changing and the brightness varying. 'You're right Shiny. He's experimenting with it,' added Stokes.

'I know that warehouse,' said Bernie. The other two look at him quizzically. Looking embarrassed he said, 'I've been to a few raves there. Legal ones of course.'

'Is there such a thing as a legal rave,' asked Shiny smiling quizzically. 'Anyway, now we know the location,' he added, 'I suggest we get on with the rest of this riveting film.'

The next frames showed a black Lincoln entering the warehouse. 'Christ that's the one used by Ryder and Brad,' remarked Shiny.

As the film progressed further, they saw the arrival of the SUV and then when the van stopped the film focused on the three men who got out of the Lincoln.

'Well, I'll be dammed. That's Captain Wilcox, our esteemed Chief of Police with them and the other vehicle is the one that attacked Francesca and Isabel.'

They watched the rest of the film which included an exchange of drugs and then money. 'Can you focus in on the drug packets,' requested Shiny. As Stokes focused, the packages could be seen stamped with an official number.

'Those numbers are from the storage facility where we keep all confiscated drugs. I'm sure of it.' Shiny wrote down the numbers and then they watched as they saw Ryder turn suddenly and fire at the camera. The screen went blank.

The three sat in silence. After a few minutes Shiny said, 'It looks like an exchange of drugs for money and unless there was some form of arrest pending and Wilcox had set up the Dwarf for a sting, this video means we have a very crooked Chief of Police.'

'No wonder he didn't want the video shown,' added Stokes. 'Surely there is enough evidence on there to bring him down.' 'Yes, but supposing it was a sting, and he had the money and had returned it to the treasury,' said Bernie.

'No chance of that. They would have stopped them getting away with the drugs and how come the poor bastard who filmed this was now in the morgue after being buried by Ryder and

Brad,' said Shiny. 'No wonder they wanted Francesca out of the way. She was and still is a key witness.'

He got out his police flip phone. 'Let's see how he reacts to this message,' as he dialled the Chief's number. 'What now?' Came the irritated answer.

'Sir, we have some good news. You know the SD card that was found that you thought was corrupted, well I had asked for a copy to be made and the IT guys have said it's OK. We are just about to watch it and thought you might like to come down and view it with .....'

The line suddenly went dead.

**

Captain Wilcox put his phone down and cursed. 'Fuck that interfering little bastard,' he shouted out loud. He grabbed a go bag which he had hoped he would never need then quickly opened his safe and took out bundles of cash. Stuffing the notes into a separate hold all he took one last look around his office. 'Hated this fucking job anyway.'

He left in a hurry, rushing past his bewildered secretary who asked, 'Is everything OK Sir.'

Ignoring her he walked quickly down the corridor that led to the exit to the car park. He glanced down the corridor and saw Shiny and Bernie walking towards his office. Turning, he ran towards the exit shoving aside a young police officer who fell to the ground. Without apologising, he left the building and ran, dragging the two bags.

As he got to his car he heard Shiny shout, 'Captain Wilcox, we need to talk to you.'

Ignoring Shiny he quickly threw the bags into his red opentopped sports car, a Porsche 911 Carrera and before Shiny or Bernie could stop him, left the car park trailing rubber.

***

Shiny went back into the building running. Bernie followed as they both hurried into Wilcox's office. The secretary was standing by the door looking confused and anxious. As Shiny entered she said. 'What on earth is going on?'

'No time for any explanations,' he replied as he rushed past her. Using one of the two phones on the desk he called the IT department. After a short delay, Stokes answered. Before he had time to say anything Shiny said, 'It's Shiny. Is it possible to get surveillance on a private car?'

'Take time. You would need authorisation, probably from the Governor and that's not easy,'

Still holding the phone, he turned to the secretary who was still standing by the door, her face ashen. 'Any idea where the Chief went in such a hurry?'

Answering in a shaky voice she said, 'he has nothing booked in his diary.'

'Where would he go for a break, does he have a holiday home, anything like that?'

'No nothing, no family just his dog.'

Shiny asked, 'How fond is he of his dog?'

'Wouldn't go anywhere without it. The only thing he seemed to cherish. He is a real loner.'

Shiny turned back to the phone. 'Stoksey, can you get CCTV on the Chief's house?'

'Now that's something I can do, hold on a second.' There was a short pause. 'Few more seconds and Bingo,' he exclaimed joyfully, 'there you go.'

'What can you see?' asked Shiny frustratedly.

'Nothing at the moment, why?'

'Just a guess, I thought if he was making a run for it, he might have gone home to collect his dog. Worth a try.'

'I'll keep an eye on it in case your hunch plays out.' 'Thanks, and if you could track a few of the other CCTV's as well, looking for a Red open-top sports car. I will put out an alert with traffic.'

'Will do, but as you know we don't have very wide coverage with our outdated system, which needs badly updating. Chief would never authorise the expenditure. Maybe he didn't want his activities tracked.'

'Agreed, keep in touch,' said Shiny and ended the call.

***

In the sports car, Wilcox drove with care. He had put the hood up and wanted to make sure he didn't draw any attention to himself. He kept to the speed limit whilst going over his escape plan. He had a bolthole in Mexico and knew that once he managed to get onto the interstate it was only a few hours' drive to the border. First, though he had to change his car and collect his dog.

He drove into a small cul-de-sac that had 16 lockups, 8 on each side all of which looked identical, then parked in front of one halfway down on the right. Getting out of the Porsche he went to the door of the lock-up, which was an up-and-over and unlocked it. Bending down he heaved on the door and struggled to open it as it groaned on the hinges objecting to having been disturbed after months of neglect. Once it had opened, he went back to the Porsche driving it into the empty garage.

The gap to the walls of the lock-up left little room to exit the car and he cursed as he struggled to get out of the open car door. Grabbing the bags he left the garage, closed the door, and did not bother to lock it. 'Never be back here, thank goodness,' he moaned as he made his way across the cul-de-sac to the left-hand line of lockups to the one nearest the end.

Going through the same procedure, he lifted the up-and-over door and squeezed past a big pickup truck, identical to the many thousands that the Texans loved. He swung the bags into the open back and after a struggle seated himself behind the steering wheel.

The truck was just 3 years old, registered and taxed under a different name from his own. He knew one day things would go wrong and they would track his car but this truck, well maintained and anonymous, was the perfect getaway vehicle. He reversed out of the garage and didn't bother to close the door, then drove the short distance to his small but comfortable apartment on the bottom floor of a modern 6story complex. Making his way quickly through the door he called out for his dog Milo, who came running excitedly. After making a fuss of him he went to the fridge and collected the dog's food and a couple of bottles of water and then, with not even a backward glance, left the apartment carrying Milo.

***

Stokes had gone to make a cup of coffee when the big truck came into view on the CCTV. He would have missed it if it hadn't been for his diet. Trying to lose the more than a few pounds he had put on since his marriage, was proving difficult. His new wife was Mexican and a devotee of the food she had been bought up on. Though delicious the calories were beginning to hit their mark. He had therefore decided to cut out sugar in his coffee and use a sweetener.

In the open office that he worked in, there was a communal coffee area. Just a small table that contained the kettle, a few mugs and sugar with milk in a small fridge nearby. After making his coffee he cursed as he realised there was no sweetener. Going back to his desk to collect some from his desk drawer was when he caught sight of a man carrying a dog walking from the apartment complex to a pickup truck. The man was tall and thin and although Stokes could not see his face he guessed, after Shiny had mentioned the dog, that this was the Chief.

Excitedly he rang Shiny after taking down the details of the truck. 'Got him,' he said as Shiny answered the phone. 'He is leaving his home in a black pickup truck.'

'The cunning old devil had changed cars. Thank goodness we guessed right about the dog. Will you be able to track him?' 'Hope so. Just keep your radio on in the car and we will try to give you directions.'

Shiny called out for Bernie who came hurrying down the corridor holding the keys to one of the Blue and White police cars. In the car park, Bernie pressed the key fob looking for the flashing hazard lights. They ran towards the car and as Shiny went to get into the driver's seat Bernie shook his head. Stunned Shiny said. 'What now?'

'Leave the car chase to me. Advanced course in pursuit driving. I know what I'm doing,' said Bernie brimming with confidence.

***

Grandma Barker was on her normal route to the shops. Her routine hadn't varied much for the past 4 years since her husband died. Three times a week she made the journey from her compact but well-maintained and comfortable flat to the small convenience store.

She had just collected her groceries and passed a few pleasant minutes chatting with some of the few people she knew before she left the store. Grandma Barker was a proud woman. Now in her mid 80's she tried to keep fit with her walking and was known by her friends as a woman of principle who did not suffer fools gladly. Outside the store, she stopped at the pedestrian crossing and as was her habit, looked both ways. The traffic was light, and she stepped out onto the black and white zebra marks with confidence.

Half a block away, the Truck was being driven fast but with care. Wilcox had no wish to bring attention to himself so kept within the speed limit. He began to feel confident that if he could make it across the border into Mexico, a drive of a few hundred miles, the contacts he had there, if well-paid, would be able to ensure his safety.

Inside the police car, Shiny sat in admiration at the skill level shown by Bernie. They received digital information on their computer screen of the whereabouts of the truck and closed rapidly. The sirens and flashing lights had opened a pathway and with the car taking corners faster than Shiny believed possible, Bernie had the gap down to just a few blocks.

Inside the truck, Wilcox heard the police sirens and his alarm bells sounded. So he put his foot down to use the full power of the Twin-turbo flat-six, which accelerated rapidly. Taking a corner at speed he was forced to slam on the brakes as ahead an old woman was crossing the pedestrian crossing. The truck slid to a halt just inches from Grandma Barker, Wilcox leaned on the horn shouting obscenities to the old Lady. 'Get out of the fucking way you stupid old bag.'

Grandma Barker was a Christian and abhorred foul language. She stared at the man behind the steering wheel and felt her temper rise. Bringing back the shopping bags she was holding, in a swinging motion, she slammed them into the front bumper of the truck.

The front sensors in the bumpers reacted instantly and sent an electrical signal to an igniter. The heat generated caused sodium azide to decompose into sodium metal and nitrogen gas. Sat behind the wheel, Wilcox was trapped as the airbags inflated almost instantly.

Grandma Barker looked on at the exploded bags and the man trapped behind the wheel and smiled. Looking both ways she continued her journey home.

Behind the stricken truck, the police car driven by Bernie took the corner in a power slide at speed before braking sharply as it nearly collided with the rear end of the truck. Parking the police car alongside, both Shiny and Bernie got out.

The airbags in the truck had deflated but had left Wilcox stunned. As he struggled to move the remains of the airbag from the steering wheel, he hadn't noticed the police car draw up beside him. As he looked up hoping to continue his escape, he heard the engine die as Shiny leaned in, turned off the ignition and removed the keys.

Shiny opened the door to the truck. Still dazed Wilcox shook his head to clear it and made a feeble attempt to push Shiny aside but to no effect. Before he realised what had happened, he was handcuffed and sat in the back of the police car. By now several other police cars had arrived.

Grandma Barker stopped when she heard all the commotion from the sirens. She turned and saw a tall man, handcuffed being led away from the car she had hit with her bags. He was placed inside a police car which sped away.

'Serves him right for swearing at a defenceless old lady,' she said satisfyingly as she turned and made her way home.

Chapter 43

S hiny arrived at the villa with Bernie. Holding a bunch of flowers and two bottles of wine. Shiny felt nervous as they walked up the driveway to the Villa.

'You all right Sir?' asked Bernie, 'you seem a little tense.' 'I'm fine,' he said trying to sound confident.

'Couldn't be that the young lady is beginning to affect you is it? She certainly affected me.'

'Shut up Bernie,' said Shiny in jest as he went a subtle shade of pink.

'I knew it,' said Bernie triumphantly, 'so the master has fallen. Can I be best man?' he ducked as Shiny took a mock swing at him.

Ringing the doorbell, the two police officers waited patiently until Isabel answered the door.

'Hi guys, what a lovely surprise. Come in. Francesca will be with us in a minute. She has just been having a long bath, relaxing after all the adventures. Coffee?'

'Yes please,' they both said as Shiny handed the flowers and the wine over to Isabel. 'This is just a thank you from both of us for all the invaluable help you gave us.'

'How lovely, many thanks.' Isabel took the flowers and wine into the kitchen and started to make coffee as Shiny and Bernie joined her.

'Any news on the two detectives?' asked Isabel.

'Yes,' said Shiny, 'and not good news. The doctor we spoke to believes they will both need extensive medical and psychiatric care for at least a year to overcome the trauma they suffered.' 'Didn't think they would be that badly affected when we came up with the plan.'

'Don't blame yourself. They are a couple of mean murdering individuals who will go down for a considerable amount of ......' Shiny stopped talking when Francesca walked into the kitchen. She was wearing a dusky rose and powder pink knee length dress that hugged her figure. Her blonde hair was flowing free and her makeup was expertly applied, exaggerating her beautiful green eyes.

'Hi guys, how lovely to see you both.'

There was an embarrassing moment of silence as both men stared at her. 'Is something wrong?' she said to break the silence.

Isabel stood behind the two men and smiled. 'No honey it's just the guys haven't seen you looking like a woman before. You have either had a face full of cuts and bruises or dressed up in leather. I think you have taken them a little by surprise.' 'I'm so sorry for staring Francesca,' said Shiny, 'but you do look stunning.'

'Yes, you look,' Bernie stumbled for the right word, 'nice,' he added feebly.

They all laughed as Isabel carried a tray of coffee cups, milk, sugar, and a large cafeteria, leading them into the lounge.

'So, tell us what has been happening?' said Francesca already curled up on the sofa. 'Have you been promoted to Chief of Police yet,' as she looked at Shiny?

Smiling he said, 'I fear that's a few years away yet, if ever.' 'I'd vote for you,' added Bernie still trying to recover from saying Francesca looked, "nice".

Shiny smiled. 'Well, the Chief of police was caught, as I believe you know, mainly down to a lovely old lady namely, Grandma Barker and,' 'Some brilliant police work by us,' interrupted Bernie.

'I was going to say by some brilliant driving by my partner here,' said Shiny giving Bernie a friendly punch on the arm. A round of applause from the others caused Bernie to go bright red.

'What will happen to your Boss?' Francesca asked.

'Well, we have enough evidence to put him away for life. You remember the giant you nearly killed in the SUV, he has spilt the beans on the exchange of the drugs for the money. He was, as you can imagine less than impressed with the way he was abandoned and decided to give us all the information we needed. The driver, Al is still on the run, but it won't be long before he is caught.' He hesitated, 'We were hoping you could stay around for another week or so, help us with witness statements and all that stuff. Could you perhaps delay your departure for a while?

'Funny old thing,' said Isabel, 'but we will be around for a while. I am taking my Granddaughter to Las Vegas for a break.' 'When was that decided?' said Francesca in delight.

'I have booked flights for first thing in the morning and a hotel for three nights. I will drop off the bike later today. So, detective if you could spare my Granddaughter for a few days?'

Shiny, sounding disappointed said, 'Yes of course. I trust you will enjoy Las Vegas.'

'Oh, I intend to,' said Francesca laughing, 'and I'm sure and hope my Gran will lead me astray.'

***

Landing at Harry Reid International, Isabel and Francesca left the departure area and took a cab to their hotel. As they booked in, Francesca looked around, awestruck at the decor and the air of excitement that seemed to emanate from both uniformed staff and guests. As they made their way to the lifts to take them to their rooms, Francesca stopped. Looking into the Casino she stared fascinated by the sight and noise coming from the variety of slot machines, their handles being pulled relentlessly in the hope of a life-changing win. Smiling, she took Isabel by the arm as they entered the lift.

After the heat of the day, the air-conditioned room was a relief. Looking around the well-equipped lounge; large flatscreen TV, coffee machine and safety deposit box, Francesca felt excited at the prospect of the next few days.

'So what's first on the agenda Gran?'

'Tonight, we are off to a casino then a show, and tomorrow we go to the airport.' 'The airport, why?'

'Wait and see,' said Isabel smiling.

***

'That was a night to remember, Gran. The show was unforgettable, just a shame we didn't break the bank at the casino, but it was fun anyway,' Francesca said as she applied some makeup whilst looking at her reflection in the bathroom mirror. 'So why are we going to the airport?'

'Just wait and see but we should get a move on. I want to be there in the next 20 minutes.'

'I'm ready,' said Francesca as she grabbed her bag before joining Isabel. After they left the room, they made their way down the elaborate staircase to the reception. Isabel glowed with excitement.

At the reception, the receptionist booked them a cab. A short drive later they arrived at the airport, Isabel leading the way to arrivals. Checking the arrivals board, she nodded after she checked her watch. 'Perfect timing,' she said and turned towards Francesca, 'any time now.'

'Any time for what?' said Francesca sounding excited. 'I'm making a few guesses here but can't imagine being right.'

Just then Isabel waved a hand and a man towing a suitcase waved back. 'Well blow me down,' said Francesca, 'none other than Bertie. Gran, you are a dark horse,' hugging her Gran.

'I have a feeling you may be in for another surprise,' said Isabel as she turned to greet Bertie. 'Good flight,' she said her voice laughing, 'and are you really going to do it here!'

Getting down on one knee and holding out a beautifully crafted diamond ring, Bertie smiled up at Isabel saying, 'Right Mrs Fordham, about time you and I got hitched, what da ya say?'

'Bertie that must be the worst American accent I have ever heard and suggest you get up from kneeling down or you may, at your age, get stuck down there. Oh, and by the way the answer is

Yes,' A few bystanders, having witnessed the event started to applaud.

Bertie pretended to struggle up and mimicked an old man staggering around, laughed, 'that's a relief,' he said as he put the ring on her finger followed up with a kiss and a long-awaited cuddle, 'was hoping the journey would be worth it,'

Francesca stood to the side and had tears running down her cheeks. Bertie went over to her and after hugging her too, asked in a serious tone. 'Francesca my love, would you do us the great honour of being a witness at our Wedding?'

Francesca unable to speak just nodded, wiping away the joyful tears.

'Thank goodness for that,' said Bertie laughing again as he hugged her, 'as the wedding is booked for this afternoon.'

Chapter 44

Shiny and Francesca sat in a Mexican restaurant struggling to converse over the music being played by the Mariachi group who circled their table. Both stopped talking to clap their hands in time to the music. As the group moved away Francesca smiled at Shiny, 'this is a wonderful restaurant, so much atmosphere,' she said before she took a mouthful of her chicken fajitas, 'and the food is wonderful.'

'There are a few good restaurants in the town, but I think this is the best,' said Shiny. 'I am so glad you decided to stay on for a few more days. I hope your Gran wasn't too disappointed that you didn't go back with her.'

Smiling mischievously, Francesca said, 'I have a feeling they will want some time to themselves.'

Laughing Shiny added, 'I'm sure you are right.'

Leaning forward towards Shiny she said, 'Now we have a little bit of peace and Bernie isn't two feet away from either you or me, can you give me an update on what has been happening.'

Taking a drink from his Margarita he said, 'Right, short version. Your witness statement and that of your Grans have been submitted to the FBI together with the evidence from the Flash drive. They are confident of a conviction that should see our ex-Chief of Police go down for at least 20 years.'

Warming to the story he continued. 'There is also another charge pending. I checked on the storeroom where all the illegal drugs are stored before being incinerated. At first, everything seemed to be in order. Correct number of packs of drugs according to the records. However, the serial numbers on the packets didn't make sense. They were random and didn't match the numbers on the manifest. So, I took one packet up to our forensic guys who thought it was hilarious when they found out it was just plain flour.'

'So, the drugs had been substituted for flour after they had been sold to keep the records straight,' said Francesca sounding amazed. 'How clever and then the packets of flour would be taken to the incinerator, burnt and no one would know the difference.'

They both continued eating and exchanging polite conversation when Shiny, sounding nervous said, 'Francesca, I know it took a lot for you to stay a few extra days when I asked you, but would you consider staying maybe for a month or so? I must admit I have rather fallen for you, and I believe if we could spend some quality time together and get to know one another,' he hesitated, 'well who knows.'

Francesca smiled and held out her hand to cover his, said,

'OK but two conditions.'

'Two! Just name them,' said Shiny.

'First, would it be possible to persuade Bernie to give us some space,' she laughed, 'he is lovely, but I have a feeling he has a bit of a crush on both of us.'